Dead Man Talking

"There's no savoring the Pepper Martin series—you'll devour each book and still be hungry for more!"

—Kathryn Smith, *USA Today* bestselling author

"My favorite ghost hunter, sassy Pepper Martin, is back in another hauntingly good mystery."

—Shirley Damsgaard, author of *The Seventh Witch*

Night of the Loving Dead

"Gravestones, ghosts, and ghoulish misdemeanors delight in Casey Daniels's witty *Night of the Loving Dead*."

—Madelyn Alt, national bestselling author

"Pepper proves once again that great style, quick wit, and a sharp eye can solve any mystery."　　　　　—*Publishers Weekly*

"Pepper is brazen and beautiful, and this mystery is perfectly paced, with plenty of surprise twists."　　　　—*RT Book Reviews*

Tombs of Endearment

"A fun romp through the streets and landmarks of Cleveland . . . A tongue-in-cheek . . . look at life beyond the grave . . . Well worth picking up."

—Suite101.com

"[A] PI who is Stephanie Plum-meets-*Sex and the City*'s Carrie Bradshaw . . . It's fun, it's 'chick,' and appealing . . . [A] quick, effortless read with a dash of Bridget Jones–style romance."

—PopSyndicate.com

"With witty dialogue and an entertaining mystery, Ms. Daniels pens an irresistible tale of murder, greed, and a lesson in love. A well-paced storyline that's sure to have readers anticipating Pepper's next ghostly client."　　　　　—*Darque Reviews*

"Sassy, spicy . . . Pepper Martin, wearing her Moschino Cheap & Chic pink polka dot sling backs, will march right into your imagination."　　　　—Shirley Damsgaard, author of *The Seventh Witch*

Supernatural Born Killers

CASEY DANIELS

BERKLEY PRIME CRIME, NEW YORK

THE BERKLEY PUBLISHING GROUP
Published by the Penguin Group
Penguin Group (USA) Inc.
375 Hudson Street, New York, New York 10014, USA

Penguin Group (Canada), 90 Eglinton Avenue East, Suite 700, Toronto, Ontario M4P 2Y3, Canada
(a division of Pearson Penguin Canada Inc.) • Penguin Books Ltd., 80 Strand, London WC2R 0RL,
England • Penguin Group Ireland, 25 St. Stephen's Green, Dublin 2, Ireland (a division of Penguin
Books Ltd.) • Penguin Group (Australia), 250 Camberwell Road, Camberwell, Victoria 3124, Australia
(a division of Pearson Australia Group Pty. Ltd.) • Penguin Books India Pvt. Ltd., 11 Community
Centre, Panchsheel Park, New Delhi—110 017, India • Penguin Group (NZ), 67 Apollo Drive,
Rosedale, Auckland 0632, New Zealand (a division of Pearson New Zealand Ltd.) • Penguin Books
(South Africa) (Pty.) Ltd., 24 Sturdee Avenue, Rosebank, Johannesburg 2196, South Africa

Penguin Books Ltd., Registered Offices: 80 Strand, London WC2R 0RL, England

This is a work of fiction. Names, characters, places, and incidents either are the product of the author's
imagination or are used fictitiously, and any resemblance to actual persons, living or dead, business
establishments, events, or locales is entirely coincidental. The publisher does not have any control over
and does not assume any responsibility for author or third-party websites or their content.

SUPERNATURAL BORN KILLERS

A Berkley Prime Crime Book / published by arrangement with the author

PUBLISHING HISTORY
Berkley Prime Crime mass-market edition / September 2012

Copyright © 2012 by Connie Laux.
Cover illustration by Don Sipley.
Cover design by Judith Lagerman.
Interior text design by Laura K. Corless.

ISBN: 978-0-425-25152-2

BERKLEY® PRIME CRIME
Berkley Prime Crime Books are published by The Berkley Publishing Group,
a division of Penguin Group (USA) Inc.,
375 Hudson Street, New York, New York 10014.
BERKLEY® PRIME CRIME and the PRIME CRIME logo are trademarks
of Penguin Group (USA) Inc.

PRINTED IN THE UNITED STATES OF AMERICA

10 9 8 7 6 5 4 3 2 1

ALWAYS LEARNING   PEARSON

For Anne and Chris

Mrs. and Mrs. Manby

happily ever after.

Acknowledgments

First things first . . . when I put the word out to readers that I needed a super title for this book, Nissa Collins came up with one that is perfect. Thank you, Nissa, for your super help!

I also would like to thank the world's greatest brainstorming group: Jasmine Creswell, Diane Mott Davidson, Emilie Richards, and Karen Young. We spent many a rainy hour in Cleveland talking about how to work through this case with Pepper. Their ideas and insights (as always) were invaluable.

Prologue

"Dearly beloved, we are gathered here today to join together this man . . ."

I'd bet dollars to doughnuts the minister had done this a couple hundred times before. He knew how to draw out the drama (not to mention earn the three hundred bucks I knew he'd been paid to perform his duties), and both his chins quivering, he paused, looked at the groom standing on his left, then swiveled his gaze the other way.

Right at me.

". . . and this woman . . ."

He raised his salt-and-pepper eyebrows, daring me to say a word. Or make a move.

As if.

It had been tough enough walking down the aisle between the tasteful white chairs set up on the flagstone patio with its sweeping view of Lake Erie. I mean, what with being poured into, mashed inside, and trussed up in a white satin concoction the likes of which until that morning I had not imagined even existed outside of animated movies about fairy-tale princesses.

Skirt a mile wide.

Strapless.

Sweetheart neckline.

Nipped waist.

I am not (and this is important to point out) anybody's idea of a Big Girl, but last minute does not leave a bride with many options. No Egyptian mummy had ever been wrapped as tight. Or with as much froufrou.

Twenty pounds of bridal gown and a train as long as a football field might make for a va-va-voom entrance, but try moving around in it. Or breathing, for that matter.

Beads, lace, sequins. In a shaft of setting sunlight that glanced off the lake, I sparkled like RuPaul at an awards ceremony. If I moved too quickly—if I even could—I'd blind half my relatives.

". . . in holy matrimony."

The minister droned on, and I sucked in a breath. No easy thing considering the underwire in my built-in bra picked that moment to poke a particularly sensitive spot. I squirmed, and maybe the minister thought it was just a case of wedding-day jitters. Instead of giving me time to collect myself, he grabbed my right hand and plunked it into my groom's.

My groom.

The words shot a tingle up my spine.

Like most girls, I'd dreamed of this day for as long as I could remember, and of the man who'd be standing at my side in front of the altar. The dewy-eyed relatives and smiling guests, the candlelight that swayed in a soft lake breeze, the flowers in shades of white and champagne . . . it was perfect. Far more perfect—in an attempt to keep a particularly irritating bead from poking me in the ribs, I lifted one shoulder, then the other—than the gown that should have been the gown I'd pictured in my mind all these years and was, instead, an off-the-rack number that was the only last-minute dress the bridal shop had in the right length for a woman my height.

"And do you . . ."

Apparently while I was busy considering all this, I'd missed something important, because when I snapped to, I found a platinum-and-diamond band on my finger and the minister giving me the sort of penetrating look that said I needed to pay attention.

"And do you," he said, a little louder this time since I'd missed this part of his spiel the first time around, "Penelope Martin, take this man to be your wedded husband to live together in marriage? Do you promise to love, comfort, honor, and keep him for better or worse, for richer or poorer, in sickness and in health, and forsaking all others, be faithful only to him so long as you both shall live?"

Did I?

I swallowed that sand in my mouth and did my best to force the traditional *I do* past the lump in my throat.

"Well, do you?" the minister asked again.

"I . . ." My voice broke over the words. "How can I not?" I asked him, and really, thinking back to the way it all started, I knew there really was no other answer.

There was no way I could possibly say no.

No way in hell.

1

The last formal dress I wore (before the wedding gown that ate Cleveland) was black. Boatneck, elbow-length sleeves, hem that hit right above the knee. It was not the zingy little number I'd anticipated wearing to the annual Garden View Sponsorship Cocktail Party. That was more in the way of a plunging neckline and halter top, but as Ella had reminded me over and over (and over) since I took her place as the cemetery's community relations manager, I had an image to project. And protect. Since she had arrived at the reception wearing an orange-and-green flowy outfit that reminded me of a tropical drink that had taken one too many spins in a blender, I wasn't exactly sure what that image was supposed to be.

Alas, by then, it was too late. Black boatneck would have to do.

What with all her talk of proper dress, Ella had forgotten to mention that by the time our three hundred invited guests arrived, I'd be feeling the exhaustion of working long hours for three solid weeks, finalizing plans for this fund-raising soiree, talking to the caterer, arranging for flowers and the kind of tasteful music that could only be provided by a harpist who (it turned out) was so high maintenance, she made even me look like a raw beginner. Run ragged was putting it mildly, and our guests had only just begun to arrive.

"Wine, cheese, fruit tray, little spinach pies, shrimp cocktails, glasses, napkins, newsletters." Under my breath, I ticked off the list of what I knew should be set artfully on the linen-draped tables on the patio outside the imposing sandstone monument where President James A. Garfield rested in peace ever since I helped him avert a national crisis that was bound to lead to all-out war with Canada.

But I'm getting ahead of myself, what with talk of ghosts, and all.

And I was forgetting—

"Newsletters!" I looked at the blank spot on the table closest to where the small white plates were stacked beside napkins the same shade as the clear evening sky, and my heart sank. Damn! I'd been in such a hurry to leave the administration building and get over here to the other side of the cemetery to get things set up, I'd left the copies of the latest issue of the Garden View newsletter in my office.

Though it would have aptly described the situation, I bit off the word I was tempted to mutter, smiled from between clenched teeth at the patrons who were lining up for their appetizers and wine, and scrambled to the other side of the patio where Ella, the newly appointed Garden View administrator, was personally welcoming each guest.

"Have to go back to my office." I stood behind the man at the front of the reception line, and catching Ella's eye, I mouthed the words and pointed over my shoulder and back toward the administration building. "Be right back!"

I'd left my car parked in front of the nearest mausoleum, and getting into it, I mumbled another curse; the primo spot was bound to be gone by the time I got back.

And I didn't have the luxury of worrying about it.

I wheeled the Mustang down the tree-lined avenue that was bordered on each side by the graves of the rich, the famous, and the common folk who made Garden View their final resting place. Whizzing past statues of angels and two-story-high obelisks, flashy mausoleums, and a smattering of plain-Jane, flat-to-the-ground grave markers, I made it to the administration building in record time, fished my keys out of my sparkly evening bag, and hurried inside.

Deadly quiet.

Why do those two words always seem to latch onto each other? And why did they occur to me when I had newsletters to worry about, and not a minute to devote to thinking that over the last few years since I whacked my head on a mausoleum and discovered I could talk to the dead, I'd been righting wrongs and investigating mysteries for those Garden View residents who weren't at peace?

"No time for you if you're around," I called out, just in case any of the disembodied happened to be waiting to waylay me. Yes, I know, this sounds heartless, but hey, what's that old saying about not judging another person until you walk a mile in her Jimmy Choos? See, on TV and in the movies, this whole I-see-dead-people thing looks like a pretty glamorous gig. In real life . . . well, okay, I admit it, in real life, I'd met ghosts I liked and even one I'd fallen in love with. Then again, there was the one who'd tried to steal my body. Her, I still haven't forgiven. In terms of weighing the positive against the negative, I guess I was lucky; I'd run into more good ghosts than bad. But that doesn't make my walk on the not-so-quiet side of death any easier. Ghosts with mysteries are ghosts who get me embroiled in murders, kidnapping, and the like, and honestly, at that moment, I didn't want to take the chance of encountering any of them. I simply didn't have time. Not when the people we hoped to schmooze that night to contribute to the cemetery's coffers were waiting back at the Garfield memorial to be charmed by the likes of little ol' me.

I hotfooted it down the hallway to Ella's old—now my new—office and unlocked the door. This office was slightly larger than the one I'd occupied (notice I did not say worked in) when I was the cemetery's one and only tour guide and for that, at least, I was grateful, even if I wasn't all that crazy about having added a whole bunch of responsibilities to my job description.

Tours. Yeah, I still did them. Along with the monthly newsletter, public relations, press liaison, and oh yeah, the Garden View Speakers' Bureau, if I ever had a moment's peace and could actually get to it.

"No time to worry about any of it," I reminded myself, shooting past my desk. "No time for anything but newsletters." That advice actually might have been easier to follow if there weren't two huge vases of flowers on my desk. The pink and white roses along with the tasteful card wishing me luck that night were from Quinn Harrison, the Cleveland homicide detective I'd once thought was the man of my dreams. That fairy tale went up in smoke the day I confessed that I talked to the dead and he dumped me.

So why the flowers?

Well, Quinn was back in my life. Sort of. Ever since he'd had his own little brush with the Other Side a few months earlier, we'd been reconnecting (in a nonphysical sort of way). One of these days if he ever finally opened up about what happened to him the night he got shot, and how he was a ghost for a few minutes and showed up in my apartment to provide me with a vital clue to the case he was investigating, we might actually move what was left of our relationship off dead center.

Dead center.

Don't think I didn't recognize the irony.

My sigh rippled the silence of the office.

Then . . . another sigh was only appropriate . . . there was Jesse Alvarez.

My gaze swung to the vase on the other side of the desk. It was a wild concoction of sunset-colored flowers studded with curlicues of ribbon in greens and purples and golds that burst throughout the arrangement like fireworks. Kind of like I'd smashed my way into the Pueblo Indian world Jesse occupied, and he'd pounded past my defenses—and into my bed.

I'd met Jesse on a ghost-related trip to New Mexico

that summer and again, I'd been fooled. See, when I met him, I thought my happily ever after had stepped out of the dry desert air and straight into my heart. But after my case was wrapped up and I asked Jesse to come back to Cleveland with me . . .

Well, there's no use rehashing what I didn't want to hash in the first place. Let's just say things didn't work. The good news? At least thinking about it didn't hurt as much now as it had when it all first went down, which meant that when the flowers from Jesse arrived and all the card said was *Good luck with the new job* instead of *I miss you, Pepper. Give me another chance*, it didn't sting. At least not much.

But then, I'd hardly had the chance to brood, what with working fourteen hours a day to get ready for the sponsorship bash.

Yeah, the one I was missing because I was standing in my office thinking about my love life.

I shook myself out of my thoughts and whirled toward the table across from my desk where the newsletters were stacked. I actually might have gotten over there without incident if I hadn't stepped into a puddle in the middle of the floor.

My peep-toe slingbacks slipped out from under me and I stifled a screech and threw out an arm. Lucky for me, I caught on to the edge of my desk. It was the only thing that kept me from falling flat on my face.

When my breathing slowed to nearly normal, I checked out the dinner plate–sized puddle on my floor.

No drips coming from the ceiling. No water flowing from the vases on my desk.

And really, did I care where the water came from? I reached across my desk for the fast-food napkins I'd picked up that day with the lunch I never had time to eat, mopped up the puddle, and tossed the napkins in the trash.

While I was at it, I figured I might as well take a moment to refresh my lipstick and check my hair, so I took care of that, too. Finished, feeling refreshed and looking fabulous, I already had the newsletters in hand when I stepped toward the door—

And nearly slipped again thanks to another puddle on the floor.

My eyes narrowed, I shot a look around the office. Sure, it was bigger than my old digs, but there was no place for anyone to hide. "Nobody here," I told myself. "No leaky pipes. No ghost cats peeing on my floor." Just to make sure, I looked behind the door and under my desk.

No nothing.

Time for an executive decision, and mine was that the puddle wasn't hurting anything but the old green linoleum. By the next morning it would be evaporated, and I wouldn't have to go searching for paper towels.

I locked up my office and the administration building and started back to the reception the way I came, on the road lined by hundred-year-old trees and streaked with the long shadows thrown by the monuments on my right and the setting sun beyond. I was just about to turn to make my final approach toward the memorial when a flash of color caught my eye.

Red and blue.

That was my first impression.

11

Casey Daniels

A man in a baggy, brighter-than-navy-blue suit, holding a bouquet of red roses.

Don't get the wrong idea, it's not like I'm a sucker for schmaltz. I didn't stop and get out of the car because the sight of the man looking wistfully at one of the grave markers tugged at my heartstrings. I am way more of a realist than that. What I did know was that if he was supposed to be at the reception, he was headed in the wrong direction. And if he was here just to visit a departed loved one . . . well, the cemetery gates were about to be locked and would remain that way until the end of the party. If he was going to get out of Garden View before dark, he'd have to do it fast.

By the time I caught up with the man, I was breathing hard. High heels. Lumpy ground. Newsletters to deliver. I think it was safe to say he didn't notice I was in a hurry. His head bowed, the man concentrated on a single pink granite gravestone and the information carved into it: *Gladys Moritz, 1920–1993.*

"Excuse me," I said, and when he never moved I figured he didn't hear me so I tried again, a little louder this time. "Excuse me, the cemetery is closing. If you stay here too long—"

"Not to worry." The man's words escaped on the end of a sigh. His head was bowed and his shoulders were stooped. His gaze stayed on the grave, but from his profile, I could see that his dark hair was touched with just a sprinkling of gray. He had chiseled features that included a strong, square jaw and a straight nose. "I'm headed over to the reception. I just wanted to stop here for a moment. When I come to Garden View, I always visit her."

One of our guests, and I knew better than to rush him. People who feel hurried are not likely to pull out their checkbooks at the end of the evening.

I stepped closer to the neatly tended grave. "Was Gladys a relative of yours?" I asked.

"Gladys?" There was a certain wistfulness in his voice I found intriguing, and I watched as he bent and laid the bouquet of flowers on the grave. "Never met her. But you know, they say Gladys was the woman who—"

Finished with the flowers, he stood and for the first time, he glanced my way, and his voice caught over a breath of astonishment. "Lana?"

The sun shone from directly over my right shoulder so I guess I could forgive him for mistaking mc for someone else. "Not Lana. I'm Pepper." I stuck out my hand. "Pepper Martin. I'm community relations manager here at Garden View."

"How silly of me!" When he reached out a hand, the sun glanced off the lenses of his tortoiseshell-rimmed glasses. His smile was both apologetic and friendly, his voice was airy. "It was the red hair, of course. For just that one instant, I thought—" Whatever it was, he shook the thought away. "I'm being rude. It's very nice to meet you, Pepper. I'm Milo Blackburne."

I might be overworked and overstressed, but that didn't mean I wasn't paying attention to the night's guest list. When it came to philanthropists we were doing our darnedest to court, Milo Blackburne was at the top of our list.

And I'd just been handed an engraved invitation to bring him into the Garden View patron fold.

I looked at the bloodred roses on the headstone and put

my best community relations manager foot forward. "You were telling me about Gladys."

"Gladys? Yes, of course." He gave his shoulders a little shake. "There's a lot of history in Cleveland," he said. "But then, you work here at Garden View. You surely know that."

True, though this wasn't the time to point out that I really didn't much care. Up close and personal time with Blackburne, that's what mattered. When Ella heard about this, she'd be so jazzed, she'd dance right out of her sensible shoes!

"Gladys Moritz played a part in a very important piece of that history," Blackburne said. "But then, you probably know that, too. Community relations manager, did you say? I'll bet you've brought people here to her grave on tours."

I hated to confess I hadn't, but lucky for me (and those dreams of dollar signs I saw dancing in my head), Blackburne didn't hold it against me. In fact, he laughed. "Well, I suppose there are those who wouldn't agree with my take on history. But Gladys here . . ." He leaned nearer, not so much as if he was sharing a secret as that he was so excited to be telling me the story, he could hardly contain himself. "She was the original model. You know, for Lois Lane."

I thought I was pretty good at covering up for the things I didn't know, but this time, I wasn't fast enough.

Blackburne stepped back and his glasses flashed at me with each unhappy shake of his head. "Lois Lane? You know, Superman's—"

"Girlfriend! Yes, of course." I fast-forwarded through

all I knew of Cleveland history. It didn't take long. "Superman was created here in Cleveland back in the 1930s."

"That's right." Apparently, Blackburne forgave my momentary lapse. His smile was as bright as the glare off his glasses. "By two teenagers named Jerry Siegel and Joe Shuster. Since then, people have said that Joanne, the woman who was eventually Siegel's wife, was the model for Lois. But I have my own theory. I've done my research."

He paused here in a way that made me think I should be impressed by this. Truth be told, I was. Research and I did not get along.

"Gladys lived in the same neighborhood as Siegel and Shuster," Blackburne said. "They all went to the same school. One of these days, perhaps you'll allow me to show you some photos of her as a young woman. Then you'll see what I see—an amazing resemblance between her and the Lois of the original stories. I will admit, I have always had something of a soft spot in my heart for Lois. Until . . ." It must have been a trick of the sunlight; I could have sworn Blackburne's cheeks darkened. "Until today, that is."

I wasn't sure what he was getting at. Or was I? Did I just not want to think about it? That might explain why when he let his gaze slide from the top of my head to my shoes and all the way up again, I pretended not to notice.

A second later, I decided I was reading too much into the look. Of course Blackburne was impressed by what he saw, but not in a creepy sort of way. If he was, he wouldn't have bowed from the waist, his smile sheepish. "I'm sorry. I'm boring you to tears with all this talk of Superman. I often have to remind myself that not everyone shares my interest in the subject and Superman's connection to Cleveland. Needless to say, I'm something of a fan."

This, I understood. I had been known to get carried away a time or two myself. At least when it came to things like shoes and purses and the other necessities of life.

"It's nice that someone remembers her," I said, glancing down to where the flowers caressed Gladys's name. "I bet Gladys would like that."

"Oh, I don't know about that." Blackburne shrugged. "All this attention from a nobody like me."

"We both know that isn't true." I kept my voice light, the way I would have if the subject had come up back at the cocktail party. Milo Blackburne was one of the city's movers and shakers. Old money, and lots of it. Deep pockets when it came to things like the orchestra, hospitals, and a whole host of charitable causes. I knew if Ella had caught wind of his Gladys/Lois obsession before this, she would have been all over him (figuratively speaking, of course, since Ella is not that kind of girl) to get him on the list of cemetery patrons. The way it worked out, that task had fallen on my slim and perfectly tanned shoulders. Since Ella had had enough faith in my abilities to not only call me back from what I thought was going to be a permanent layoff but to promote me, too, the least I could do was make the most of the situation.

I offered Blackburne a ride back to the reception and as we walked over to my car, I scrambled to make the sort of small talk a man like him might appreciate. "You're doing something special. I mean, for Gladys. There aren't many people who would bring flowers to a woman they never met."

Big points for me; the corners of his mouth twitched into a smile. "I like to think so. You know, you're going to think it's crazy for me to even say it, but I like to think that the dead have a kind of grapevine. That they talk to each other. You know, about people who were kind to them in this life, and the ones who remember them now that they're gone, too."

He had no idea how true that was!

We kept up that sort of chatter all the way back to the memorial, and when I walked back into the reception and I introduced Ella to Milo Blackburne, she just about fainted from excitement. I signaled her to play it cool and excused myself so that I could put the newsletters where the newsletters should have been all along.

After that . . .

Well, I quickly learned that at events such as these, things are not easy for a community relations manager. Schmoozing is a required skill, and I schmoozed for all I was worth. Lucky for me, Milo Blackburne knew everyone in sight. Mover and shaker, remember, and when I ran into him a time or two (or three) at the reception, he was more than willing to introduce me to the other members of the country club set and tell them what a worthy cause Garden View was and how he was planning on donating, and donating big.

After that, was there any way I could say no when he came over to say good night and asked if I'd have lunch with him sometime soon?

More money than Bill Gates, and Blackburne was still the shy, retiring type. He looked at his Italian leather wingtips before he dared to glance up at me again. "I don't mean to sound too personal," he said. "I hope you understand. I just thought we could meet somewhere casual. The Ritz, perhaps. And talk about my donation to the cemetery."

See what I mean about not being able to say no?

We set a date for the following Wednesday and when Blackburne left, I turned and nearly ran right into Ella, who was glowing like a Christmas tree.

"What?" I asked her.

"He likes you," she purred.

"I don't want him to like me. I only want him to contribute to the cemetery."

"Of course." Ella's cheeks were a shade of pink that didn't go with her tropical outfit. She hid a smile. "But the fact that he likes you—"

"Is completely irrelevant. He's not exactly my type."

"Rich isn't your type?"

I did not dignify this question with an answer. Instead, I bustled around, helping the caterer with cleanup, saying good night to the prima donna harpist, and collecting the issues of the newsletters that hadn't been picked up. I was just stashing them in my car when a big, shiny black Jag rolled by and Milo Blackburne waved.

And yes, I was busy, and tired, to boot.

That must have been why I could have sworn I heard him call out, "Good night, Lana."

2

There are still times when I catch a glimpse of Quinn and my whole body sizzles as if I've touched a power line.

This was not one of them.

Yeah, even through bleary eyes I could see that he looked great standing there near the door to my apartment building. Dark suit. Blinding shirt. Killer tie.

But it was late, and I was dog-tired.

Then again, if he suggested a martini at one of the nearby cafes, I just might perk up.

"You're not going to believe it." Quinn pushed off from the wall where he was leaning and he was talking even before I was out of my car. "I tried calling to tell you, but you didn't answer your phone."

So much for the obvious signals sent by a little black dress and a sparkly evening bag. Not to mention the dark smudges of exhaustion I feared might be under my eyes.

I unlocked the door to the lobby and pushed it open. "I was a little busy."

"But I called, and you didn't answer your phone."

I got my mail out of the box just inside the door and turned toward the stairs. "Busy," was all I said.

Something told me Quinn would have taken the steps two at a time if I wasn't dragging up them in front of him. The way it was, he was so close behind me, his breath brushed my neck when he asked, "Too busy to talk? To me?"

By the time I got up the energy to actually glance over my shoulder at him, we were at the second-floor landing. "Sponsorship reception."

"Oh yeah. That. I—"

"Forgot?" If I'd been with anyone else, I might have gone for a withering look here. There was no use wasting the effort on Quinn. He wouldn't notice, anyway, and even if he did, he is not the withering type. "You sent flowers."

"I did, and you know I meant it when I wished you good luck with the evening. But that was before—"

"Before you forgot I just got my job back, and a huge promotion, too." I unlocked the door to my apartment. "And that I was in charge of the biggest cemetery event of the year even though I've only had my job for a few weeks. And—" When it looked as if he might try to say something, I stopped him cold. "That I've been working like mad to make sure everything went off without a hitch."

"I didn't forget." When he pushed open the door, he let me step through first. "I just—"

"Forgot." I turned on a light and tossed my keys on the table near the door. "It was kind of a big deal."

"And I'll bet you did a great job."

I set my purse next to my keys, the better to fold my arms over my chest. "I'll bet you don't really care. If you did, you wouldn't have forgotten."

"You know that's not true. It's just that—"

"What?" I pinned him with a laser look. "It's just that it doesn't matter that I might have pulled off the biggest coup in Garden View Cemetery history? And maybe roped in the biggest donor around? All because I was able to make the most of a chance meeting?"

"Really?" There was a momentary flash of admiration in those impossibly green eyes of his, otherwise I would have taken the comment personally, and not well.

"Really." I headed into the dining room and from there, to the kitchen for a bottle of water. "None other than Milo Blackburne," I called out so he could hear me. "Big bucks, and I charmed the socks off him."

"I don't doubt it for a moment."

Good thing I had my head in the fridge when he said that. Otherwise, I might have seen the look I knew went along with that last comment. Believe me, I knew it well. Hotter than lava and just as deadly. See, Quinn didn't get it. He thought that just being his old sexy self was enough to get things back to the way they were when we slept together on a regular—and very satisfying—basis. Oh yeah, typical guy. He was completely missing what I'd figured out since then—it wasn't about the sex, it was about the relationship. And a relationship with a guy who's been dead and refuses to talk about it . . . well, that doesn't say much about trust and sharing and all those other important things a relationship should be based on, does it?

It was no wonder I'd fallen into Jesse's arms without a moment's hesitation. Jesse accepted me for who I was, ghosts and all.

While I was in the kitchen, I'd grabbed a bottle of water for Quinn, too, and back in the dining room, I shoved it at him and kept walking. I plunked down on the couch, kicked off my shoes, and after a long, cool drink, tilted back my head and closed my eyes.

"They put me on desk duty."

I knew I hadn't fallen asleep, but I must have been in some la-la land just next door to dreaming because I sat up, startled, and looked at Quinn, who was standing in the doorway between the living room and dining room. "What did you say?" I asked him.

"They put me on desk duty." He marched into the living room and sat in the chair across from me. "I went back to work today and—"

"They gave you a desk job?" This was crazy talk. Quinn was hard-charging, smart, and successful in his job as a homicide detective. Okay, I was biased, but when it came to Cleveland's finest, I considered him at the top of the list. He'd just gone through months of grueling rehab, and he'd finally been cleared to return to work. They wouldn't have done all that and then saddle him with—

"A desk job? Are you sure?"

He hadn't opened his bottle of water. He set it down on the coffee table. "I got down to headquarters this morning and was told to get right back in the car and report to the Second District."

"A neighborhood station?" The fact that he'd forgotten all about the sponsorship event suddenly made sense, and I felt like a moron for not picking up on his mood sooner. "After you took a bullet in the line of duty?"

He got up and paced to the far side of the living room. "Kind of what I was thinking," he said, and since Quinn is not usually into sarcasm, his words were all the more acid. "My captain told me they wanted to make sure I was one hundred percent before they gave me back my old job. One hundred percent! Hah!" He held out his arms at his sides as a way of telling the world to take a look and dare to tell him he wasn't in perfect shape.

He was. Perfect. Trust me, I knew.

"And they've assigned me to the Community Services Unit. You know, as a district liaison."

I didn't need him to tell me that stung. I could see it in his eyes. I leaned forward. "You mean like you're supposed to go to schools and tell kids they shouldn't do drugs?"

"And work with school crossing guards, and hold meetings to listen to neighborhood complaints." Too antsy to keep still, he crossed the room and plopped back down. "My first duty assignment? They've got me acting as the contact between the police and some convention that's coming to town and setting up shop at a hotel not far from the station." He folded his arms over his chipped-from-granite chest. "I've got half a mind to quit."

"You wouldn't. You couldn't. You don't know how to

be anything but a cop. It's in your blood. Maybe if you just wait—"

"For what? The doctors have cleared me. They say I'm as good as new. I'm going to get lost out there in the boonies and never make my way back to Homicide."

"You don't really believe that." I'm not very good at rah-rah cheerleading, which might explain why the words were encouraging enough, but even I didn't sound like I believed them. "They'd be nuts to lose you in Homicide." This I did believe, so it wasn't hard for the statement to pack a punch. "You're good at what you do. Better than good. Besides, you're bound to have people who will go to bat for you downtown. When word gets out that they've banished you—"

"Yeah. Banished. That's exactly what it feels like." For a few, uncomfortable minutes, we stared across the room at each other, me, trying to come up with the words to take away some of the hurt and him, too angry to listen even if I could find them.

"Maybe you're right." The words escaped him on the end of a sigh. "There are a couple of guys who I know will put in a good word for me. Until then . . ." He stood. "I've ruined your evening, and I didn't mean to. I'll just put this away." He grabbed the water bottle. "And I'll get out of your hair."

He walked out of the room and a few seconds later, I heard the fridge open and close.

"Hey!" He paused on the way back and poked a thumb over his shoulder. "Did you know there's a big puddle on your dining room floor?"

Do I need to say how this bit of news made me grumble?

I dragged myself off the couch and went to check it out.

It was a puddle, all right. Just like the puddles I'd found in my office earlier that evening.

"I'll clean it up," I told Quinn, even though he hadn't made a move to beat me to the task. I went into the kitchen for paper towels and when I came back, Quinn wasn't alone.

"What?" He looked from me to the puddle and back again. "Why is your mouth hanging open? It's just a puddle."

"A puddle and a ghost." I looked over the guy standing not three feet to Quinn's right. He was sixty, maybe. Short-cropped hair, khakis, golf shirt. Not as tall as Quinn, but his chest was broader. Like he worked out with weights. His face . . .

I hadn't turned on a light in there, and I leaned forward for a better look, gasped, and jumped back. Hoping the shadows were playing tricks on my eyes, I flicked on the light above the dining room table and then was sorry I had. The blood drained from my face.

Above the piece of silver duct tape slapped over his mouth, one of the ghost's eyes was swollen and bloody. His jaw looked like he'd shaved with a cheese grater, and there was a rusty streak on his shirt that was particularly gruesome against the yellow cotton. His hands were lashed behind his back with one of those big plastic ties, and his legs . . .

I gulped.

The ghosts legs were bound up in heavy rope, one end tied in a sturdy knot just above his ankles and the other laced through the square opening of a cinder block he dragged behind him.

His clothes were soaked.

And the puddle on my floor was getting bigger and bigger.

"You're kidding me, right?" Quinn looked where I was looking, but obviously not at what I was looking at. That didn't stop him from taking a step to his left. "What's this ghost doing, watering his ghostly garden or something?"

"Or something." I dared a step closer to the horrible apparition, unable to look away. "You don't see him?"

The noise Quinn made wasn't exactly a tsk. That would have been too polite. "What, you think that I've suddenly got an inside track on the woo-woo just because I was dead myself for a while?"

Pikestaffed, I pivoted toward him. "What did you say?"

Quinn's shoulders shot back. "Nothing."

"You said you were dead. You finally admitted it."

His chin came up. "Now you're having auditory hallucinations as well as visual ones. I never said that."

"And you're trying to rewrite history. I know what I heard. I know what you said."

"I said—"

"That you were dead for a while. Your exact words."

When he shook his head, Quinn's inky hair glimmered in the overhead light. "You obviously heard me wrong."

"I did not. You said—"

"That you're talking crazy. There's no ghost here with us. And even if there was . . . even if there was such a thing to begin with . . . you couldn't see it."

"And you—" I pointed a finger at Quinn. "You're trying

to change the subject. And I'm not going to let you. It's about time you admitted it. You were dead. You were a ghost. When you were, I saw you and I talked to you. Right here in this apartment. You need to come clean about those couple minutes, Quinn, or—"

"Hmhm Mmm. Mmmmnm."

The words—if they could be called words—came out of the ghost and I swung his way.

"What did you say?" I asked.

Quinn's mouth thinned. "I said—"

I put out a hand to shush him. "I wasn't talking to you. I was talking to him." I pointed toward the ghost and the puddle. "He said something."

"Hmhm Mmm. Mmmmnm," the ghost repeated.

"Only I can't understand him," I said, for Quinn's benefit as well as for the ghost's since he kept mumbling whatever it was he was mumbling and he needed to realize it was getting us nowhere.

Quinn took another look at the blank space next to him. "I don't see anything."

I tossed my head. "Of course you don't see anything. You're not the one who sees dead people. I'm the one who sees dead people. Although since you were dead for a while . . ." This was a new idea and I cocked my head, considering it. "Maybe if you tried," I suggested to Quinn. "You know, if you sort of thought back to what it was like when you were a ghost and how it felt. You might be able to connect with the Other Side and see what I see."

"Only there's nothing to see." I think he actually believed this, but he took another step back, anyway. "Why is the puddle getting bigger?"

"The ghost is . . ." I did my best to demonstrate, fluttering my fingers in an "Itsy Bitsy Spider" sort of way. "His clothes are wet. They're dripping. And you know, he must have been at Garden View today. There were puddles there, too."

The ghost nodded.

"Yeah," I said, interpreting. "The ghost says I'm right. He was the one who left the puddles in my office this evening."

"Right." Correct word. Not so much a correct look from Quinn, which was more like mouth twisted and eyes screwed up with disbelief. "What else does the ghost have to say?"

"Hmhm Mmm. Mmmmnm."

"He can't exactly say anything. I mean, he's trying. But . . ." Demonstrating, I patted my hands against my mouth. "He's got a piece of duct tape over his mouth. He's trying to talk, but I can't understand anything he's saying."

"Hmhm Mmm. Mmmmnm," the ghost said, confirming my statement.

"Duct tape." Obviously, the comment came from Quinn. I mean, what with the ghost only being able to mumble and all. "Who dies with a piece of duct tape over their mouths?"

"Well, obviously, this guy." I pointed toward the ghost again before I realized I was really wasting my time and energy and brought my hand back to my side. "His hands are tied, too. And there's this rope around his legs that's attached to a big block. Ohmygosh!" The thought hit and so much for keeping my hands at my sides; I clutched them to my throat in a feeble effort to contain the bile that rose there. "He was murdered. Drowned!"

The ghost nodded.

"He says he was," I told Quinn. "Well, he nodded when I said he was. That explains why he doesn't look like the other ghosts have always looked."

Quinn's eyebrows did a slow slide upward. "And that is . . . ?"

"You know, like they must have looked when they were laid out at the funeral home. All clean and well dressed. This guy must have been drowned and I'll bet his body is still in the water someplace. That explains the puddles, right?" I looked at the ghost, who nodded to confirm my theory.

"And that explains why he looks the way he does, too. Like he got worked over before he died."

Nod. Nod.

"And dumped in the water."

Nod.

"That's just awful." I am not usually the emotional type. I mean, unless there's something worthwhile to get all emotional about. But the thought of the horrifying way the man died and the fear that must have gripped him when he hit that water . . .

I coughed away the knot in my throat at the same time Quinn asked, "So what does this ghost want?"

I thought I knew the answer, but I put a hold on considering it. At least until I dealt with the more pressing issue.

"You're asking me about the ghost," I said to Quinn. Ms. Obvious, yes, I know, but something told me it wouldn't hurt to point it out to him. He was a man, after all. And hardheaded went along with the hard-charging. "So you must believe I'm really talking to a ghost."

His shoulders shot back another fraction of an inch. "I never said that."

This time, he was actually right. But . . .

"You didn't have to," I pointed out. "You wouldn't have asked me what the ghost wanted if you didn't think I was talking to a ghost. Therefore—"

"Therefore, nothing. I'm just . . ." Quinn glanced away. "I'm just making conversation. Just being polite."

"Since when are you worried about being polite?"

"Hmhm Mmm. Mmmmnm." Apparently, the ghost was not a patient man. He hopped forward (cinder block, remember) and poked his head in Quinn's direction. "Hmhm Mmm. Mmmmnm."

"I think he's trying to say something about you," I told Quinn. "Maybe he just wants to remind you that you said you were dead. You know, because he heard you say it, too."

"That's it!" Quinn whirled around and headed for the door, sidestepping the puddle on the way. Call me perceptive, but I noticed the little shiver that crawled along his shoulders when he walked by the ghost.

"Chilly?" I asked him.

He was already at my front door. "Just a draft."

"Or a ghost. You know, like the kind of ghost you were when you—"

"There's really no talking to you when you get this way." He opened the door and stepped out into the hallway. "I'll give you a call."

I tried for some really good comeback, but before I could come up with one, Quinn was gone.

When I walked back into the dining room, the ghost was, too.

Fine by me. Two annoying men out of my life. At least for now.

And didn't it figure, they left me with a puddle to clean up.

3

After all these years, I know how ghosts think. It goes something like this:

Pepper Martin.

Private investigator for the dead.

Need her.

Find her.

Bug the heck out of her—and threaten to haunt her forever—until she agrees to help.

Was it any wonder that I arrived at the office the next morning fully expecting to find the drippy ghost in there waiting for me?

Turns out I was right. Sort of. Sure enough, there was a ghost behind my desk.

It just wasn't the ghost I was expecting.

"About time you showed up, sister." This ghost was short, square, and puffing on a fat cigar. He was wearing a gray double-breasted suit with wide pinstripes and huge shoulders, and he had a hat jammed way back on his head. While I was still trying to process who he was and why his pudgy ectoplasm was in my desk chair, he pointed at a paper on my desk.

"We gotta talk," he said. "Don'cha know anything about a lead?"

I hadn't quite recovered from the exhaustion that was the sponsorship party, not to mention my encounter with the wet ghost and my head-to-head with Quinn. I went over to my desk, deposited my purse in the bottom drawer, and stepped back, fists on hips of the black pants I was wearing along with a sweet little schoolboy blazer in a mossy green that looked especially good with my red hair.

"I know about leave," I said, emphasizing that last word in hopes that he'd get the message. When he didn't, I rolled my eyes. "All right, get it over with. What do you want?"

"Want? Me?" He took the cigar out of his mouth, studied the mushy end of it, then stuck it right back where it came from in the first place. "I don't want nothin', sister. You're the one who should want somethin'."

"Like a little peace and quiet?" No way he was moving, so I went around to the other side of the desk and sat in my own guest chair. "Or to be left alone so I can actually try and get some work done?"

"Work. Exactly." Again, the cigar came out of his mouth. This time, he used it to point at that paper on my desk. Gray ash floated down like snow and vanished into nothingness before it landed. "I been lookin' at your work. Don't they teach you kids nothin' these days?"

I'm not very good at guessing games, so I leaned forward to see what he was looking at. It was the latest edition of my newsletter, the one I'd taken to the cocktail party the night before. There was only one question appropriate to the occasion. "So?"

"That's all you got to say for yourself?" The ghost hauled himself out of my chair, and I saw that he was just about as round as he was tall. "You need some passion in your writin', kid. Some oomph. You know what I mean? How you gonna get anybody to read this rag of yours if alls you talk about is humdrum, ho-hum hooey? What's sensational is what sells newspapers!"

Far be it from me to take my work personally. At least my work at Garden View. But hey, I'd spent a lot of time on that newsletter. And a lot of effort, too, to get it written and printed in time for the cocktail party. I couldn't help but feel the teensiest bit defensive.

"First of all, it's not a newspaper, it's a newsletter," I pointed out. "And second, I'm not selling it, I'm giving it away. To anyone who visits the cemetery and wants one. Or anybody who calls and asks for one. Those people aren't looking for sensational. They just want information. You know, about when we're open and what there is to see here and—"

"You've sure got a thing or two to learn." The ghost stalked around to the front of the desk. He smelled like stale cigars. My nose twitching, I leaned back in my chair.

"People always wants what's sensational," he said. "Murders. Robberies. Colorful characters. Affairs of the heart." His bushy eyebrows twitched. "They want the nitty-gritty, you know, the lowdown. The scoop! And you . . ." He pointed at me with that fat cigar and thank goodness those ashes disappeared right before they landed, otherwise they would have polka dotted my black pants and I would have been even unhappier than I already was. "You, sister, are the one that's gonna give it to 'em."

"But I don't want to give it to them. Don't you get it? I don't care."

"Not care? About gettin' the story?" His face went as white as a . . . well, I don't have to say it. "The news is the only thing there is worth caring about," he said. "Gettin' the story. Knowin' the facts. Diggin' deeper than anybody else for all the dirt."

"There is no dirt. Not in cemeteries." All right, even I realized how dumb that sounded. But not until I'd already said it. Rather than have this ghost point it out, I barreled right on. "In case you haven't noticed, the facts around here aren't all that interesting, anyway. Nothing ever happens at Garden View that anybody would go out of their way to read about." Not technically true since once upon a time, one of our volunteers had been murdered, a photographer had once been mugged, I'd body-snatched a famous Native American, and there had been any number of attempts on my life within the cemetery walls. I edited my last statement.

"Well, nothing happens around here that the cemetery would actually want anybody to find out about," I said. "I'm the community relations manager, remember. That means I have to make people think this is a great place to visit. That's why I . . ." I leaned over and poked a finger at my newsletter. "I have to stick to the facts."

"That's because there are facts"—another twitch of those so-needing-a-good-tweezing brows—"and there are facts. If you get my meaning."

I didn't.

With his cigar, the ghost waved away what was, apparently, my complete stupidity. "What I'm tellin' you, sister, is sometimes those facts are out in the open for you to see right away. And sometimes, they're a little more slippery. You gotta run and catch 'em. And then there's the times when you gotta make 'em up. But that's only when you got no other choice, you understand. Or when addin' a little . . . you know . . . color . . . when addin' a little color gives you better headlines than them other newspapers have. Headlines grab attention, kid, and attention grabs readers, and readers—"

"Grab advertising dollars." I wasn't jaded, just practical.

"Quit talkin' like a nincompoop! Advertisin', that's a problem for the boys upstairs. Down in the newsroom, alls we care about is readership. There's nothin' like the thought of people sittin' around their kitchen tables, readin' your story. Or picturin' 'em listenin' to some dope on the radio talk about the news and them thinkin', 'That's not the way it happened. That ain't the way Chet Houston wrote about it.'"

"Houston." The name was vaguely familiar and I shuffled through my mental Rolodex of Garden View's permanent residents to place it. "Chet Houston, as in the old-time Cleveland newspaper reporter?"

"Ain't you a perceptible one?" Chet laughed. He had a gap a mile wide between his two front teeth.

"I've taken people to your grave," I told him and

watched him puff with pride. "I remember the story. You were alive back in the thirties."

"Pretty and smart." He flicked ashes on the floor and one by one, they morphed into sparkly clouds, then burst like tiny fireworks. "Maybe you ain't a lost cause after all."

"I'm not a cause at all. I'm just trying to get to work. So why don't you . . ." I shooed him out of my way and went to sit down behind my desk. "If you could just go back to wherever it is you came from . . ."

"Well, that's just the problem, ain't it, sister?"

Here it comes.

The words echoed through my head and I knew what they meant.

I plunked my elbows on my desk, cradled my chin in my hands, and said, "All right. Get it over with. This is the part where you tell me what I have to do to help you move to the Other Side. Then I tell you I don't want to get involved. Then you tell me I have no choice because you need to right some wrong or whatever, and then I finally give in and take your case."

Chet had a pencil behind one ear and he grabbed it, scratched the side of his bulbous nose, then put it back. "You got me all wrong," he said. "I ain't askin' nothin' from you. Well, hardly nothin'. But I am offerin' to do you a big favor."

This was a new wrinkle on the ghostly visitor game, and I sat up and, yes, my look was a little dubious. Like anyone could blame me? "What do you have in mind?" I asked him.

"Well, that newsletter of yours for one thing." Chet

looked to where the newsletter sat on my desk and shook his head slowly. "It could be really good. You know what I mean? It could grab readers by the throat and drag them in. If . . ." He hauled in a mouthful of smoke, then let out a perfectly formed ring. "If you'd let me write it for you."

Did I say new? This wasn't just new, it was monumental.

Which is exactly why every skeptical cell in my body started to tingle.

"You're willing to do my work for me? And write the newsletter?" That little warm curl I felt around my heart was something very much like hope, and I dared not get too attached to it. No doubt, there was a catch. I'd bet anything I wasn't going to like it.

Chet crossed one stubby finger over his nonfunctioning heart. "Every issue," he said. "And I guarantee each and every one will be jam-packed with stories that will knock your readers dead."

"I think we've already got enough dead here to go around," I said, and when that didn't get a laugh out of him, I bagged the humor and went straight for the details. "Why?" I asked, leveling him with a look. "Why would you do that for me?"

His answer was simple enough. "Well, for one thing, your newsletter stinks. And for another . . . well . . ." Chet took off his hat. His head was as round as a tennis ball and he scraped one hand through the few strands of mousy brown hair he had left. "It's kind of boring. I mean, this being dead and all. If I could just get back into the game—"

"And write my newsletter for me?" I thought about the

dreary hours I'd spent cobbling together the latest issue of
the newsletter and about all the others I'd have to write in
the future. It took more self-control than I knew I had to
harness the smile that threatened to erupt, but I did it. See,
if I'd learned anything in my years as the world's only PI
to the dead, it was that ghosts are a cagey bunch. Oh, they
might be willing to help, all right. But they always want
something in return. I slid my gaze to Chet. "Why?" I
asked him. "What do you want?"

He shrugged. "Not much. Hardly nothin' at all. It
wouldn't take a dame with your smarts more than a few
minutes to arrange the whole thing."

"Which is . . . ?"

He pulled at the loose skin under his chin. "Just a new
headstone."

I guess my astonishment showed, because he rushed in
to explain.

"The one they gave me after I kicked the bucket . . . it's
just about the darned ugliest thing I ever seen. Angels.
Imagine puttin' angels on the headstone of a guy like me.
And flowers. Makes me want to puke every time I look at
it. My sister done it. I guess she was just tryin' to pick out
somethin' nice and respectful. You know, on account of
how people get all mushy when somebody dies."

"And you'd like something a little more appropriate."

Chet grinned and gave me a wink. "Like I said, smart
and pretty."

I looked from him to the newsletter, and oh boy, I was
tempted. But before I could agree to his plan, the door to
my office popped open and Ella breezed in.

"Oh my!" She waved one hand in front of her face. "It

smells like old cigars in here. Pepper, you haven't been smoking, have you?" She thought this was pretty funny so she laughed. "Ugh! You really need to open a window."

Ella marched across the office and she would have walked right through Chet Houston if he hadn't stepped aside. Apparently, he'd watched Ella at work before. He knew exactly what I knew: with Ella, there was no such thing as a quick conversation. When Ella threw open a window, Chet puffed away in a cloud of cigar smoke that whooshed out the open window and vanished.

"That's better." Still fanning for all she was worth, Ella plunked down in the guest chair I'd recently vacated. "You did a great job last night, Pepper."

Sure, Ella was cemetery geek number one, but she was also my boss and my friend. Her praise meant a lot to me, and I smiled.

"You are . . ." Ella's little cough had a nervous edge. "You are going to continue, aren't you?"

"With my job? I just got it back, Ella. I'm not going to—"

"Oh, that's not what I meant." Ella's apple cheeks were rosy. "I meant . . . well, you know. Milo Blackburne. You are going to keep that date with him next week, aren't you?"

So much for that smile. "It's not a date, it's lunch," I reminded her. "And it's not a friendly type lunch, it's a lunch to talk about his donation to the cemetery."

"Yes, of course." Ella smoothed a hand over her ankle-length black skirt and tugged at the lace-edged sleeves of her white blouse. "I completely understand. Of course I do, Pepper. It's just that—"

Just that, nothing, and I wasn't going to sit there and listen to it. I pinned her with a look. "Maybe you'd like to come along. You're the cemetery administrator. That would impress the hell out of Blackburne."

"No, I don't think so." That day, only Ella's earrings hinted at her sparkly side. They were pink rhinestones, and when she stood, they twitched and caught the light. "I wouldn't want to intrude and to . . . you know . . . distract Mr. Blackburne."

My sigh should have said it all. Just in case it didn't, I pointed out, "It's business, Ella."

"Yes, of course it is." Too bad she didn't look like she believed it. "But he's not a bad-looking man, and he's just about the right age for you. And you know, he's got money out the wazoo. Old Cleveland family. Very well respected. I hear he's got a huge house on the lake and—"

"Earth to Ella." I waved my hands to stop her before she could get carried away. Or maybe I should say more carried away. "I'm not interested in Blackburne. Not in that way, anyway."

"Of course not." Her smile was swift and sweet. "But I could tell he was interested in you. You know, *that* way."

I wanted to say *no duh*, but bit my tongue. When she gets like this, there's no use encouraging Ella.

"I know you're smart and professional, Pepper, and I'd never suggest that you would actually throw yourself at any man."

"But . . . ?"

"But . . ." Ella's smile dissolved into a grimace and she flopped back down in my guest chair. "Getting Milo Blackburne on our patron list would be . . . well, I won't mince words. It would be something of a feather in my cap, and you see, I sort of need that. After that whole austerity program we worked under earlier in the year, then finding out that our revenues would have been just fine if our last administrator wasn't cooking the books . . . well, you can understand, a lot of our long-time donors are nervous. The board is a little antsy, too. And it's not that I blame them or anything." Ella held up one hand as a way of signaling that really, she understood where they were coming from. "Of course, they're gun-shy. Of course, they want proof that things here can run smoothly."

It made sense, I just hadn't thought about it before, but . . .

I narrowed my eyes and gave Ella a careful look. No easy thing since I was suddenly trembling. "Are you telling me . . . You mean to say . . . Those idiots on the board are actually making you go through some sort of test run? Like you're in a probationary period or something? They're questioning whether or not you can do the job?"

"Now, Pepper . . ." Ella slipped into motherly mode. Raised eyebrows. Soft voice. That little flicker of sympathy in her eyes that warmed my heart at the same time it brought home the fact that she was way too kind and understanding for her own good. "Of course the board wants proof."

"From you?" I slapped a hand on my desk. "You've worked here practically forever. Nobody knows Garden View like you do. Every headstone, and every tree, and every statue and—"

"That doesn't mean I can run the place." Ella, the voice of reason.

"Yeah? Is that what those fools think? Then they've got their heads up their butts. They're missing out on the fact that you're also smart and organized and that everybody who works here loves you so you know they're going to work harder for you than they ever did for Jim. And the board should know that, too, and—"

"Thank you, Pepper." When she reached across the desk to pat my hand, Ella's eyes were misty. "I knew you'd understand." She lowered her voice. "Nobody else knows. About the ninety-day trial period, I mean. I didn't want anyone to worry, or to question my competence. Not that I care what they think of me personally!" The color in her cheeks got a little brighter. "But I don't want anyone to think less of Garden View or of our trustees and board members."

No, Ella wouldn't. That was the one thing about Ella. She was a geek, all right, a bighearted, dedicated, sincere, loyal geek.

A geek who kept her gaze on her round-toed black flats when she added, "So if there was any way you could actually work your magic and bring us Milo Blackburne as a patron and if you could make it happen within the next couple months . . ."

Bighearted, dedicated, sincere, and loyal, huh?

It looked like Ella could also be sneaky.

I sat back, my head cocked, the better to give her a look that told her I was onto her. "So you're willing to dangle me in front of Milo Blackburne like a fat worm on a hook. All so you can get him to donate to the cemetery."

Ella looked up at the ceiling. "I could never think of you as a fat worm," she said.

"You know there's a name for what you're doing," I reminded her.

She didn't dispute it.

In fact, all she did was stand up. "You'll do it?"

"I was going to even before I knew how stupid the board is."

Her smile blossomed.

"It's just lunch," I reminded her before her imagination could run away and take her common sense along with it. "A business lunch with a man I hardly know and who I am not in any way, shape, or form interested in."

"Yes, of course." Ella bustled over to that table where I'd had the newsletters stacked the night before. Some of the things she'd always kept in the office and had yet had time to move were stacked there, too. "I just came for my pictures," she said, gathering the framed photos of her three girls. She already had her hand on an arrangement of silk flowers that featured giant white daisies, pink carnations, and very bright blue snapdragons. "These flowers have always added just that right touch of color in here. If you wanted to keep them . . ."

I looked at the two giant vases of fresh flowers on my desk as a way to tell her I didn't.

"You might not always have handsome men sending you flowers. Then you'll be sorry." Ella's warning came along with a smile. She added the silk flowers to the pile she was carrying and headed for the door.

"Oh, I almost forgot." She turned back to me. "I didn't want to bother you with it, what with all of us being so busy getting ready for the sponsorship party and all. But we'll be meeting next week. You know, about department budgets for next year."

"Budgets?" The word was not in my vocabulary so it was no wonder it felt too big for my throat.

"Not to worry." She hugged the framed photos closer to her chest. "It's all a part of the community relations manager's responsibilities. You'll get the hang of it in no time."

"Get the hang of it? Like actually do the budget?"

She let out a silvery laugh, but even that wasn't enough to convince me. I needed clarity. Especially when it came to the *b* word.

"You don't actually expect me to play with numbers, do you?" I asked her.

"Oh, Pepper, you're so funny." Apparently I was, because she laughed again. "It's all a matter of looking at what your department spent last year, comparing it to what you anticipate spending next year, doing some tweaking, and . . . voila!"

"Voila." After she was gone, I echoed the word though without the note of triumph Ella had added to it. Then again, it was a little hard to sound upbeat when my stomach was doing flip-flops. "Budgets?" The word soured in my mouth. "They don't actually expect me to—"

"I might be able to help ya, sister." Along with the stale-peanut smell of old cigars, Chet Houston was back. He was standing on the other side of my desk and when he leaned nearer, his eyes twinkled. "See, I know this guy who knows numbers."

"A dead guy?" Yeah, a no-brainer, but like I said, clarity.

Chet nodded. "Albert's a little bored, too, ya see, and he's got this crazy woman buried right next to him. Some dame with a big, noisy family and she's been dead for years, but they still keep comin' to see her. Go figure. They do a lot of talkin' and a whole lot of cryin'. You know the types."

I did, though I couldn't imagine what I was supposed to do about it. "And Albert's looking for . . . ?"

"A little peace and quiet is all."

I doubted I could make that happen. Then again, if Albert was all he was cracked up to be . . .

"He's good with numbers?" I asked Chet.

A grin softened his pug-ugly face.

In that one instant, I made up my mind. Since ghosts are incorporeal and can't touch things, I'd need to get Chet a tape recorder so he could dictate the stories for the newsletter and I could enter them on the computer.

As for Albert . . .

"I'll need to check it out," I told Chet, leading the way to the door. "But if this guy's as good as you say he is . . ."

"God's honest truth! I seen him work wonders with numbers," Chet said. "And the crazy part is, it all makes sense to him."

Numbers and sense. Not a likely pairing of words, but I wasn't about to argue. Budgets, lunches with potential donors, no sign of the drippy ghost, and two new ghosts in my life and still, it was turning into a not-so-bad day. Suddenly, I had staff. Yes, they were dead, but a girl like me can't afford to be picky.

4

I should have saved the especially cute outfit for the next day because the next day, Quinn was taking me to lunch. That day—the day I met Chet and acquired my ghostly peeps—I spent most of my time slogging from one end of the cemetery to the other, which meant, obviously, that the cute pants and schoolboy blazer look was totally wasted on everyone but the dead.

The good news is that I didn't let the disappointment that comes along with a fashion letdown stop me. In fact, I was at my brilliant best that afternoon.

Chet's headstone, as it turned out, was as schmaltzy as he described it. Unfortunately, though it had been carved and put in place nearly eighty years earlier, it was also in perfectly good shape. Let's just hope no one saw me when I went into a nearby groundskeeping shed and borrowed a hammer so that I could do a little damage, write up a report about the vandalism I'd discovered, and order a new headstone sans angels and flowers.

As for Albert, the numbers man, his problem was a little easier to solve and didn't involve any malicious mischief and hardly any lying at all. Those noisy visitors he complained about were there when I arrived to check out Albert's grave, and the solution was clear to me the moment I heard them reminiscing about the dearly departed. That afternoon I put in a request to have a row of hedges planted between Albert and his popular neighbor. Sure, it was out of the realm of my responsibilities, but Ella's handwriting isn't all that hard to copy and Silverman is easy to spell.

Those two missions accomplished, I found one of those voice-activated tape recorders and got it set up for Chet. It would have been easier if he had been able to do his own typing, but a girl can't have everything.

That left me free to take care of work, which pretty much consisted of touching up my nails (vandalizing a headstone does nothing for a manicure) and figuring out what I was going to wear to the next day's lunch.

I probably shouldn't have bothered putting so much thought into it. When Quinn came to the cemetery to pick me up the next afternoon, I don't think he even noticed my slim black mini, white cami, or that mossy green schoolboy blazer I had slung over one arm. Yes, I know, it's a fashion faux pas to wear the same article of clothing two days in a row, but believe me, there was a method to my madness: (1) I left the blazer in my car and kept it there until Quinn pulled his unmarked police vehicle into the parking lot outside the administration building so really, no one at Garden View had an inkling that I might wear the jacket again, and (2) I might need it if the restaurant Quinn was taking me to was chilly.

I paused just outside the door of his car, the better to give him a chance to look me over, and when all he did was lean over to the passenger side of the car and shove open the door, I gave up with a sigh.

"Nice to see you, too," I said, getting into the car.

"I left my cell phone at the station," he grumbled.

"Nice to see you, too."

"I said I left . . . Oh." He wheeled out of the cemetery and glanced at me out of the corner of his eye. "I get it. Of course it's nice to see you. You know that. But I just realized I left my cell phone back at the station and I hate not having it."

"In case someone needs to call about a meeting with school crossing guards or something."

Another grumble from the driver's side of the car. "Not funny."

"Wasn't trying to be. Just pointing out that you probably haven't missed any important calls."

"Also not funny."

I wasn't sure where we were going to lunch, but I had suspected Little Italy. It is the closest place to Garden View for good food. Which is why I was surprised when Quinn didn't head that way. "You've got something else in mind."

"We'll get lunch. After I pick up my phone."

This, I could understand. At least to a point. I felt naked

without my cell, too. But there was something more to Quinn's bad mood. And it had nothing to do with school crossing guards.

Ghosts don't call me smart for nothing. I turned in my seat, the better to see his reaction when I said, "You're up to something. Otherwise you wouldn't be so pissed about your phone."

He slid me a look. "Maybe."

"Probably. And it has nothing to do with the job you're supposed to be working."

This time the grumble contained a couple words I will not report. "Community liaison. I was over at that hotel where the convention's going to be held. You know, the one I'm supposed to work on as a go-between for the police and the community. Can you believe it? It's a comic book convention!"

"Comic books? Like the Smurfs?"

"More like Batman. And the Avengers. And Superman."

Superman.

It wasn't the first time in the last few days that the superhero's name had come up in conversation. At the sponsorship cocktail party, Milo Blackburne had mentioned Superman. Superman and Lois Lane. "So what are you supposed to do with these comic book people?" I asked Quinn.

"Darned if I know. Make sure no one decides to put on a cape and tights and take a leap off the roof of the building, I guess."

"No doubt you'll handle that part just fine." I sat back and stretched out my legs, the better to look relaxed and catch him off guard when I added, "But you're doing something else, too."

It was midafternoon and traffic was heavy so I guess I could excuse Quinn for keeping his eyes on the road and not answering me right away. Then again, Quinn is the careful type. He thinks—twice—before he commits and gives too much away. We were blocks closer to downtown and the bridge that would take us across the Cuyahoga River to the west side of town, where Quinn's new station was located, when he said, "There was a murder a few months ago—"

"And you're investigating!" I slapped a hand against the fake leather seats. "I knew it."

"You don't know anything. Not for sure. Not officially. I didn't say I was looking into the murder. I only said there was one."

"Because you're not supposed to be investigating. You're supposed to be working with the comic book crowd."

"Will you quit reminding me!" Good thing we were at a red light because he plunked his head down on the steering wheel.

I waited until we were driving again before I asked, "So who got killed?"

"Plenty of people. It's a violent city."

I wished he wasn't concentrating on traffic, otherwise he would have noticed the acid look I shot his way. "Who got killed that you're not supposed to be looking into the murder but you are anyway?"

"If I was . . ." Another quick glance. "It happened a while ago, before I got shot."

"And ended up dead."

He ignored the comment. No big surprise there. "Small-time thief, guy named Danny Ackerman. He was known on the streets as Dingo."

The name—either name—didn't ring any bells.

"And we care about Dingo because . . ."

"Because back when he got himself shot in the head and his body was dumped in a landfill, I was working Homicide and Dingo was one of my cases."

"And you can't let it go."

"I shouldn't have to."

I agreed with him, so I didn't argue.

"So what have you found out?" I asked instead.

"Nothing much." We were at another red light, and Quinn drummed his fingers against the steering wheel. "Dingo was a nobody scumbag."

"But there's something about his case that interests you."

Another quick look, but then, Quinn was waiting to turn left so he had the time. "Has anybody ever told you you're too nosy?"

"Plenty of times. Mostly you."

"You're not going to tell me there's some ghostly connection and so you've got to find out all there is to know about Dingo, are you?"

"Hey, you're the one who brought up the ghosts." I shouldn't have had to point it out.

"So why do you care?" he asked.

I shrugged. "I don't. Not really. Except that you do."

The driver behind us beeped his horn and Quinn was forced to look away from me and get moving.

"If your bosses found out you were still working Dingo's case—"

"I'm not. Not technically."

"But you're nosing around."

"Maybe. A little."

"And if your bosses found out—"

"They'd remind me I have other things to do these days. Like work with school crossing guards and worry about comic book conventions."

"But you're not ready to let go of Dingo's case. And there has to be a reason. I mean, a reason more than that you're working on other things now and you're not happy about it."

We were through downtown, across the river, and into a working-class neighborhood where the houses were set one next to the other and trees shaded the streets, and Quinn passed up a car wash and pulled into the parking lot of a low-slung redbrick building. He parked the car, turned off the ignition, and turned in his seat.

"There's been some talk . . . about a cop named Jack Haggarty. Black Jack, that's what we all called him. There's a rumor that there might be some connection between him and Dingo's murder."

"Dirty cop, huh?"

Quinn slapped the steering wheel and, startled, I sat up like a shot.

"Not a chance," he growled.

"Sensitive subject."

"No, it's not. Sensitive subjects are only sensitive because the people looking at them can't be objective. And as always, I'm plenty objective." Quinn pulled in a long breath and let it out slowly, and I could just about see the debate going on behind that chiseled face of his. To tell or not to tell. That was the question. Lucky for me and the curiosity that made me feel like I was going to crawl out of my skin, he decided to fess up.

"Jack and I were partners once. A long time ago. When I first got onto the force. We worked a patrol car together over on the east side."

Somehow, I had always pictured Quinn the way he was now: sophisticated, well-dressed, superior detective. The thought of him in a blue patrolman's uniform . . .

"What are you smiling about?" he asked.

"I wasn't." As if to prove it, I wiped the smile away and promised myself that one of these days, I'd ask to see him in his uniform. I'd bet anything he was as cute as a button. "So you worked with Jack and you know he was on the up-and-up. I get it." I nodded. "So what does he have to do with Dingo's death? And why don't you just ask Jack about it?"

Quinn scraped a hand through his inky hair. "Believe me, I'd love to talk to Jack. But nobody's been able to get a hold of him. And nobody's seen him. Not since a couple days after Dingo's body was found. As for Jack's connection to the murder . . . there was some evidence . . ." A cop Quinn recognized walked out of the station and he lifted a hand in greeting.

I guess that was enough to remind him that he was sharing, maybe a little too much. Remember how I said that Quinn is careful? Well, the not sharing goes along with the careful. Or maybe it's the other way around. No matter. He changed the subject in a heartbeat.

"I'm going to run inside for my phone," he said, sliding out of the car. "I'll be right back."

I suppose if he had been, I would have stayed where I was. The way it was, Quinn was gone too long for it to qualify as *right back*. And I was hungry. Not to mention bored.

I sashayed into the station, told the sergeant behind the desk that I had an appointment to speak to Detective Harrison, and was ushered back into a dull bullpen area packed with gray metal desks. Quinn's was in the far corner, he was talking on the phone and as I made my way over there, I saw a number of raised eyebrows and heard a couple of mumbled comments. My response was a sparkling smile that didn't waver even once.

Not even when Quinn caught sight of me and rolled his eyes.

I sat down in the gray metal chair next to his desk and waited.

"I can stop by this afternoon." Quinn said this with another roll of the eyes that made me think maybe the first one might not have been meant for mc after all. "How long?" He looked at the clock on the wall. "Fifteen minutes or so. Yes, I'll find you. Ycah, see you then."

I smiled as sweetly as I could, considering that my stomach was growling. "Got a date?"

"Yeah, with a security guard over at the hotel where that convention is being set up. He says he's got something he needs to talk to me about."

"Does that mean we have to wait for lunch?"

"There's a vending machine out in the lobby."

Not the answer I was hoping for, but before I had a chance to point that out, a uniformed cop walked into the room. "Got another one," she said, waving something small and rigid in the air. "Another postcard from Jack Haggarty."

An hour earlier, I wouldn't have known or cared. Now, my ears pricked right up. So did Quinn's. In fact, he jumped out of his seat, closed in on the cop, and plucked the postcard out of her hands.

"Come on, Harrison, get over it!" one of the other detectives sitting nearby called out to Quinn. "Just because Haggarty's sending postcards doesn't mean he's not—"

I guess the cops in this new station already knew Quinn pretty well. One scathing look from him and the other detective shut right up.

When he sat back down, I leaned nearer to Quinn, careful to keep my voice down. "I thought you said nobody has talked to Jack Haggarty, not since a couple days after Dingo's murder."

"That's right. Nobody's talked to him. And he doesn't answer his phone when we try to call. That doesn't mean we haven't heard from him." Quinn looked over at the bulletin board on a nearby wall and I saw that there were three other postcards stuck onto it with pushpins. From this distance it was hard to tell exactly where they were from, but I thought I recognized scenes of Las Vegas, Seattle, and Chicago.

"This one's from New York," Quinn said, checking out the picture of the Statue of Liberty before he turned over the card and looked at the postmark and the cramped letters written in blue ink. "*Wish you were all here instead of working like dogs.*" He read the message with something very like acid in his voice. "Same as always. And just signed *Jack*. Same as always."

"So this Jack guy is somehow connected to a murder. Maybe. Then he disappears. And now he's sending post-cards from all around the country?" It was so weird, I had to try to talk it out, just to get it to make some kind of sense. "Why would he do that?"

"Because Haggarty's pulling our chains." The voice of the cop at the next desk startled me, and I jumped. I guess I hadn't been talking as quietly as I thought. The guy was middle aged and beefy, with short-cropped sandy hair, a square jaw, and the beady-eyed gaze of a Doberman. "He's practically daring us to prove he was involved in Ackerman's murder."

"Or he's doing exactly what he always promised he'd do." Quinn set the postcard down on his desk. "Jack always said that one day, he'd just walk away from the job. That he'd travel and finally get to enjoy life. Maybe he's just reminding us that while we're slaving away, he's getting to live his dream."

"Whatever." The cop at the next desk went back to reading a stack of reports.

This time I made sure my voice was even quieter. "Do you believe that? That he had something to do with Dingo's murder? You said there was evidence."

"And I'm sure not going to say any more. Not here." Quinn tucked his cell in one pocket, the postcard in another, and led the way out of the station.

Out in the car, I was finally able to give voice to the questions that had been bugging me. "Why do all those other cops think Haggarty was involved in the murder? And who's this guy we're going to see over at the hotel? And when . . ." Since this was the most important question of all, I paused to give it all the drama it deserved. "When are we going to get lunch?"

Like most cops, Quinn is logical and methodical. He answered my questions in order.

At least I think he did.

"Candy bars," he said. "Vincent. And eventually."

Yeah, that was supposed to satisfy me.

Turns out the hotel where the convention was set to begin in just another week's time wasn't all that far from the police station. That was bad news for me, because it didn't give me time to ask Quinn what the hell he was talking about. It was good news for him, because it didn't give me time to ask Quinn what the hell he was talking about.

Since he didn't tell me to stay in the car, I followed him into the hotel, one of those generic places concerned more with efficiency than style that are always built close to interstates. This one had a good-sized lobby with shiny floors the color of autumn leaves, a trickling fountain outside the bar, and tan couches scattered here and there where travelers waited for the airport shuttle, their suitcases on rolling carts nearby. Across from the front revolving door was a wide corridor and a sign that pointed to the ballroom. Even from where we stood near the registration desk, I could hear the sounds of sawing and hammering coming from that direction.

The girl behind the desk had a bright smile when she looked from me to Quinn. "Checking in?" she asked.

It was an all-too-obvious reminder that there was a time when there wouldn't have been any question about it. Quinn would have looked at me, I would have looked at him, and we would have scooped up the first available room and been in the sack together in record time. It said something about our relationship that these days, all he did was flash his badge.

"Detective Quinn Harrison," he said, oh so professional in what could have been a too-hot-to-handle personal situation. "I'm the department's liaison with the comic book convention. You have a security guard here, Vincent Bagaletti. Is he around?"

The girl was maybe nineteen and she either had never had to deal with cops before or she was just stunned by Quinn's gorgeousness. Her mouth hung open for a couple seconds before she shook herself back to reality and pointed down the corridor and toward the ballroom.

Vincent, as it turned out, wasn't much older than the girl behind the desk. He had spotty skin, hair that hung past his collar, and a silver stud in his left earlobe. His khaki-colored uniform shirt hung from scrawny shoulders and I guess Quinn had run into similar types before, because he didn't waste any time. He introduced himself and got right down to business.

"You said there was something you needed to talk to me about."

When Vincent gulped, his Adam's apple bobbed. He glanced over his shoulder to where a couple guys in jeans and flannel shirts were fitting together what looked to be some sort of painted backdrop of a city skyline. "Not here," he said. "They might hear."

Since it was hard to hear even my own voice over the construction noises that echoed off the crystal chandeliers and glossy wallpaper, it didn't seem likely. Still, I couldn't help but be intrigued. "Who?" I asked Vincent before Quinn could.

"We need to . . ." Vincent took another quick look around and even though none of the workers in the ballroom was paying the least bit of attention to us, he shuffled his black sneakers against the green-and-maroon plaid carpeting. "We can't talk here. We need to . . ." He never finished; he was too busy scrambling for the door.

Quinn and I followed and a minute later, we found ourselves out on the loading dock behind the hotel. There was a semi parked nearby, but no one was in it, and to our right and over by the corner of the building, a couple women in housekeeping uniforms were puffing on cigarettes and chatting in Spanish.

"Who was going to listen to what you had to say, Vincent?" This time, Quinn asked before I could. "And why would they care?"

"They always listen." Vincent's gaze darted from the door behind us to the far corners of the parking lot. "They keep an official record, you know. Of everything I say and do."

Quinn did not seem to think this was as interesting as I did. In fact, when he stepped back, I practically saw the starch go out of his white shirt. "They," was all he said.

Vincent nodded like a bobblehead on the dashboard of a car speeding over railroad tracks. Maybe I have a more trusting face than Quinn; when he lowered his voice, it was me Vincent looked at. The moment might have packed more drama if his breath hadn't smelled like Doritos. "The ninjas," he said.

"Great." Somehow, Quinn's grumble sounded almost

professional. "Then there's really nothing you need to talk to me about, is there Mr. Bagaletti? If that changes any-time soon . . ."

He'd already started to walk away when Vincent latched onto Quinn's arm.

So not a good idea, even in the best of circumstances. Coming on the heels of being shot dead the way it did, this sort of physical contact was bound to make Quinn testy.

But then, Vincent learned that quick enough when every muscle in Quinn's body tensed, he spun, grabbed the kid by the throat, and had him up against a wall before Vincent had a chance to catch his breath.

"I didn't . . . I couldn't . . ." Vincent went as pale as a ghost—and I should know, right?—and gurgled like a swimmer who's been under water too long. But then, Quinn's hand was a little tight around the kid's skinny neck. "I didn't mean . . ."

"No. Of course you didn't." Three cheers for Quinn; a couple seconds of staring into Vincent's eyes as a way of sending an unmistakable message, and he backed off and backed away, giving Vincent room to shake in his shoes. "You'd better be careful, or you're going to find yourself—"

"What Detective Harrison means to say . . ." Me, the great smoother-over. "Is that you caught him by surprise. I'm sure you didn't mean that, did you, Vincent? So why don't you just tell us why you called us here."

Yes, the *us* was stretching the truth a tad, but this was no time to explain about my personal stake in this interview—which was pretty much that I wanted to get it over with as quickly as possible so we could eat.

"It's . . . It's like I said, the ninjas. I heard them talking. And when the convention starts—"

Quinn's eyes sparked and when he took a step closer, Vincent folded himself against the wall. "What's going to happen when the convention starts?" he asked the kid.

Vincent ran his tongue over his lips. "I'm not supposed to know. I'm not supposed to tell. But I heard the voices. I heard them talking. The ninjas are going to break in. Through the morgue."

Predictably, after that, the interview wound down pretty quickly. Quinn held it together until we were all the way back to the car. Shaking his head, he unlocked the door. "The guy needs meds."

This was hard to dispute.

"He's seeing things. And hearing things." Quinn got in the driver's door and I opened the other. "I can't stand it when people make things up."

"Make things up?" I'd already slid into the car on the other side and I patted the empty seat between me and Quinn. "You mean like this?"

His jaw tensed. "Not you, too! You're as bad as Vincent. Wet ghosts and wet spots and—"

Because I knew he wouldn't do it on his own, I took Quinn's hand and pressed it to the empty seat between us.

"It's wet," he said.

"Yeah." I glanced into the backseat. It was empty. "Wet spot, but no wet ghost. I wonder what that means."

5

Thank goodness the drippy ghost didn't show up while we were in the car.

Fake leather upholstery, remember (standard in unmarked police cars), and so not good at absorbing moisture. If that soggy spirit had popped up in that seat between me and Quinn, my schoolboy blazer might have gotten soaked, along with the rest of me.

As it turned out, he never made his entrance until we were already at Heck's, one of the restaurants that's an institution in Cleveland, partly because it's been around for practically forever and mostly because the food is so good. We'd just been seated at one of the round bistro tables in the open, airy room in the back where dozens of hanging plants and pots of flowers caught the afternoon light and the terra-cotta-tile floor gleamed.

That's when I noticed the puddle on the floor near our table.

Quinn was reading the menu so I reached across the table and poked him.

"He's back," I said.

Since I was the one who was starving to death, Quinn shouldn't have been the one concentrating on the menu. "He who?"

"The ghost of course. Look."

He did, saw the puddle, and grimaced. "I thought this mojo of yours was some sort of magical, secret thing. Is it supposed to happen out in public?"

"So you finally believe me, huh?" I grinned and leaned forward so he couldn't escape my penetrating look—or my question. "You're willing to admit I have—"

"An overactive imagination." He flapped his menu shut and set it down on the table. "What are you ordering?"

"I haven't had a chance to even look at the menu yet. Ghost, remember."

"Puddle," he corrected me.

"Puddle." My arms crossed over my chest, I sat back. "But you know what that means. First the puddle, then the ghost. He's bound to show up sooner or later."

Turns out sooner was a little too soon. Because no sooner had Manny, our way-cute waiter, arrived to ask what we wanted to drink than the ghost was standing right next to him.

"Water," I said, pointing to the ever-growing puddle so that Quinn couldn't ignore it.

"With or without lemon?" Manny asked.

"No. I mean . . . I'll have iced tea."

"With or without lemon?" Manny asked.

I went with the lemon, waited while Quinn ordered the same, then when Manny left to get our drinks, I tipped my head to my left to where the ghost was waiting—and dripping.

"He's here now," I told Quinn. "Not just the puddle. All of him."

He glanced from the puddle on the floor to the row of windows set high up on the wall and beyond that to the ceiling. "Or the construction here is lousy, and the roof has a hole in it. It is a pretty old building."

A passing busboy caught sight of the puddle, grabbed a rag, and sopped up the water, shivering when he stood. Mumbling, "It's cold in here," he disappeared into the kitchen.

"Did you hear that?" I leaned my elbows on the table. "The kid said it was cold."

"It's not."

"Or it is. Because he felt the chill from the ghost."

"Or he's coming down with something and we better hope he doesn't touch our food."

I grumbled and plunked back in my chair. "You just won't stop being stubborn, will you? Why don't you just—"

Manny slipped up to our table and deposited our glasses of tea. "Ready to order?"

"Yes," Quinn said, at the same time I said, "No," offered Manny a sleek smile and told him to give us a couple more minutes.

"I thought you were hungry."

"I am," I told Quinn. I snapped open my menu. "If you'd quit interrupting me—"

"Which I'm not."

"Like right now." I gave him one telling glance and went back to studying the menu.

I was just reading the description of the chargrilled chicken breast (it came with spicy blue cheese sauce, crunchy potato wedges, and asparagus—yum) and my stomach was growling when—

Drip, drip, drip.

"Oh, come on!" I groaned.

From across the table, Quinn gave me a vacant look. "Come on where?"

"Not you. The ghost." I tipped my menu in Quinn's direction so he could see the spots of water on it. "He leaned over my shoulder when I was reading about the chicken with blue cheese sauce and—"

"She'll have the chicken with the blue cheese sauce." Quinn nabbed Manny just as he buzzed by. "I'll have the Cajun burger."

"Maybe I didn't want the chicken with blue cheese sauce," I pointed out at the same time Manny scooped up our menus and walked away.

"Sure you did. That explains how your menu got all wet. You were drooling on it."

Not so hilarious that it deserved such a big laugh from him.

"So . . ." Still grinning, Quinn took a sip of tea and sat back. "What does the ghost want?"

I looked at the apparition. "You heard the man. What's shakin'? And what do you want?"

"Hmhm Mmm. Mmmmnm," the ghost replied.

I grumbled a word best not used in public. "This isn't going to work."

"He wants us to know what's not going to work?" Quinn asked.

"He doesn't want us to know anything's not going to work. This . . ." I motioned back and forth between me and the ghost as a way of signaling communication that really didn't communicate very clearly.

Manny thought I was calling him and hurried over to refill our iced teas.

I waited until he slipped back into the kitchen. "This trying to talk to the ghost," I said, continuing right back where I'd left off. "He can't talk, remember. He's got duct tape over his mouth."

"Hmhm Mmm. Mmmmnm," the ghost said.

I decided it meant that he agreed with me.

"So how am I going to figure out what you want?" I asked him,

He shrugged as much as he was able, which wasn't much since his hands were tied behind his back.

Thinking, I drummed my fingers against the table. "I could ask questions," I said, sliding a look at the ghost. "And you can answer them."

He nodded.

Feeling a little more in control, I sat up. "We know you were murdered. Am I right?"

The ghost nodded.

I rubbed my hands together. "He says yes. Now we're getting somewhere. And you came to me because you want me to figure out who killed you."

"Does he?" Quinn asked.

The ghost shook his head.

"He says he doesn't," I reported. "Which is weird, because that's usually what they want. You know, justice."

"And you're the one they pick to get it for them."

I might have taken offense at Quinn's comment if there wasn't a green spark in his eyes that made me think that maybe—if he actually believed I talked to the dead—he'd be impressed.

Just in case that wasn't what the look meant, I made it clear. "Yes, I get justice for them. Only this time . . ." I took another look at the ghost and at the water already puddling around his feet. "You don't want me to find out who killed you?"

He nodded.

"You do want me to find out who killed you?"

He shook his head.

I grumbled some more.

"Let's start again," I suggested because I was getting confused. "You got murdered."

"Are you talking to me or the ghost?" Quinn asked.

"I'm talking to the ghost because you didn't . . ." Another groan. "Of course you did. You got murdered, too," I said to Quinn. "But I'm not talking about you getting murdered . . ." I swung back toward the ghost. "I'm talking about you getting murdered. You . . ." Another look at Quinn. "You were brought back. This guy . . ." I took another gander at the apparition, at the way his hands were tied and his mouth was covered, at the gash on his jaw and the blood on his shirt. "This guy stayed dead."

The ghost nodded.

"Are you sure you don't want me to find out who did it?" I asked again. I know, I was being a little obsessive-compulsive, but it never hurts to get things straight with ghosts. Or with cops, so I added for Quinn's benefit, "That's what they all want."

The ghost shook his head.

Manny showed up with our lunches and Quinn took a bite of his burger and wiped juice from his chin. "Maybe he doesn't need you to find out who killed him because he already knows who killed him."

I looked toward the ghost, who nodded enthusiastically.

"He says he does. I can't tell you how much easier that makes this for me. If he knows who killed him—"

"Just tell him to get me some suspects," Quinn suggested, "a motive, and oh yeah, evidence, and I'll be happy to take care of it for him."

"Not so easy since he can't talk."

Quinn thought this over while he took another bite of burger. "Why doesn't he take the duct tape off?"

"His hands are tied, remember."

"Then why don't you take it off for him?"

I bit back my irritation at having to explain this most basic of ghostly concepts, but only because I remembered that when it came to ghosts, Quinn hadn't been dead long enough to learn the rules. "They can't touch stuff," I explained. "Not like we can. That's why they need me to do things for them. And I can't take it off," I added, because I knew that's what he was going to bring up next. "Because if I do, I'll get frozen to the bone." I did not point out that I knew this for a fact because I'd once made the mistake of kissing a ghost. Instant lip freeze, and I talked like Elmer Fudd for hours.

It was kind of hard to tell if Quinn was buying any of this or not, what with him munching on french fries and all.

"Do you believe me?" I asked him.

"I believe you believe it."

"Not what I asked." I was suddenly not as hungry as I was irritated by his attitude. I poked at a crunchy potato wedge with the tip of my fork. "I shouldn't have to prove it. If you were any other guy—"

"Like that cop in New Mexico?"

Yes, there had been some phone calls between me and Quinn while I was visiting the great Southwest, mostly in regard to the case I was working that involved the kidnaping of a friend. Yes, Jesse had been in the room a time or two and no doubt, Quinn had heard his voice in the background. As for him jumping to the conclusion that there was something going on between me and Jesse . . .

Even though I hadn't eaten the first one, I stabbed another potato wedge. Hard. "That's old news."

"Love 'em and leave 'em, huh?"

"Oh no!" With my fork and the potato wedges stuck on it, I pointed at Quinn. "You're the one who did that. You're the one who walked out when—"

"Hmhm Mmm. Mmmmnm," the ghost said.

I swallowed the rest of my accusation along with those potatoes. They were as delicious as advertised, but one taste and I knew my lunch was getting cold fast, so I got to work on the chicken. "It's bad form to fight in front of strangers," I told Quinn between bites.

He glanced at the people seated around us. "I'll say. From the looks we got when you pointed your fork at me, I think they were a little worried that you were going to lunge across the table and attack me."

"Not them." I spared hardly a look at the dozen or so occupied tables around us before I pointed at the ghost. "Him."

"The ghost who doesn't want us to find out who killed him?"

"Because he knows already," I reminded Quinn. "But that still leaves a big question." I turned to the ghost. "What do you want?"

"Hmhm Mmm. Mmmmnm," he replied.

Thinking, I got to work on the asparagus. "You want me to right a wrong?" I asked the ghost.

This time, he didn't shake or nod. Instead, he sort of tilted his head from side to side—right ear to shoulder, left ear to shoulder.

"So what you're telling me is you're not sure? You don't know if what you want me to do is going to right a wrong?"

The ghost hopped up and down.

"So whatever it is you want me to do . . ." I was at the end of the logic train here, and I cut into the chicken breast, dunked it in the blue cheese sauce, and chewed thoughtfully. "It's not exactly righting a wrong."

The ghost nodded.

"But it's not exactly not righting a wrong, either." Even I knew I was in danger of muddying the waters way too much, so I waved away the question. Manny showed up with more iced tea and while he was there, I asked to see a menu again.

"We don't have time for dessert," Quinn said.

"Not dessert." I opened the menu. "Information." I held the menu so that the ghost could see it. "Maybe there are some words you can point out," I told him. "You know, to tell me what you want from me."

He nodded and read over the day's specials and when one caught his eye, he did a little shuffle step toward me and tipped his head.

"What you want me to do involves tuna in citrus sauce?" I said, and when the ghost shook his head, I tried again.

Drip, drip, drip.

The water droplets plunked down on one word.

Cooked.

Both Quinn and I thought it over.

"He's hungry," Quinn said.

Considering it, I wrinkled my nose. "I don't think ghosts get hungry."

The ghost confirmed this by nodding.

"He wants to learn to cook," I said, grabbing at straws and thinking out loud.

"He wants you to learn to cook."

I gave Quinn's comment the glare it deserved.

"Maybe he was killed by a cook," I suggested, to which the ghost indicated that I was way off base.

"Cooked." Quinn repeated the word. "Cooked as in dead?"

The ghosts eyes lit. At least I think they did. It was kind of hard to tell since they were so swollen. He looked toward Quinn and nodded.

"He says you're right," I reported. "Cooked meaning dead. But we already know you're dead."

The ghost waggled his head.

"So it's not you we're talking about."

Nod, nod.

"That means it's . . . ?" I did my best to encourage him.

To which the ghost responded by looking all around the room.

"It means everybody here is going to die?" This sounded pretty strange, and my disbelief rang through my words.

The ghost gave me a look that said it was a pretty pathetic guess. Again, he looked around the room.

"He's looking at everybody here," I told Quinn.

"Everybody." Quinn shook his head just like the ghost had been doing. "That doesn't seem likely. Unless the place is going to explode or something."

The ghost said no, then took another look around the room and when I still drew a blank, he dragged himself and that cinder block attached to his legs over to the table closest to ours.

He looked down at a woman eating her salad, then over at her companion, a middle-aged man who was sipping a martini.

The ghost raised his eyebrows in question.

He did the same at the next table, and the one after that.

"Everybody," I mumbled. "You're saying everybody here . . . But no, that's not what you mean," I added because I knew the ghost would only tell me I was wrong. "You don't mean everybody. You mean that lady, and that man and that lady . . ."

The ghost leaned forward and bobbled his head.

I was getting close, the look said. Warmer and warmer.

I leaned forward in my seat. "So if you don't mean that lady or that man specifically—"

Warmer.

"Then maybe what you're saying isn't everybody. It's anybody."

Hot!

"Somebody."

He jumped up and down.

"Somebody and cooked." The truth hit. "What you're saying is that you need my help or somebody else is going to die!"

I hadn't even realized I'd jumped out of my seat and yelled the words until I saw every mouth in the room drop open.

No worries, when the hostess hurried over, Quinn took care of things by flashing his badge along with his credit card, telling the woman he had everything under control, and waiting barely long enough to sign his name to the bill before he dragged me out the door.

I didn't manage to untangle myself from him until we were almost out to the car. "You could have given me a chance to ask for a doggie bag," I said. "That chicken was fabulous."

"This is what you do?" I guess it was a good thing he wasn't holding on to me anymore. It gave Quinn a chance to throw his hands in the air. "This is how you communicate with the dead?"

"Well, they're not usually bound and gagged," I said.

"And you expect me to take you seriously?" He unlocked the car, got in, and slammed the door.

I considered walking away, but the prospect of public

transportation back to the cemetery was not a pretty one. I got in the car and slammed the other door.

"It's plenty serious. Weren't you listening? Or do you just not get it? They want to cross over to the Other Side. Ghosts, I mean. It's always what they want. And they can't because they have some sort of unfinished business. My guess is that's why this one is talking about somebody else who's going to die. We're going to have to save that person. You know, so this ghost can accomplish his good deed and cross over."

"Put on your seat belt," Quinn rumbled.

In fact, it was the only thing he said all the way back to Garden View.

6

All right, so Ella wasn't far off when she said Milo Blackburne was a moderately attractive man. Nice hair. Decent features. Great suit.

None of that meant I was thinking about anything other than fund-raising as we sat across the table from each other at Johnny's Downtown, one of those unassuming little restaurants that Cleveland is famous for. Fabulous food. Service that's way above and beyond. Prices . . . well, let's just say that if Milo hadn't insisted on treating we (a) wouldn't be there or (b) would be eating only the bread our attentive waitress brought to our table.

"Wine?" Milo asked me before the waitress could walk away.

I was tempted. But. "I've got a tour coming to Garden View at two," I told him, leaving out the not-so-inconsequential fact that it was one of the reasons I'd chosen that afternoon for our lunch. Quinn had accused me of having an overactive imagination and maybe he was right, because every time Milo Blackburne looked at me, I could have sworn his eyes glazed over like a Krispy Kreme doughnut. Honest, if we were two characters in a cartoon, I was pretty sure I'd see his heart thump, thump, thumping its way right out of his chest and little Xs and Os floating around his head.

I shifted uneasily in my chair at the same time I told myself to get a grip. It was business, I reminded myself, and so what if the guy was attracted to me? He wasn't the first, and he wouldn't be the last. Guys, I knew how to handle.

Except for one.

"You're lost in thought." I snapped out of my daydream to find Milo with one elbow on the table and his chin on his fist, all moon-eyed like some sappy hero in a romance novel. "No doubt, you're occupied with all the details for that tour."

"The tour. Yes, of course." It was a better answer than telling him my mind was playing over my last encounter with Quinn. Damn the man for being so stubborn! Quinn claimed to be all about wanting the truth, didn't he? And yet when I gave it to him and admitted that the wet, murdered ghost was hanging around because he needed my help . . .

Well, there was no use stirring up the ugly emotions all over again.

Suffice it to say I hadn't seen or heard from Quinn since our lunch at Heck's.

Which was fine by me, I reminded myself, since I was still mad about the no-doggie-bag thing, not to mention the way he'd minimized my Gift and my talent for helping ghosts make it safely to the Other Side.

Then again, I hadn't seen the wet ghost since that afternoon almost a week earlier, either.

Just to make sure I wasn't saying too much too soon, I checked the spotless floor of the restaurant. Spotless being the operative word. As in no puddles. This, too, was fine with me since I didn't relish the thought of another round of charades. Especially since I was in no position to explain what was going on to Milo.

Who, I realized, was still staring at me from behind those tortoiseshell-rimmed glasses of his so intently, I wouldn't have been at all surprised if they started to steam.

"I'm glad you're considering a donation to Garden View," I said, hoping to get him to keep his thoughts on money, not on me. "Our donors are the lifeblood of the cemetery. Without them, we wouldn't be able to effectively get our message to the community through our tours, or our speakers' bureau, or—"

"You don't have to give me the spiel." Milo sat back and laughed. "I'm going to give, and generously, I promise. After my visit to the cemetery last week, I realized there are many wonderful and valuable and beautiful things there. They need to be preserved. And nurtured."

If we were talking about headstones, I wouldn't have felt so queasy. The way Milo's gaze ranged over me and the too-prim-for-my-liking black pantsuit I'd bought especially for the occasion sent a clear message: he wasn't as concerned with the dead as he was with the living. Provided the living we were talking about was me.

I pretended not to catch on. Years of dating, and nobody could play the game like I could.

"Garden View is an amazing place," I said, my smile bright. "But then, you know that. You visit Gladys regularly."

"Who?" No sooner was the question out of his mouth than Milo remembered. His cheeks darkened. "I'm afraid I haven't been to pay my respects to Lois . . . er, that is, to Gladys lately. You see, I realized something very important the night of the sponsorship event. About Lois. And Lana."

He'd tossed around both those names before, but at least this time, I knew who Lois was. Before I could ask about Lana, though, our waitress arrived with our entrees and for a few minutes, I was so busy tucking into my Caesar salad with grilled shrimp, I didn't worry about conversation.

That is, until Milo hit me with, "So, are you seeing anyone?"

There is no tightrope quite as narrow, taut, or wobbly as the one walked by a community relations manager with her hand out and her boss's job on the line.

"I'm sorry," Milo said before I could even think of the best way to handle the situation. "I know I'm being forward. It's just . . ." He gave me another one of those sappy looks. "You look so much like Lana."

"Which doesn't mean I am Lana." I shouldn't have had to point this out, but when guys get this way, sometimes it's best just to lay things on the line. "And who is this Lana chick, anyway?"

"Lana!" Milo's sigh was pure seventh heaven. "Lana

Lang. She was Superman's girlfriend. You know, back when he was a teenager and lived in Smallville with his adoptive parents, the Kents."

"And you think I—"

"Well, it's only natural," Milo said. "Like you, Lana is a beautiful redhead."

I didn't mind being called beautiful. Especially by a man who was never going to get the chance to lambaste me about my Gift because I was never going to tell him about it.

But I didn't want to give Milo the wrong impression.

That would explain why I didn't so much change the subject as I bumped it in a slightly different direction.

"There's a comic book convention coming to town," I said. "I bet they'll have Superman stuff there."

"Who told you?" At least Milo wasn't giving me moon-eyed looks anymore. In fact, he leaned forward and studied me, so intent, his eyes were closed nearly to slits. "What do you know about the convention?"

Since I didn't know what I'd said wrong, it was kind of hard to figure out how to fix it, but I knew instinctively that mentioning Quinn and my connection with him and with the police wasn't going to help. "I . . . I read about it. In the newspaper. I just thought—"

"Of course. Yes, of course you did." His smile shimmied at the edges and he concentrated on his veal ravioli for a few minutes before he dared to look my way again. "I have a modest collection," he said. "Of Superman memorabilia. I'm afraid when I hear people talk about things like comic book conventions—"

"I get it. You're not into that goofy stuff."

"Quite the contrary. I find it all fascinating. But some people belittle my interest, and I'm afraid I get defensive when that happens. I thought you might—"

"Never!" It was true. I'd never call Milo a comic book geek. At least not in front of him. "I think it's interesting."

"Really?"

Damn! We were back to moon-eyed.

"Just thinking about Superman and his marvelous powers . . ." Again, Milo's cheeks darkened and I think this time, maybe he realized he was sounding a little too much like the crazed fanboy he expected me to make fun of, because he bit back his words and looked down at the ravioli on his plate. "I must confess, I sometimes wish I could be just like him."

"Him? As in Superman? But he's—"

"I know. It's just a pipe dream."

I was going to say *make-believe* so I bit my tongue.

Milo shifted his gaze to his sterling and lapis cuff links. "I've never confessed that before." He lifted his head to look into my eyes. "Not to anyone."

"Wow, look at the time!" Lame, yes. It was incredibly lame. But for the first time, I think I understood how Quinn felt when I started carrying on about ghosts. Like I didn't know where to look. Or what to say. In my experience, when that happens, pulling back is the best course of action. I pushed my chair away from the table and thank goodness I had the smarts to meet Milo at the restaurant. That meant my car was in the parking lot right around the corner. "I'm afraid I'm going to have to be getting back to Garden View," I told Milo. "You know, for that tour."

I thanked him, told him we'd talk again soon (I figured

I had to say that and besides, I still needed to collect a check from him), and got the hell out of there.

This time, I was so busy beating a hasty retreat, I never even thought about a doggie bag.

I should have been relieved to make a clean break from Milo Blackburne and those telling looks of his. I should have been grateful, and proud of myself for not being too obvious. I hope.

Instead, all I was by the time I got back to the office was pissed.

Pissed at men in general, a couple specifically, and one in particular.

And since I wasn't particular about which particular one it was, the first thing I did when I got back to Garden View was get rid of both those vases of flowers on my desk. They were well past their prime, anyway, and dropping petals in musky little piles that I'd been ignoring for the last few days and were now officially getting on my nerves.

It wasn't until after I'd deposited both bouquets in the flower room where someone would reuse the vases for some cemetery event or another and got back to my office that I saw the ghost sitting behind my desk.

Not the wet ghost. Or Chet, either.

This was a woman, neat, petite, wearing a gray suit and a white business-y type shirt that was buttoned all the way to up her throat. Her hair was dark and pulled back, the top teased into a poofy round beehive and hairsprayed to within an inch of its life. No way one hair on that head was going to move. Ever. Her shoulders were rigid, and she was shuffling the papers on my desk.

"Excuse me?"

No, I am not particularly territorial when it comes to my workspace, but reread the above sentence. Shuffling. The ghost was shuffling papers.

I pointed a finger her way. "You shouldn't be able to—"

"You're forgetting." She tapped the papers into a neat little pile, set them down exactly in the center of the desk, and sat back, her hands folded on her lap. "In the first days after a person passes away—"

"They *can* touch things. Until the first full moon after they die!" I'd learned that lesson back in Chicago when a bitch of a ghost stole my body and I was invisible myself for a while and way more than grateful that I could still touch and feel things so I could get myself out of that jam. "So you just recently—"

"Expired. Yes." Her expression was serene. "Just this morning. It's quite a unique experience, and there's so much to learn! I'm afraid it will take me a while to get up to speed, but of course, I will do my best. In the meantime, though, word on the Other Side travels fast, and they talk about you, Miss Martin. Oh yes, they do talk about you."

I hoped my shoulders didn't sag too much when I realized the subtext of what she was saying. I already had a murdered ghost on my hands, someone else who was going to die if I didn't help, and no idea whatsoever of how I was going to figure out where to begin my investigation.

"You were murdered," I said.

"Oh dear, no. That would be . . ." Searching for the right word, she blinked rapidly. "That would be simply too sensational, wouldn't it? And I have always been . . . that is, I always was . . . anything but. I went quite peacefully at one of the nearby senior care centers. I assure you of that. Ninety years old. Quite an accomplishment, don't you think?"

She didn't look a day over forty. But then, I'd learned that was part of the mojo on the Other Side, too. Ghosts could choose to appear as they had when they were alive, and happiest.

I slipped into my guest chair. "So if you weren't murdered, why are you . . . ?"

"Oh, how I've missed it all." She took a deep breath. Well, not literally since she wasn't breathing, but if I didn't know better, it would have fooled me. "You see, I've been over at the retirement village for years. That would be thanks to Denice and Benny, my niece and nephew. They determined that I wasn't capable of taking care of myself. Imagine!" Her sniff was small, and no less monumental because of it.

"They managed to get legal custody and I got locked away with all the other old, forgotten people. But this . . ." When she glanced around my office, her eyes lit. "How I've missed this! The schedule. The routine. The satisfaction of making coffee first thing in the morning and the smell of mimeograph ink."

I eyed her with suspicion. "Are you telling me you actually enjoyed your years of working?"

"Enjoyed?" She tipped her head and studied me as if

I'd just stepped out of a UFO. "It's not a matter of enjoying, is it? It's a matter of doing what needs to be done."

"And you did what needed to be done."

"Well, certainly." She stood and walked around to the front of the desk and I saw that her skirt skimmed the bottom of her knees and her shoes had thick, low, and very sensible heels. We hadn't even officially met, and I wasn't surprised. "We each have our place in the Universe, Miss Martin. Those of us who are lucky find that place early on and settle into it."

"And your place was in an office?"

"You make it sound dreary, and I assure you, it was anything but. Yes, I began my career in the steno pool, but I quickly showed my worth. I'm Jean Tanneman." She stuck out her hand, and I forgave her. After all, she was new to the dead game. When I waved her off, she took it in stride. "I was executive secretary to Mr. Martin Farquand. You must know the name. Everyone in town knew Mr. Farquand. He was once the head of the largest bank in Cleveland."

"And you were his right-hand man."

I wasn't imagining it; her top lip actually curled a bit. That is, right before she realized she might be giving too much away. Jean's shoulders shot back a fraction of an inch. "I've never liked that phrase," she said. "After all, though men do all the truly important work within any corporation, without their secretaries . . ." A smile twitched her lips. "Well, you know as well as I do. Without their secretaries, men would get nothing accomplished."

We would need to have a talk about that truly important work comment, this ghost and I. Right now . . .

I glanced at the clock on the wall. In just twenty minutes, a whole bus full of old folks from the Brecksville Senior Center would be arriving outside the door of the administration building, and I would have to be there to greet them.

"That's terrific," I said because there didn't seem to be any point in saying anything else. "But what are you doing here?"

She swiveled her gaze to my desk, and to the papers now neatly piled there that had been on my desk chair when I left the office. From there she looked toward the manila folders tossed on top of the file cabinet across the room and the half dozen or so issues of *Marie Claire* I'd brought to the office with me for those off times when I could put my feet up and do some serious thinking about what I'd be wearing once fall officially arrived.

Jean clutched her hands together at her waist. "Right before I retired, that's when all the crazy talk started. You know, about equal rights for women. Equal pay. Equal job responsibilities. That's all well and good when the women who are promoted to positions of authority are capable of handling them."

"And you think I'm not." Don't worry, I didn't take this personally. We were talking about my job at Garden View, after all, and in all honesty, I wasn't sure I couldn't handle it, either.

"I think you need someone who can get you organized."

Like Jean, I didn't like giving too much of what I was thinking away, but I couldn't help myself. I sat up like a shot. "You'd do that? For me?"

"It would be a welcome diversion after all these years

of inactivity. And my goodness, Miss Martin, I hate to be the one to tell you so frankly, but you certainly do need it."

It was more than tempting, especially when I glanced at the calendar on the wall (Ella had left it there, and that month's picture featured white kittens with pink bows around their necks) and saw that Jean had died on the best of all possible days. The full moon had been just two nights previous. I'd have Jean's help for nearly another month and in that time . . .

I thought about the speakers' bureau I'd never had time to work on.

And the mail that needed to be answered, and the email that seemed to multiply whenever I wasn't looking.

I thought about Chet taking care of the newsletter. And Albert who, when he popped in for a minute the day before, said he was well on his way to getting my department's budget in order.

And I smiled the smile of a woman who loved the thought of having staff.

Until . . .

"What do I need to do in return?" I asked Jean.

Her jaw went stiff. "Hardly anything at all."

"That's what Chet and Albert said."

"And you handled their requests handily. Except for the vandalism, of course. I cannot condone that sort of tomfoolery. Still . . ." She puckered her lips. "It did show a certain amount of creativity on your part. And the ability to think on your feet. Just don't get any ideas"—her voice hardened along with her look—"about trying such nonsense when I'm around. If you want my help, you'll follow the rules."

"Done," I said, even as I wondered how doing that might hamper whatever it was Jean wanted me to do for her. And let's face it, what she wanted me to do for her is what it all came down to.

I pinned her with a look. "So . . . ?"

"So . . ." She cleared her throat and her shoulders were stiff, but that didn't fool me. When Jean turned her back to me, I knew for sure this was one subject that made Miss Efficient and Organized mighty uncomfortable. "Before you came into the office this afternoon," she said, her voice low, "I was here, waiting, and there were flowers on your desk."

The sound I grumbled was halfway between a swear word and a harrumph.

Jean looked over her shoulder at me. "You didn't like the flowers?"

"I did," I admitted.

"Then you didn't like the men who sent them, that Quinn and Jesse."

I hate shilly-shallying. I shrugged, anyway. "I like them both, but—"

Jean turned back to me. "But?"

"Well, Quinn doesn't believe in ghosts, and he doesn't believe that I believe in ghosts. Or that I talk to them."

"I wouldn't have, either," Jean mumbled. "Before today."

"Yeah, I get that. Really, I do. Only Quinn was dead for a while a couple months ago and when he was, he actually came to see me. Well, his ghost did. So you'd think he'd get it, you know?"

Jean nodded. "I know this whole business of being

dead takes some getting used to. And I've got eternity to do it. If this Quinn had only a little while . . ."

"I guess I never thought of it that way," I admitted.

"And Jesse?"

I looked at the bare spot that once held the flowers from Jesse and damn it, I shrugged again. "Whoever it was who said absence makes the heart grow fonder, never took into account a couple thousand miles and a phone call now and then. Don't get me wrong," I pointed out fast. "I'll never forget Jesse. But now that I'm home, it's getting harder to remember why I thought I was in love with him."

"It sounds like you have a decision to make," Jean said.

"You mean between Jesse and Quinn."

She shook her head. "Don't be silly. You already know you don't want Jesse. If you did, you'd be off to wherever it is he is, and you wouldn't think twice about it. When it comes to men, you've already made your choice. Now you just have to decide if you can live with the fact that he doesn't believe in your Gift."

As insights went, this was a pretty powerful one, and I chewed it over while Jean went back behind my desk and took a seat.

"How'd you get to be so smart?" I asked her.

She sloughed off the compliment. "There were always young girls in the office. You know, before they got married and left the bank to raise their families. There was always drama, and a broken heart or two."

"I'll bet you broke a few hearts along the way yourself!"

She fingered the high, stiff collar of her blouse. "That's just it, you see. There was never time . . ."

"No love life?" I didn't mean for it to sound quite as brutal, but let's face it, it's hard to comprehend anybody living the life of a cloistered nun. Unless . . .

I studied Jean with renewed interest.

"You gave it all up, didn't you? You gave it all up for your work."

She sighed. "And I never once regretted it. Not when I was at the bank. But all those years of retirement . . . well, I had plenty of time to think, to second-guess the choices I made. Seeing your flowers today, that made me aware that when I was alive, I never got so much as a single bouquet of flowers. Not from any man."

"You want—"

"Flowers. On my grave. Oh, not all the time or anything. But once in a while." When she glanced up at me, Jean's eyes were moist. "Pink."

"You got it," I assured her and watched her face light with a smile. When she bustled over to the file cabinet and started rooting around in there, she was humming.

And me? I was thinking about that tour that was about to pull in. I'd already taken a step to leave the office when another thought occurred.

"I know you haven't been dead for long, Jean," I said, "but you did say that word travels fast on the Other Side. I was wondering if you'd heard anything about a man who was murdered. Drowned, I think. He was trying to get me to help him out, but I haven't seen him for a while, and he says someone else is going to die if I don't help."

"My, that is serious." You could have fooled me since Jean never once stopped leafing through the files in the drawer. "But I'm afraid I can't help. Haven't seen the man. Haven't heard anything about him, either. But if I do . . ."

I didn't wait for her to finish the sentence. I had a tour waiting for me, and Jean was too engrossed in being blissfully busy.

That evening, I left the office at the stroke of five. No wonder. I had staff, and my staff was taking care of all the details I usually stayed late to handle. With an entire evening beckoning, I promised myself a trip to the mall, but on the way there . . .

I tapped a disgusted tattoo against my Mustang's steering wheel.

Instead of driving to the mall without a care in the world, I found myself thinking about the wet ghost and how someone else's life was in danger.

And I couldn't help it. Thinking about the wet ghost made me think about Quinn.

And thinking about Quinn made me think about how I hadn't seen him in a week.

Or the ghost, either.

And all that made me realize—

I would have slapped my forehead if I didn't need both hands on the wheel to steer my way around the traffic lined up outside Beachwood Place Mall and head to the freeway.

Within a half hour, I had found a parking place (okay, so it wasn't technically an official parking place, but it was sort of legit and who was going to care about one little extra car, anyway?) outside of the refurbished (and very pricey, by the way) factory building that housed Quinn's seventh-floor loft.

I was talking practically before he opened the door.

"He only shows up when we're together," I said at the same time I scuttled inside and stationed myself near the floor-to-ceiling windows with their killer view of the river and the downtown skyline and far from the door so Quinn couldn't shut it in my face when he pushed me back into the hallway. "The wet ghost only shows up—"

"You haven't seen him again?"

For any other couple, it would have been an odd sort of exchange of greetings, but for me and Quinn, it was pretty much par for the course.

"I haven't," I said, tossing my purse down next to the sleek leather couch. "And it never occurred to me, you know? But then I was in the car and I was thinking about it and . . ." I had no choice at this point but to stop and haul in a breath. I did my best to follow the logic that had led me here in the first place. "The first time I saw the puddles, those flowers from you were in my office, and the first time the ghost showed up, you were at my apartment. And then I didn't see him again until we were at lunch together and now . . ." I threw my hands in the air. "No sign of his drippy ectoplasm. Not since last week when I saw you."

"Interesting." Quinn was dressed in faded jeans and a T-shirt that had the logo for a band called Silverlights on it. On any other guy, the outfit would have looked homey and casual. On Quinn, no surprise that it was homey, casual, and sexy as hell. He was holding a file folder and I saw that the amber-colored handblown glass pendant lights above the kitchen breakfast bar were lit, and that there were more files and papers scattered over the black granite countertop.

"I'm interrupting you," I said.

"Just going over some papers." He led the way through the living room and the attached dining room and over to the kitchen space where more windows revealed even more glorious views of the city and from this direction, a sliver of the Lake Erie shoreline. "I'm kind of busy."

As brush-offs went, it stung like hell.

I wasn't about to let that stop me.

"I get it," I said. "I know you're upset about what happened at lunch the other day, and I understand. The dying thing, it takes some getting used to, and most of the ghosts I meet have had plenty of time. You never did. I understand that now, Quinn, and I swear, I'm not going to make a big deal out of it or bug you about it anymore. But don't you see, us fighting, that means the ghost isn't going to show up. And we can't let that happen. Not when somebody else's life is on the line."

He considered this for a moment or two before he said, "You want a glass of wine?"

"Wine?" I stepped closer to the place where he'd been working. "Sure, I—"

My words disappeared on the end of a gurgle of surprise, and I scooted closer to the countertop to take a better look at the papers and newspaper clippings scattered there.

"This . . ." I grabbed the nearest newspaper clipping and held it up for Quinn to see. "This is—"

"Jack Haggarty." He had already opened a bottle of Shiraz and was reaching for two wineglasses. "You remember. The cop I used to partner with. The one who sent that postcard from New York last week. Every once in a while, I pull out the old files and go through them again, looking for something that will explain that murder everybody thinks Jack is connected with. I know, I'm wasting my time, but—"

"But nothing." I shook my head, and because he was pouring the wine and not paying any attention, I added, "Jack Haggarty didn't send that postcard. Not last week, anyway."

To say Quinn's expression was incredulous is to underestimate the word. He handed me my wine and took a sip of his own before he asked, "And what makes you say that?"

"Because last week, Jack was busy being dead. That wet ghost I've been talking to? It's Jack Haggarty."

7

"You're trying to tell me—"

"I'm not trying to tell you anything." I set down my wineglass, but not before I took a sip. When something like this shakes up my world, a little calming libation is not a bad idea. "This is the guy," I said, waving the newspaper article and the picture of Jack at Quinn. "This is the ghost who's been leaving puddles all over the place."

A few months earlier, I knew he would have blown me off instantly.

Apparently, we were making progress in our relationship because now, it took about fifteen seconds. But then, Quinn was busy opening and closing his mouth, struggling to find the words.

As it turned out, the words that managed to come out were pretty much, "You're kidding me, right?"

Grumbling seemed a better option than telling him it was a stupid question. "Why would I kid you about this?

And, oh!" I was so darned pleased with my thought process, I jumped up and down. Have no fear, the people in the apartment below had heard far more interesting sounds coming from Quinn's place when I was visiting.

"That explains it," I crooned. "That explains why the ghost only shows up when we're together. Jack was your partner. He knows you. He wants you to help."

While I'd been busy gloating about my brilliance, Quinn had downed his wine. He poured himself another glass and flopped down on the couch with it. "Maybe," he said.

Maybe.

One word.

And it said so much.

A thread of warmth tangled around my heart, I hurried over to where he was sitting. "Are you saying you believe me?"

"I'm saying . . ." As if he was worried about what he might see, Quinn took a quick look around the loft and when he didn't see anything (well, of course, he didn't see anything; I didn't see anything, either), he sat back. "Jack can't be dead. He's sending postcards."

"Somebody's sending postcards. Come on, Quinn." Since he was doing his best to ignore this incredible deduction, I whacked him on the knee. "It's been staring us right in the face and we haven't seen it. Jack is dead. And somebody's—"

"Trying to cover it up by sending those postcards and making us think that Jack has left town. Which means—"

"That maybe he didn't have anything to do with that murder you're investigating. Maybe he was a victim, too."

He scraped a hand over his jaw. "But no one reported Jack missing. And you don't know . . . you don't know Jack. He's a real tough guy. Street-smart and savvy. The ghost . . ." I guess the word must have tasted funny in his mouth, because Quinn had to take another sip of wine to wash it down. "The ghost you talked about was obviously murdered. No way. Jack is a larger-than-life character. No way he ended up dead."

While he'd been working his way through this little mental exercise, I'd taken the chance to look around the loft again. I gave Quinn another poke and pointed across the room. "If Jack's not dead," I said, "explain that."

Certain instincts are impossible to resist. Even for a hardheaded detective. Quinn looked toward the fireplace. "There's a puddle on the floor."

"Uh-huh. And a ghost standing right in the middle of it."

He finished his glass of wine.

Me? I wasn't about to waste any time. I hopped to my feet and closed in on the ghost. "You're Jack Haggarty," I said.

It wasn't a question, but Jack nodded.

"He says he is," I told Quinn. "And maybe he'll tell us—"

"Ask him how long we were partners."

Oh, I knew what was going on here. I was being tested. By a man who should have taken my word for this whole woo-woo thing. I was just about to point this out to him when I remembered something Jean had said earlier in the day. It took some time to get used to being dead, and—thank goodness—time wasn't what Quinn had on the Other Side.

I turned to Jack. "Quinn's having a little trouble," I said, even though I suspected Jack already knew it. After all, cops are a perceptive bunch. "He doesn't believe you're here. He doesn't believe I can talk to you, either."

Behind the duct tape, Jack's mouth pulled into a smirk.

"I think Jack is saying that he's not surprised," I said. "I bet in the time you worked with him—"

"And how long was that?"

I rolled my eyes and turned back to Jack. "Let's make Mr. Skeptical happy. How long?"

Jack jumped up and down three times.

"Three," I told Quinn. "I'm guessing that means three years."

He got up from the couch.

"How many times was Jack married?" he asked.

Jack jumped up and down four times and I told Quinn that, too.

"And divorced?"

Another four jumps. Along with a look that was as bitter as unsweetened chocolate.

"Four," I told Quinn. "And my guess is he got taken to the cleaners each and every time."

I looked over my shoulder to where he still stood near the couch, his arms loose at his sides, his head cocked, as if he was listening for something. Or trying to think through everything I was telling him and decide if I was Gifted. Or just one lucky guesser.

I threw my hands in the air. "You still don't believe me, do you?"

Quinn crossed his arms over his chest. "It's my job to ask questions."

"Yeah, when you're dealing with scumbags. But this is me."

"And there is such a thing as the Internet."

As if he'd punched me in the stomach, I sucked in a sharp breath. "You don't think I—"

"I didn't say you did. I just said it's possible."

"That I would do research about Jack Haggarty and then try to get you to believe I was talking to his ghost? Why?" I took one step in his direction before I realized my hands were already curled into fists and I'd better stop right where I was, or I was going to do something I'd regret. Like smack that gorgeous face of his. "Why would I do that?"

As if it would somehow deflect the anger coming off me in waves, Quinn put his hands out. "I don't know why. I only know—"

"That this is for real. You know that, Quinn, because you were part of it. You were a ghost. That's pretty powerful. At least it would be if you were anybody else. But you're you, and you're stubborn and afraid to admit to something that makes you seem weaker than you really are. News flash, Detective, being dead doesn't make you weak, it just makes you dead. And just because some creep shot you—"

"I never should have given him the chance." Quinn's voice ricocheted against the hardwood floors, and maybe the passion in it surprised him as much as it did me. Maybe that's why he turned away, and left me with a view of his shoulders (too rigid) and his head (too high).

"I was in that warehouse and I knew I was tracking a killer. I never should have let him get the drop on me. I should have been more careful. I should have been smarter. I should have been less—"

"What? Less human? Is that what this is all about? You're not afraid to admit you were dead. But you sure as hell hate to admit somebody got the best of you. Don't you see, Quinn, it doesn't matter. All that matters is that you're here. Now. That they were able to bring you back. And even if they weren't . . ." It was one of those things I hated to think about, mostly because every time I did, my knees buckled and I couldn't catch my breath. "Nobody ever would have said it happened because you were sloppy or stupid, because you're not. And I'll bet the same thing is true as far as Jack is concerned. He didn't die because he did something wrong. He died because he caught a bad break, and now he's a ghost and if you don't start believing that, somebody else is going to die. If we don't help—" My voice shook so much, I had to pull in a breath and give it another try. "If we don't help keep that person alive, that's something you can feel guilty about. You dying, not so much."

I'm not sure what I expected Quinn to say. Or maybe I am sure. I expected him to slap his forehead, admit he'd never thought about it this way before, and tell me I was right. When all he did is stand there, his shoulders heaving with each deep breath he took, I lost it.

"You want proof that Jack's here?" This time, my voice, too, echoed through the loft.

"You don't believe the stuff about how long you were partners or how many times he was married? That isn't good enough for you? Then tell me something else about

Jack, something I couldn't find on the Internet because it wouldn't be in a newspaper article."

He made a small motion with his right hand. "No. You don't need to—"

"Oh yes, I do." I closed in on him, and when he still didn't turn around, I did an end run and came up at him from the other direction. He's taller than me, and I had to tilt my chin to glare at him. "Did Jack have a scar? A tattoo?"

I didn't expect him to answer. Not now. Not ever.

"A tattoo." Quinn's voice was no more than a whisper. "Yeah. Jack had a tattoo on his right upper arm. But—"

By the time he made a grab for me, I was already on my way to the other side of the room.

Quinn was only a couple steps behind me. "How do you expect to prove that?" he demanded. "You said he was wearing a golf shirt and you told me once that you can't touch a ghost."

"Wanna bet?" I'd already reached out for Jack so even if I'd stopped to think about what was about to happen to me, it wouldn't have mattered. The way it was, thinking was something I was way beyond doing. I was working on instinct, along with a big ol' dose of mad as hell. Before I could stop myself, I had one hand on Jack's arm and with the other, I was pulling up the right sleeve of his shirt.

I guess if I'd thought about it, I would have expected the cold to hit in waves. But that's not how it happened. The sensation crashed over me in one quick burst. Icy. Complete. Terrible.

Along with the freezing cold, a pain shot through my fingers and up my arm. I didn't let even that stop me.

"It's . . ." My voice sounded as if it had been folded into a Jell-O mold, the words suspended and thick. "It's a hula dancer," I said in between the chattering of my teeth. "She's wearing a blue flower lei and it has the name Estelle written under it. And . . . and . . ."

Somehow, my brain finally connected to my hands. Maybe it was the frigid pain that prickled through my body and made my bones ache. Or the frostbite that nipped my skin. By the time I realized I'd made a terrible mistake, it was too late. The cold flowed from my arms into my torso. It hit my heart like a hammer. Slowed it down. Froze it.

When Quinn yelled, "You told me once if you touched a ghost, it would freeze you," I wanted to say *no duh*, but the words, too, were frozen inside me.

I couldn't move. Or blink. Or breathe.

I stood suspended in some boundless, arctic place where the seconds ticked by like hours and as each one passed, another cell in my body turned icy and died.

"Pepper? Pepper?"

Quinn's voice. Far away.

"Pepper!"

It wasn't until he wrapped both his arms around me and dragged me as far away from the fireplace as he was able that I realized what had happened.

Quinn pulled me close and chafed his hands up and down my arms. "You're frozen."

Another *no duh* moment, but I couldn't point it out. I

couldn't do anything but stand there and savor the heat of Quinn's body, chasing away the cold inch by inch.

"Come on." He lifted me into his arms and carried me across the living room. "I'm going to run a lukewarm shower and get you in there. That's the only thing that's going to help."

There was a master bath just beyond his bedroom, and in the doorway between the two rooms, he stripped off my black suit jacket and unbuttoned my shirt.

"It's going to be okay," he crooned, his hands slipping inside my shirt and playing over my ribs. He skimmed them down to my waist and back up again. "I promise you, Pepper, you're going to be all right."

He left me long enough to start the shower and little curls of steam tickled my skin. Slowly, the heat penetrated. I blinked back to consciousness and that's when I started to shiver.

"Okay, just a couple more seconds." Quinn darted out of the bathroom and folded me into an embrace. "We'll get you warmed up and tuck you in bed under some blankets. I'll make you some tea and—"

"Just hold me." I settled my head against his chest. "You're nice and warm."

I didn't exactly see him smile (head to chest, after all), but I felt some of the tension go out of his shoulders at the same time his arms tightened around me.

"How's that?" Quinn rested his chin on my head. "You ready to get into the shower?"

I shook my head and when he put a finger under my chin so he could lift my face to his, I smiled. It hurt a little.

But then, I was pretty sure there were ice crystals on my lips. "I think I need a kiss first," I said.

Here's the thing about Quinn: he can be a royal pain in the butt, and as pigheaded as anyone I'd ever met, but when he's willing to oblige . . .

I melted into the kiss, savoring not just the warmth but the taste of Quinn's lips against mine. This was something that had been missing in my life for too long, and now that it was back, I decided right then and there that I wasn't going to move. Not ever again.

Which meant when Quinn pulled away, I started shivering all over again. He looked over my shoulder and out the door. "Is Jack still there?" he asked.

I had to bend a little backward to see. "Yup."

Quinn didn't say a word. He didn't have to. His arms still around me, he back-stepped me across the room and closed the bedroom door.

Quinn made tea, all right. But not until after he made sure—personally—that I was warmed through and through.

He's that kind of guy.

He is also the kind of guy who when we were done with all that warming up, served the tea in bed along with gooey grilled cheese sandwiches. By the time we were finished (with dinner and with everything else), I was feeling pretty much back to normal.

With a sigh of satisfaction, I burrowed down under the sheets and the extra blankets Quinn had piled on top of me and watched him clear away the dishes. On a personal level, all was right with the world. When it came to my investigation, though, there was plenty bothering me, and it all started with—

"Candy bars."

Quinn had just come back into the room. He'd put on his jeans but not his T-shirt, and hey, I wasn't complaining. In the light of the single lamp next to the bed, his skin was burnished, and his muscles were as well-defined as if they'd been sculpted by an artist with a really good eye whose sole purpose in life was to make me crazy.

"You still hungry? I don't have any candy bars. But we can pick up some when we go out."

"I don't want any candy bars. You said candy bars."

He left his T-shirt where I'd tossed it when I took it off (okay, *ripped it off* was more like it) of him, and he got a collared shirt out of the closet and slipped it on. "Hey, I've missed being with you," he said. "And I might have gotten a little carried away. But I'm pretty sure I didn't say anything about—"

"Candy bars." My clothes were on the bed and I sat up and tugged them on. Not that I'm psychic or anything, but even before he said something about going out, I figured something was up. Smart girl that I am, I knew if we were headed out at this time of the night, it had something to do with our case, and with Jack's murder. I was comfy. I was content. I was very, very satisfied. As much as I would have liked to stay exactly where I was, there was no way I was going to miss out.

"Not today," I said, buttoning my shirt. "The other day when I asked you why the cops thought Jack was involved in Dingo's murder, you said candy bars."

Quinn reached for his shoes. "Jack's second wife was a woman named Margo. She was a Brit, and she got him hooked on these English candy bars. Topic, they're called. As far as I know they're not sold in this country. Jack used to have them shipped from some shop in London."

I zipped my pants. "And buying English candy bars means Jack killed somebody?"

"No." When he hurried past me, Quinn dropped a kiss on the top of my head. If he'd stopped and lingered for a while, I wouldn't have objected, but he kept right on, got his weapon out of the gun safe in his closet, and strapped on his shoulder holster.

Like I said, psychic had nothing to do with it.

We were definitely heading out.

When that was all set, he put on a jacket to cover up the gun. Yeah, like anybody with half a brain couldn't take one look at Quinn and know he was a cop. "There was a candy bar wrapper found with Dingo's body."

"A Topic candy bar wrapper."

He nodded.

"But Jack can't be the only one who—"

"Obviously." Quinn walked out of the bedroom and by the time I found my shoes and caught up to him, he was waiting for me at the door. "There are plenty of people in the department think it does, and they're talking trash about Jack." Quinn opened the door and let me walk out ahead of him. "He was my partner, Pepper, and now he's dead. I owe it to him to find out what really happened, just like I owe it to him to make sure whoever killed him pays for it."

We started at Jack's house.

Since it was already after ten at night, I was a little afraid we'd bother whoever might be home, but Quinn told me we didn't have to worry. For one thing, after four marriages, four divorces, and countless girl-friends (some of the girlfriends overlapped the marriages, hence the divorces), Jack had learned his lesson; he lived alone. For another, seeing that it was late, Quinn's plan was to get into—and out of—the house before any of the neighbors saw us nosing around.

On the way over, he told me that Jack had joined the force back in the day when Cleveland police officers were required to live within city limits. Then again, so had Quinn himself. But one look, and I knew Jack's neighborhood was about as far from Quinn's—aesthetically speaking—as the Earth is from the moon.

We parked about a block away from our destination, in

front of a house with an overgrown lawn and boarded windows, and we walked up a sidewalk that was cracked and heaving thanks to the roots of the trees that someone with more of an artistic streak than good sense had once decided to plant on every tree lawn. The houses were planted close together, too, on mini-lots with just a driveway between each. Lucky for us, it was a cool night. Otherwise, I suspected the neighbors might have been out on their front porches watching the world go by, and keeping under the radar would have been a lot harder.

"That's the house." We'd already walked by the burgundy-colored bungalow with a squat front stoop and white shutters when Quinn tipped his head back and to the left to point it out. Before I had a chance to ask—nicely, of course—why, if we were going to Jack's, we'd passed it up, I realized what he had in mind. We strolled past five more houses, crossed the street and came back the other way to Jack's. Just so we could take a good look around and make sure no one was paying any attention to us.

At the house opposite, he poked me as a way of telling me to get a move on, and I darted across the pitted blacktop, up Jack's driveway, and into his backyard.

"I'm not in the mood to get arrested." I knew better than to talk too loud, so when Quinn joined me, I kept my voice to a whisper. "We're not going to break in, are we?"

"We don't have to." While I stood near the back door, Quinn covered the ten feet or so over to the garage. "Jack always kept an extra key out here." He reached around a withered plant that might have once been a geranium and into a flowerpot, and when he was done rooting around, he came up smiling and flashed the key.

A minute later, we were standing in Jack Haggarty's kitchen.

"No lights. I brought flashlights." Quinn pressed one of those pen-sized ones into my hand. "But not here. Not until we can close some curtains."

Lucky for us, when it came to decorating, Jack didn't believe in a lot of extras. I banged my knee on a kitchen chair, but made it through to the pint-sized dining room without further incident. It wasn't until I was in there that I realized Quinn hadn't followed.

I retraced my steps—carefully—and found him standing in front of the fridge. He inched the door open.

"Ohmygod!" I slapped a hand in front of my nose almost before he slammed the door shut again. "It smells awful! That food must have been in there forever."

In the sliver of light that came in the kitchen window, I saw Quinn's mouth thin. "Not exactly what somebody would do if they were thinking of leaving town for months on end, is it?"

He opened the freezer. Thank goodness there were no bad smells coming from there, but even so Quinn didn't look any happier.

I scooted around the open freezer door and saw why.

"Topic candy bars," I said, shining the narrow beam of my flashlight into the freezer. "A dozen Topic candy bars."

"Yeah." Quinn shut the freezer, and from there, we made our way through the dining room and into the living room where the flat-screen TV was covered with an inch of dust and the fifty-gallon aquarium had a layer of scum floating on the top along with six dead and mostly decomposed fish. Rather than risk catching a whiff of any more rotting things, I took the steps two at a time and waited for Quinn to join me on the second-floor landing.

Jack Haggarty was already there waiting for us.

I didn't need to tell Quinn. He squished into the puddle in the middle of the beige Berber and made a face.

"What's Jack telling us?" Quinn asked.

In response, Jack poked his head toward the end of the hallway.

We followed him to a room that featured a king-sized bed (unmade), another flat screen, a chest of drawers, and another, smaller, aquarium. Apparently, Jack was just setting this one up when he went missing. No water. No dead fish. Thank goodness.

The room was the size of my closet back in the day when my dad had yet to go to prison and we were one of the most better-off families in our way-more-better-off-than-most-to-begin-with neighborhood. When Quinn edged over to the window, I had to stand back against the wall. I waited until he lowered and closed the blinds and pulled the curtains shut over them before I flicked on the lamp beside the bed.

"Ew!" This from me when I saw that the base of the lamp was made from two deer legs and the shade featured outdoor scenes of romping moms and baby deer. They wouldn't have been so happy if they knew that eventually, their pieces and parts would be turned into household furnishings. "That's gross."

Quinn spared barely a look for the lamp. He was already digging through Jack's dresser.

"Jack liked to hunt," was all he said.

While we were busy with all this, Jack made himself at

home on the bed, and as Quinn poked through drawers of socks and underwear and ties that looked like they hadn't been worn since sometime in the last century, Jack shook his head. I knew what this meant; there was nothing there, nothing interesting, anyway. I did not, however, report this to Quinn. He was back doing what he did best (well, second best), and I wasn't about to break his little investigatin' heart.

"Nothing." Disgusted, Quinn banged the drawers closed and pushed away from the dresser. "Why did Jack want us in here?"

I looked to the ghost. "Why this room? What's so special?"

When Jack got up from the bed, he left behind a wet spot. He walked over to the closet and with a telling look, steered me that way, too.

"There's something in the closet," I told Quinn.

He came over to check it out. "Did Jack say what?"

If Quinn had taken the time to glance my way rather than poking his head into the closet, he would have seen the look that should have reminded him that Jack wasn't able to say much of anything. "He's . . ." I wasn't sure how to describe the ghost's gyrations, which pretty much consisted of jumping and poking his chin toward the closet. "It's definitely where he wants us to look."

Quinn pushed the clothes on the rod to one side and pulled the chain for the overhead light. "Nothing but clothes and shoes," he grumbled.

"Jacks says no." The ghost made a move to get closer, but I stopped him in his spooky tracks. "I've had enough freezing for one night. Quinn! You get over there." I

111

grabbed his arm and sent him back across the room. "That way, Jack and I will have a little more room to maneuver."

When Quinn vacated his spot, Jack took his place. He poked his chin toward the closet.

"But Quinn says there's nothing in there," I told him.

Jack poked some more.

The beige Berber there in the bedroom matched the carpeting in hallway and had probably been last vacuumed when that stuff had—when I was back in college. I wasn't particularly happy about it, but I got down on my hands and knees and scooted as far as I could into the tiny closet. "Well, I couldn't live in this house, that's for sure," I said, though I wasn't sure Quinn could hear me since my head and shoulders were in the closet and he was back over by the bed. "I'd need to make one of the other rooms into a wardrobe room. There isn't space in here for half of what I own."

Jack, apparently, did not share my concerns. When I craned my neck to look over my shoulder, all I saw was him poking some more. Faster and faster.

I scooted even farther into the closet, turned on my flashlight, and skimmed it along the walls.

It wasn't until just about all of me was squeezed in there that I saw that the edge of the carpet in the farthest corner was turned back a little.

I poked my head out (try doing that gracefully in a closet the size of a postage stamp) and told Quinn I'd found something.

Needless to say, he did not let Jack's icy presence keep him away. He hurried over, stopped where the air was chilliest, told Jack to take a hike, and squatted down to peer where I was shining my flashlight. "Pull back the carpet," he said.

I did, and found a loose floorboard underneath. Remember, no room to move, and I'm not exactly tiny (though it is important to point out that I am perfectly proportioned), so it took a while—and a broken fingernail—before I was able to grab the edge of the floorboard and tilt it up and out of the way.

"Go on, see what's under there," Quinn urged when I hesitated to stick my hand into the dark place below the floor. "What? Something's going to jump out and get you? You already talk to ghosts. What could be scarier than that?"

"Spiders." My hand over the hole, I hesitated. "Dirt. Creepy crawlers. Dead things." I squeezed my eyes shut and felt around below the floorboards. "Paper," I said when my fingers connected with something. I couldn't quite get a good hold on it, so I took a deep breath, wedged my shoulders into the corner, stretched, and—

I grasped a corner of the paper and pulled.

"It's an envelope," I said and crawled out of the closet, said envelope clutched in one hand. I sat down with my back to the wall, set down the envelope long enough to scrape one spiderweb-encrusted hand against the leg of my pants, then took a closer look.

It was nothing more than one of those manila envelopes with the little metal clasp on them, dirty as all getout and about the size of a piece of typing paper. It was fat and squishy and when I looked at Quinn and he didn't object, I undid the clasp and peeked inside.

"Holy shit! There's money in there, and plenty of it."

When Quinn motioned for it, I dropped the envelope in his hands.

"How much—"

He answered with a shake of his head. "Hard to say, but thousands, that's for sure. Way more than any cop should have stashed away." His jaw went rigid. "At least any honest cop. Ask Jack what the hell's going on."

I would have, honest, but by the time I pulled myself to my feet and looked for him, Jack had vanished.

"You have money."

"It's not the same thing."

"Of course it is."

It was the next morning, and I had to leave for work from Quinn's extra early if I wanted to get over to my apartment and change clothes. Which I obviously did so that I didn't wear the same thing to the office two days in a row and because my black pants hadn't fared very well from that excursion into Jack's closet. Quinn was just cleaning up the espresso/cappuccino/latte machine that I knew cost more than what I paid for one month's rent, and that alone should have been a reminder to him that when it came to simple living, he was not exactly a candidate for poster boy.

"I bet the cops at the station talk about you, too," I said.

"So what if they do?" Quinn came over to the countertop and sat on one of the high stools pulled up to it. He'd toasted one English muffin for himself and one for me, and he slid mine over along with a jar of raspberry preserves. "It's nobody's business."

Raspberries dripped onto my chin and I wiped them off with one finger and licked them away. "So when your fellow cops see you in your fancy suits—"

"They're not all that fancy."

"And your expensive ties."

"I'm a very careful shopper."

"But that's not the point. You find money at Jack's so you assume he must have been up to no good. That's exactly what the other cops are probably saying about you. And since we know it's not true about you—"

"I don't want it to be true about Jack, either." Quinn was just about to bite into his muffin, and he tossed it down. "I worked with Jack every day for three years. I knew him pretty well. Sure, he could be abrasive. He had this whole Dirty Harry thing going on, thought he was the toughest lawman in town, and he wasn't afraid to let everybody know it. I've never met another cop who managed to pull off that kind of macho nonsense and actually get away with it."

Quinn paused here, and because I was afraid I was supposed to say something, and I knew if I did that something would have been *look who's talking!* I took a giant bite of muffin and chewed for all I was worth.

Thank goodness he was on a roll and didn't notice. "And obviously," Quinn said, "Jack's personal life was a mess. Sure, I saw him bend the rules. Plenty of times. But I never saw him break them. Even after we stopped partnering . . . we didn't see a lot of each other. He stayed in uniform, and I went on to the detective bureau. We weren't exactly good friends. But we kept in touch now and again. I always thought he was a solid cop." He washed away the thought with a sip of coffee. "And here I've spent all these months defending him, telling anybody who would listen that there's no way he could have been involved in Dingo's murder."

"That hasn't changed. Just because we found money—"

"It was thirty-five thousand dollars, Pepper." We'd put the money back exactly where we'd found it, partly because Quinn wanted to figure out where it came from before he presented the money to the authorities and partly because we knew it would be safe there, especially after we wedged that floorboard down nice and tight and shoved a couple pair of Jack's shoes into the corner to hide the loose carpet.

"You don't just keep that kind of money tucked away for a rainy day," Quinn said. "And you don't hide it in your closet, either. Not if it's honest money."

"Maybe Jack didn't trust banks."

Quinn's look was as bitter as my espresso would have been if I hadn't loaded it with sweetener.

I let him think about all this while I polished off half my muffin. "Okay, so the bank thing, that's not exactly a strong argument. But just because he had that kind of money, that doesn't mean Jack had anything to do with Dingo's murder. Come on." Quinn was next to me so it was easy to give him a playful poke in the ribs. "Facts are facts. Admit it. Maybe it's not honest money. I'll give you that. But that money and the murder aren't necessarily tied together."

"No, they're not." I guess this realization actually made him feel better because he chomped into his muffin and washed it down with more coffee. "It's still mighty strange, though."

"I'll give you that."

"And I still want to look into it."

"Of course you do."

He got to his feet. "I'd ask you to come along, but I know you need to get to the cemetery."

I was about to concede that this was true. Until I remembered Jean. And Chet. And Albert.

"Good news." Smiling at the prospect of a day free of cemetery woes, I grabbed my purse. "Everything I need to work on at Garden View is taken care of. We can spend the day investigating. After I change clothes."

He was about to slip his suit coat over his shoulder holster when Quinn's cell rang.

"Hey, Vincent!" Good thing that geeky security guard over at the hotel couldn't see Quinn frown. "What is it this time?"

Quinn listened.

I put on a fresh coat of lipstick.

"The morgue, huh?" He shook his head in a gesture of infinite patience. "Yes, I remember that, Vincent. You told me all about it when I came over to the hotel to talk to you. And when you called me yesterday, and the day before, and the day before that. What's that? You think it's going to happen at the convention? Yeah, you told me that, too, Vincent, and I really appreciate your help. I'm going to keep checking into this. I'll get back to you."

When he snapped his phone shut, his teeth were gritted.

I gave him a peck on the cheek when I breezed by. "Bad day at the office, honey?"

He wrapped his fingers around my arm to stop me in my tracks and pulled me close so hard and so fast, I couldn't have stopped him if I wanted to. And believe me when I say, I didn't want to. "At least it was a good night at home."

The kiss he gave me to remind me of this was slow and deep and made my head spin.

"First we'll head out and see what we can find out about Jack and Dingo," he said when he was finished. "Then I'm thinking we need to come back here for some serious getting reacquainted time."

I didn't argue about that, either.

After all, I knew a good thing when I saw one, and what I'd seen—and felt—from Quinn the night before was as good as it gets. Still . . .

Oblivious to what I was thinking, he headed for the door, whistling softly.

And I wondered if he'd still have the same swagger in his walk if he knew a couple sessions of really good sex hadn't changed anything. Not really. It was easy to forget that when we were in bed together. And when we weren't?

When I walked out of the loft, my sigh rippled the air. When we weren't in bed, it was impossible to forget that there was still a gulf between me and Quinn.

And it was about a million miles wide.

First stop, my place, and since I wasn't planning on making an appearance at the office and I didn't have to worry about looking business-y, I put on jeans and long-sleeved wheat-colored T-shirt and grabbed a jacket.

Second stop . . .

I have made many a sacrifice in the name of investigating. Sleepless nights. Grimy places. Dead people. Still, I had through luck (not to mention the whole ick factor) always managed to avoid places that had anything to do with tattoos and piercings.

Until now.

"Let me guess." The girl behind the counter at Crazy Lady Body Art shopped in the large-sizes department. She was wearing a black tank top and a very short skirt, and every inch of skin I could see (and believe me, there were plenty of inches) was covered with tattoos. When she looked back and forth between me and Quinn, the silver stud in her eyebrow flashed. "You . . ." She grinned when she looked my way. "You want to get a stud in your tongue. And you . . ." The look swiveled toward Quinn, only this time, she added a come-and-get-it smile. "You're looking for—"

He flashed his badge. "Gretchen," he said.

The girl went a little pale. I mean, I guess she did. It was kind of hard to tell because she had a whole bunch of colored stars tattooed across her forehead, nose, and cheeks. Her smile fell right along with her hopes. "Gretchen!" she called out. "There's a cop here who—"

"That's fine." Quinn marched through the shop toward the back room. "I'll find her myself."

Find her, we did. Gretchen had as many tattoos as the counter girl, and way more piercings. Call me squeamish, but I couldn't look at her eyes and the studs in her eyebrows. Or her nose and the fake diamond that winked there. Or her lip and the gold hoop looped through it. If we weren't on unofficial official business, I would have grabbed Quinn's hand and told him to get me the hell out of there before I barfed.

The way it was, I stood behind him in the cramped Crazy Lady office and rather than look at Gretchen, I tried to focus on the calendar on the wall, but since it showed a tattooed torso, that wasn't exactly successful. Neither was looking at the photograph on her desk, the one that showed a smiling Gretchen with her arms around a just-as-tatted-up guy with a bald head and a beer gut.

Dingo. I'd stake my reputation as PI to the dead on it.

"You." Gretchen wasn't happy to see us. She'd been standing, and now she flopped down into the chair beside a beat-up metal desk. Like the girl at the front of the shop, she was dressed in an outfit that showed off her body art to best advantage. Black bustier. Jeans cut off so short, I had to wonder why she bothered with pants at all. "Told you everything I know about Dingo last time you came around asking."

"That was a while ago. The way I figure it, you've had time to think, and you remember a lot more now than you did then."

"Think so?" She had a smoker's laugh, and the cough to go along with it. "You're wrong."

"And you're on probation for that robbery you and Dingo pulled off at the convenience store a couple years ago." Quinn didn't so much lean toward her as he closed in. "You don't want to get on my bad side."

Her laugh was meant to be seductive. Pardon me for passing judgment, but I just couldn't tally seductive with all those nasty piercings. She glided a look from the top of Quinn's head to the tips of his shoes. "You don't have a bad side."

At least she was a good judge of . . . er . . . character.

Just in case Gretchen had forgotten I was there, I spoke up. "I think what the man means to say is that you'd better stop messing around and start talking," I said. "He's not very patient. Trust me, I know. That stuff he said about probation, he wasn't kidding."

"She's kind of touchy for a partner." Gretchen only had eyes for Quinn and she was doing her best to make the most of it. Which would explain why she spared me less than a nanosecond of a look. "Unless there's more to the two of you than just two cops trying to roust me."

Neither Quinn nor I corrected her. There wasn't much point, and besides, it didn't make any difference.

"What we're trying to do. . . ." I began.

"Is find out exactly what happened to Dingo," Quinn finished.

"And since you were supposed to be his girlfriend . . ." Yeah, I know. This was way too touchy-feely a tack to take as far as Mr. Tough Homicide Detective Who Wasn't in Homicide Anymore was concerned, but hey, speaking as a woman, I thought I knew how to get to Gretchen. When I looked at that photograph on her desk and she looked that way, too, I saw the way her eyes got misty. "If you really loved Dingo, I think you'd want to find out what really happened to him."

Touchy-feely time over. Quinn stepped forward. "And while you're at it, you can tell me if Dingo knew a cop named Jack Haggarty."

I wasn't imagining it. Gretchen really did catch her breath. "I don't know," she said. "Not for sure."

"But . . ."

Quinn and I spoke the single word together, but it was me Gretchen looked at when she answered. See, sometimes it pays to go for touchy-feely.

"Dingo, he said once that he'd met this cop named Haggarty. It wasn't . . . it wasn't like a social meeting or anything. Haggarty nailed him. You know, when Dingo was doing a job."

"Haggarty caught Dingo during a robbery?"

I was glad Quinn asked the question because I wasn't sure what Gretchen was getting at.

She nodded. "I'm guessing you cops never proved nothing, because nothing ever happened because of it. I mean, Dingo didn't do no time or nothin'. He never even went to court."

"Then there should be something in Dingo's record," I said to Quinn. "You know, about Jack arresting him. You do keep track of that kind of thing, don't you?"

I knew we'd discuss this later, but for now, it was clear he didn't want to let Gretchen in on too much of his thought process. He waved aside my question with one hand and concentrated on Gretchen.

"Where did it happen?" he asked.

When she looked up at him, her eyes were so big and moist, her mascara ran. "Dick's," she said. "You know, over on the west side. Dick's Comic Book Shop."

9

Dick's wasn't exactly what I expected, though what I expected, I really couldn't say, never having been to/ thought about/imagined a comic book shop. The store occupied the corner of a strip of stores in a decent part of town. Clean, well-lit, organized. But then, I guess when you have thousands of comic books in your inventory, organization is the name of the game.

There were other customers already browsing when we arrived, all adults and all guys. Two of them were looking through a display of new releases and three more were checking out a bookshelf at the back of the store. They looked like regular people. Who knew comic book buffs could be so normal! Or at least so normal-looking.

No browsing for us. We went right over to the front counter, a glass display case that held what was obviously the store's most unique and valuable inventory: a Dick Tracy watch, a vintage Wonder Woman lunch box, a

Spider-Man figurine, a display of postage stamps that featured superheroes.

There was a middle-aged pudgy guy behind the counter. His nametag was a giveaway. We'd found Dick.

As I had learned over the years, when it comes to business (and other things, come to think of it) Quinn isn't much for small talk. He flashed his badge.

Dick slapped a hand on the counter. "I've been calling you guys for months. It's about damn time somebody listened and came to see me."

"Have you? Been calling?" Quinn pulled out a little leather notebook and clicked open a pen. "About?"

"The robbery, of course." The three guys who'd been looking through the bookshelves came up front with a hardcover book about graphic novel artists, and Dick took care of the purchase. "That's gotta be what you're here about, right?" When he was done with his customers, Dick turned his attention back to us. "That kid you picked up here a few months ago."

"You mean Danny Ackerman."

Oh yeah, cops are sneaky that way—well, at least Quinn is. He made it sound like he knew exactly what he was talking about even though I knew he wasn't really sure. It's a great investigative technique. I should know. I'd used it myself a time or two.

"Yeah, yeah. Ackerman. That was his name." Dick settled himself comfortably, his stomach resting on the glass counter. "I know that, because the kid came in here a couple times. You know, before the robbery. He bought a couple small things and we got to talking. Figured he was just a regular kind of guy, but now that I think back, he must have been taking a look around, you know? Checking things out to see what we had and what was worth ripping off. But hey . . ." He waved a hand in the air and bonked an inflatable Iron Man hanging from the ceiling tiles above the counter. "It's that whole twenty/twenty hindsight thing. If I knew then what I know now. Only I didn't. And that's why I never thought nothing of it the night Ackerman came in here just before closing time and robbed me. I mean, I knew the kid, right? I figured he was okay people."

The two guys who'd been checking out the new releases—a skinny kid with a head full of curly black hair and an older, beefier guy with a gold stud in his ear—came over to look into the display case, and Quinn and I moved aside. Dick told them he'd be right nearby if they had any questions, came around to the front of the counter, and ushered us over to a corner where a colorful sign advertised a comic book club for kids and weekly Saturday morning meetings. There was a display there, too, one of those spinning racks that had flyers on it for other comic book shops as well as conventions and events from all over the country. Good host that he was, Dick plucked one of each flyer off the stand and handed them to me.

"Lots of fun, Officer," he said, making the same mistake the girl at Crazy Lady had in assuming I was Quinn's partner. Police partner, that is. "Comic book conventions are perfect family entertainment."

"Like the one that's coming to town?"

His smile told me I got points for knowing this. "It's gonna be great. Lots of Superman stuff there. In fact, they're doing a whole tribute to the Man of Steel. You know, on account of because—"

"Superman was created right here in Cleveland."

Could it be that I'd actually impressed Quinn with this snippet of trivia? The way he pulled his mouth into a wry smile, I think it was possible.

Dick thought this commendable, too. He excused himself around the two guys looking into the display case, raced around the counter, and came back smiling. "You get a prize," he said, pressing something small into my hand.

It was a gold ring. Well, it was a plastic ring painted gold. It had a fancy, curlicue pattern in the band and a big green stone (well, a plastic stone) in the center.

"It's what I give every customer who has the smarts to know Superman originated here in Cleveland. You know, just for fun. I tell everybody it's genuine kryptonite."

Quinn explained. "Kryptonite is a meteorite that was created when Krypton, the planet Superman came from, exploded. It's Superman's one weakness, the only thing he's powerless against."

I knew that. Sort of.

"Hey, you can wear that, Officer." Dick laughed. "Maybe it will protect you from the bad guys."

Wear? Plastic? I thought not. But rather than break Dick's heart, I thanked him with a smile and tucked the ring in my purse along with those brochures he'd given me.

"So, Danny Ackerman . . ." Quinn eased us back into the conversation.

"Ackerman, yeah. Like I was saying, he came in here that night and since it was late, I was the only one here. We chatted for a while, just like we always did. Then the

next thing I know, he's got a gun pointed at my belly."
Dick laid a hand on his round stomach. "It's a big belly. I
knew he couldn't miss."

"You must have been scared to death."

Okay, so it was more of a civilian thing to say than a
cop comment, but Quinn didn't need to look at me that
way.

"Sure, I was plenty scared." Dick nodded. "I put my
hands up just like he told me to." He demonstrated, both
hands high enough in the air to reveal the sweat stains
under his arms. "And I backed away . . ." He did that, too.
"And hey, I wasn't about to argue; I let him rifle through
the stuff in the front case. When he was done . . ." Overhead florescents, do nothing for anybody's coloring, but
they weren't the reason Dick looked a little green. Not
that I blamed him or anything. I'd been on the wrong end
of a gun a time or two in my day, too, and I knew just
thinking back on the experience was enough to unsettle
anyone. "I figured he was going to pop me right then and
there. Thank goodness that cop just happened to walk in."

I don't think people's ears actually prick. I mean, not
like a dog's or anything. But I'll tell you what, Dick sure
got Quinn's attention. His hand poised above his notepad,
Quinn shot Dick a look. "And the cop was Jack Haggarty."

"Sure. Yeah. That's right." The guys who were looking
in the front case decided to get a move on to check out the
older issues of comic books Dick kept toward the back of
the store. They excused themselves around us and while
they went one way, we went the other, wandering back
toward the front counter. "I knew Jack from around, you

know? I'd see him over at the diner across the street once in a while, or driving around the neighborhood in his patrol car. Kind of a prick."

When Dick realized he might have said something he shouldn't, that green hue in his face spread. "What I mean is that he was kind of a tough guy. Not really friendly. You know, the way some cops are." He glanced at me when he said this. No doubt, he was looking for an ally.

"But I'll tell you what." Dick ran his tongue over his lips. "That night when he walked in on the robbery, I could have grabbed Haggarty and given him a kiss. That's how happy I was to see him. That kid . . . Ackerman . . . he took one look at Haggarty and dropped his gun like it was on fire. I kicked it away so he couldn't try to go for it again." Dick was particularly proud of this. His chin came up.

No big surprise that Quinn isn't much for props. "What happened after that?" he asked.

Dick shrugged. "Haggarty took the kid away. That was months ago, and like I said, I've been calling since. I mean, I figured they want me to testify, but . . ." Another shrug. "Never heard nothing from nobody. I've called Haggarty about fifty times."

"He's been a little busy," I said without adding *being dead*.

"Yeah, well, I can understand that. I mean, hey, the city's not getting any safer, is it? I know you guys—and girls—" He gave me an apologetic smile that was supposed to make me feel better. "I know you're overworked. But hey, I haven't heard a thing. If nothing else, I'd like my merchandise back, you know? I figured you guys have had plenty of time to do whatever you need to do with it. That's what I keep calling Haggarty about. All I want is my stuff back."

"And that stuff. . . ?" I glanced at Quinn as a way of telling him to be ready to take notes. "How much did Danny Ackerman take?"

"How much?" Dick made a face. "The kid had good taste, that's for sure. But like I said, he must have been in here scoping things out. That's how he knew exactly what to go for."

"And that was . . . ?" Quinn, the essence of patience.

"Well, it's like I've told Haggarty in every single one of the messages I've left him. You know, so he won't forget. The one thing Danny Ackerman stole from me that night was a platinum number seventy-five."

When we stared at him, waiting for more, Dick's mouth pulled into a bittersweet smile. "I guess I can't expect everyone to know what we comic book aficionados know. Number seventy-five. It's from the nineties, and a real classic comic if ever there was one. Not one of the ones in the black-and red bag. I've got those around here, too, and I'm asking thirty bucks apiece for them. This comic was one of the platinum ones and I had a price tag of eight hundred bucks on that baby. You know, *The Death of Superman*."

Superman.
     One guy I'd never even met, and I was already sick of hearing about him.

Not that I'm all that into obsessing about stuff like that, or even thinking about it when there are so many other things to occupy my mind. (Like what Quinn and I would be up to later in the evening because he texted me bright and early the day after we visited Dick's and said he hoped to see me that night.) But when I arrived at Garden View at nine, and a gigantic vase of flowers arrived for me from Milo Blackburne at ten, I couldn't help but do a little grumbling.

After all, Milo Blackburne had admitted that he was a fan of the Man of Steel.

And the mystery surrounding Jack Haggarty and Dingo had something to do with a Superman comic book.

What's it that psychology types call it when you focus on one thing because you don't want to think about another?

Transference?

All right, I admit it, rather than think about how I wanted Blackburne to open up his checkbook and give to the cemetery, but how I didn't want to give him me in return, I concentrated on the whole, crazy super-theme mojo that had suddenly popped into my life.

Hence, the grumbling.

"Not going to do it," I said, looking over the three dozen red and white roses in a vase the size of my apartment. "Not going to sell myself in exchange for Milo Blackburne's money, and I'm going to tell him exactly that. And I'm going to tell Ella, too. It will be kinder to her in the long run. And better for me, that's for sure. And—"

"Oh, Pepper!" Of course, Ella had no idea how I was preparing to cut off our potentially biggest donor at the knees. That would explain why she sounded chipper when she breezed into my office just a few minutes after the flowers arrived.

Her cheeks rosy, Ella stopped inside the door and looked over the arrangement, and her eyebrows climbed up her forehead. "Someone's trying to impress you," she said, her voice a singsong that told me she thought she knew who that someone was. "Those flowers must have cost a fortune."

She was right. And I was impressed. To a point, anyway.

But not impressed enough to sell my soul.

Or any other part of me Milo Blackburne might have his eye on.

"It's not what you think," I told her.

"Oh, I'm pretty sure it is." Her grin said it all.

In fact, it said so much, I couldn't stand to even look at it. I went around to the other side of my desk and sat down. That flower arrangement was so big, I could barely see Ella on the other side.

"They're from Milo Blackburne," I mumbled.

"Oh." The way she said it, I had to sit up, part the flowers, and take a gander at Ella. What I saw was that the color in her cheeks had ebbed, at least for a moment. "I thought they were from Quinn and that maybe you had something to tell me about the two of you. But . . ." Color or no color, her eyes twinkled. "But this news is just as good, isn't it? I mean, in a whole different way."

"No, it's not." I was tired of trying to make eye contact through the forest of flowers, baby's breath, and ferns so I rose to my feet. "He thinks—"

"Of course he doesn't." Maybe I was better off sitting down. At least with thirty-six roses placed strategically between us, I didn't have to see Ella rocking back and forth, her excitement uncontainable. "No doubt he thinks you're smart and beautiful, Pepper. Because you are smart and beautiful. But he'd never overstep the line. Give the man a break. He's good-looking, rich, and available. It's only natural that Milo Blackburne would—"

"But I don't want him to," I wailed.

Ella clutched her hands together at the waist of her trim navy suit.

Ella. Navy suit. Sedate pearls at throat matching the pearl studs in her ears.

For the first time since she sailed in I took a minute to look Ella over.

And another to wonder what the hell was going on.

"What are you up to?" I asked her. "You look—"

"Businesslike and in control, I hope." Ella fanned a hand in front of her face. "We've got a board of trustees meeting this afternoon and I didn't want to come across as too flighty. Or too casual. Or not serious enough. I thought I'd be better off showing them my no-nonsense side. You know, so they don't get any ideas about making my probation period even shorter than it already is."

"Not a chance." I believed this with all my heart so it wasn't hard to put some oomph behind the statement. "They know you're the best person for the job. That's why they gave it to you in the first place. Besides, who else could they possibly find who would love Garden View more than you do?"

"It's true." Ella pulled in a breath. "This cemetery is in

my blood. Just like I'm sure it's in yours, Pepper. But you know how some people can be, and you know what they told me when they gave me the job." My office door was closed so it wasn't like anybody was going to hear, but she leaned closer, anyway. "You know, about how I won't keep the administrator's job if I don't bring in some serious donations."

I tried not to look, but I couldn't help myself. My gaze automatically went to the flowers and an iceberg settled in my stomach. "Like Milo Blackburne's."

"I hope you don't think—" This time, the color that shot into Ella's cheeks was the exact shade of the red roses in the vase. "I hope you don't think I'm asking you to . . ." She lowered her voice to a whisper. "To prostitute yourself. I mean, figuratively speaking. If there's something about Mr. Blackburne that's making you uncomfortable, Pepper—"

"No, there isn't. Not really." It was the truth, and I told myself not to forget it. Maybe then I wouldn't be so queasy. "I just don't need a guy hanging around right now."

"Oh?"

How can anybody utter that one little syllable and make it pack the punch of so many suspicions?

Ella's grin ratcheted up a notch. "It is Quinn, isn't it? You two . . . are you back together?"

"Maybe," I told her, because really, I wasn't in the mood for a million questions I wasn't going to answer, especially when I wasn't sure of the answers, anyway. "We've been seeing each other."

"I knew it!" Ella clapped her hands together. "I told

you years ago, Pepper, you two are meant for each other. I knew he'd come around eventually. Oh, I just love a happily ever after."

"And Milo Blackburne?"

She clicked her tongue and headed back across the office. "All you have to do is be pleasant. And get me that donation. Nobody's telling you to marry him." She stopped just as she got to the door. "Oh, I almost forgot what I came in here for. I was looking over that list you left on my desk yesterday. The one about the speakers' bureau."

I braced myself for more questions, and this time, they wouldn't be ones I didn't want to answer, they'd be ones it was impossible for me to answer. Apparently while I was out investigating, Jean had been hard at work.

"The list." I said this with as much enthusiasm as I could muster and scrambled for a half-truth that would satisfy Ella. "Let me explain."

"No need." Ella opened the door and scurried into the hallway. "I just wanted you to know that it's absolutely perfect. You've paired some of our most knowledgeable volunteers with the subjects they're best qualified to talk about. It's brilliant, Pepper, and you put the whole thing together so quickly and so professionally. I'm impressed, and you can be sure I'm going to mention your good work to the trustees this afternoon."

She left smiling.

And after that, I was supposed to call Milo Blackburne and tell him to stick his flowers?

Okay, yeah, I was tempted. But before I could, my phone rang.

"Hey."

Mr. Small Talk.

"Thought you should know I did some digging around," Quinn said. "You know, about Jack and Dingo."

"And . . . ?"

"And nothing." Quinn did not sound happy to report this. "Nobody knows anything about it. Not unofficially. Not officially."

"But then how—"

"Yeah. Exactly what I've been asking myself. But I've done all the digging it's possible to do and I'm coming up empty. We know what Dick told us, but there's no record of Jack Haggarty ever having arrested Danny Ackerman for that comic book store robbery."

10

B y the time I was done talking to Quinn, I was grumbling again.

Jack arrested Dingo but he didn't arrest Dingo?

It made no sense at all, and besides, I knew that if my
newest ghostly acquaintance showed (which he didn't, but
then, ghosts have the annoying habit of never being
around when I need them), it wouldn't help much. Playing
guessing games while Jack tried to signal what he wanted
me to know was not high on my list of things to do at the
moment.

And even if it was, I wouldn't have had the luxury. The
latest issue of the Garden View newsletter was due on
Ella's desk in just a couple days, and in an effort to get it
done—but without the effort part—I'd set Chet Houston
up with one of those voice-activated tape recorders in a
mausoleum that I knew hadn't had a visitor in years. I was
supposed to pick up his dictated newsletter articles that

morning so that I'd have time to enter them in my computer, and still thinking about Jack and Dingo and what the arrest record that wasn't meant, I climbed into my car and drove to the other side of the cemetery.

As soon as I parked the Mustang, I was reminded that this was still an active part of the cemetery. In graveyard lingo, that means people were still being buried there. There was a freshly dug grave between the road and the mausoleum where I was headed, and a backhoe waiting to finish the job once the casket was finally in place. I wound my way through the folding wooden chairs set up for the mourners around the gaping hole and made up my mind: Chet and I would have to make this meeting short and sweet. I might not be a cemetery geek, but I wasn't a total loser when it came to understanding grief and the respect due mourners. I didn't belong, and I'd need to be long gone by the time the funeral procession arrived.

With that in mind, I ducked into the mausoleum and wrapped up my business with Chet in no time at all. For the record, his new headstone had been put into place, and he was thrilled. No angels. No flowers. I had a friend and a ghostwriter—literally—for life.

That taken care of, I'd just stepped outside and locked the mausoleum door behind me when a prickle like icy fingers touched the back of my neck.

You can't be a private investigator for the dead for as long as I have and not know what this means—someone was watching me, and since Chet had disappeared into the nothingness where ghosts go when they're not bugging me, it wasn't him.

It wasn't the funeral goers, either. One quick look

around, and I didn't see any cars but my own and no one walking through the vast expanse of headstones or visiting at one of the nearby graves. At least no one I could see.

But still, those icy fingers danced across my skin, chilling me to the bone.

"Hello!" Anyone else would have headed right to the car, but hey, see above and the whole PI to the gone but not departed bunch. The someone I knew was hanging around could be someone who wasn't really a someone anymore. Catch my drift? If that was the case, it was best to get things over with.

"Are you looking for me?" I called out into the still air. "Because if you are, make it quick. I've got stuff to do back at the office."

No answer.

No sounds.

No nothing.

Nothing but that sensation that trickled down the back of my neck and seeped into my spine. Somewhere along the way it soaked into my bloodstream, too. My legs locked, and my stomach clenched. The quiet settled against me like unseen hands.

Adrenaline is a funny thing. At the same time it exploded through my body and rooted me to the spot, it tickled my brain and sent out a warning.

Run.

Great advice if I could make my feet move.

Run.

I gulped in a breath that hurt going down around the ball of panic wedged in my throat.

Run.

I did. Or at least I tried.

For one thing, it was hard to take those first few steps on account of how my legs were heavy and I couldn't breathe. For another, I hadn't planned on doing anything more strenuous that day than going out to the nearest Chinese takeaway for lunch so I'd worn a new pair of platform-soled, peep-toe pumps. Black patent leather upper, python heel (okay, fake python heel, but it looked like the real thing). They were as cute as can be, and they might have been serviceable when it came to covering a short, flat span in a reasonable amount of time, but the ground in cemeteries is lumpy and there were dozens of headstones—and that newly dug grave—between me and my car. I dodged around an angel with a sad face, did a two-step scurry (it was more like a shuffle) past an urn atop a monument that was a full twelve feet tall, stepped over a flat stone half hidden by grass.

And tripped.

Desperate to keep from smacking into the nearest headstone, I threw out a hand and, hallelujah, connected with one of those chairs set up for the funeral. For a second, it held. That is, until the chair folded and went down and I went down with it.

My knees thwacked against a flat headstone and I cursed my luck and my dry cleaning bill since I was wearing linen pants in a sage color that was sure to show the dirt. The good news was that after a few seconds, the pain in my knees subsided and I knew I wasn't seriously hurt.

The bad news?

It turned out to be a few seconds too long.

Before I could pull myself to my feet and long before I realized someone had come up behind me, two hands went around my throat. I wedged my fingers under my attacker's, fighting to loosen the grip, but even I knew it was a losing cause. His fingers digging into my windpipe, the man (who else would be that strong?) lifted me clear off the ground.

I kicked. And thrashed. I would have screamed if I could get so much as a peep out of a windpipe that was slowly being crushed.

My attacker hauled me to the lip of that open grave.

I'd like to say that the last thing I heard before he threw me into the hole were the sounds of my own feeble screams.

Too bad that wasn't true.

See, the last thing I heard was that backhoe chugging to life.

Right before it rolled over to the hole and dropped a load of dirt on top of me.

I would have tried screaming again if I wasn't afraid of getting a mouth full of dirt.

The way it was, I propped my hands over my head and fell to my knees under the weight of the first load of dirt.

"No, no, no." My voice was small and muffled in the confines of the grave. "Not going to die like this."

Finished with the load, the backhoe pulled away, but I didn't dare breathe a sigh of relief. I knew what it meant— my attacker was going for more dirt.

"It's really not such a bad thing, you know."

In a morning filled with surprises, hearing the sound of another voice down there in some stranger's grave was par for the course. I brushed soil off my face and opened my eyes to find Albert, my personal accountant, standing in the corner opposite from me, as calm as can be.

He could afford to be calm. He was already dead.

"Are you crazy?" Hard to believe my voice could be so shrill, what with nearly having my trachea crushed and all. "Dead is very bad. It's . . . it's dead."

Albert was a full head shorter than me, anorexic-looking, and I suspected, as pale in life as he was now when he floated over the first load of dirt toward me. He had a pair of wire-rimmed glasses pinched to the bridge of his nose, and they winked at me in what little light made its way to the bottom of the hole. "You'll be fine in a minute," he said.

"I'll be dead in a minute."

The beeping of the backhoe proved my point. "He's coming back," I wailed. "Albert, I got those bushes planted for you. You've got to do something!"

"Me? Oh dear." Behind his glasses, Albert blinked. "I'm afraid I wouldn't know how. I'm just an accountant, after all."

"Then get somebody else. Somebody who can help."

"I'm afraid there isn't anyone else. I can't fetch help because you're the only one who can see and hear me."

"Then what about . . ." The whirring of the backhoe's engine got closer, louder. "Get Chet. Maybe Chet will know what to do."

He did, all right. When Chet popped up next to me, he was holding a pad of paper and the stub of a pencil.

"I'll get the details," he said. "You know, of your last moments."

This was supposed to make me feel better?

Rather than argue, I screamed, and when I was done, I screamed some more. At the same time I was doing that, I dug my cell out of my pocket and tried Ella's number.

Just for the record, it's impossible to get a cell signal in a grave.

Time for a Plan B, and I needed to come up with it fast.

"I do hate to bother you at a time like this, Miss Martin." This time, it was Jean who showed up. Three ghosts and a hole that was no bigger than a couple feet across and six feet deep. It was getting crowded in there, not to mention chilly.

Jean clutched her hands at her waist. "I was just planning. You understand. For any . . . contingencies."

"Contingencies." I had to yell to be heard over the sounds of the backhoe. The motor birred and I knew my assailant was raising the bucket, getting ready to drop the next load. "You mean contingencies like me being dead?"

"Well, I should go over your schedule with you. Just in case. I'd hate for cemetery business to suffer. You know." Jean gave me a level look. "Just in case."

Her words were brought home when the second load of dirt rained down on me.

Pebbles bonked me in the head. Dirt splattered into my eyes. Instinctively, I folded myself into the corner of the grave and luckily, my attacker couldn't see me from his seat in the backhoe; he dumped the dirt in the center of the hole.

Spiders on my shoulders.

Worms stroking my arms.

Muck that oozed up from the bottom of the grave and squished between my toes.

I ignored it all, keeping my place and holding my breath while the dirt spilled into the grave and flew around me in a gritty cloud. When it settled enough for me to see again, what I saw was that my three ghostly assistant were gone and Jack Haggarty was down in the hole with me. He was standing in the center of the grave, right atop that dirt pile, and he was jumping up and down.

"Yeah. Right. Thanks." I made the mistake of running my tongue over my lips, then ended up spitting out a mouthful of soil. "I'm kind of not in the mood for games, Jack. A little busy here getting buried alive."

Jack jumped up and down some more.

He looked down at the dirt. Jump. Jump. Jump.

He looked up at me. Jump. Jump. Jump.

And for a woman who earlier in the day swore she didn't want to engage in another round of charades, I decided suddenly and completely, that pantomime was my favorite thing in the world.

Because, see, I knew what Jack wanted me to do.

It wasn't easy and, thank goodness, there never were and never would be pictures. But I climbed right on top of that dirt pile and did exactly what Jack was doing. I jumped up and down for all I was worth.

Slowly—too slowly—the dirt beneath my feet packed down. It wasn't hard to figure out why I couldn't move faster. I said good-bye to the peep-toe pumps and kept hopping for all I was worth.

Little by little, that dirt pile at the bottom of the grave

got harder and taller, and I wasn't so deep underground anymore. One more load . . .

I glanced at Jack, who looked relieved that I'd gotten the message. "If it doesn't cover me completely and smother me to death," I told him, "one more load and I should have enough dirt to pack down to climb out of here."

If.

In what seemed way too short a time, the backhoe's yellow basket filled with soil hung directly above me again.

Dirt rained down, and I scrambled down the hill I'd created and mashed myself into the corner. By now, even this far from the center of the grave, the dirt was nearly up to my waist, and I had to fight my way through it to get to the higher spot I'd stomped into existence. I fell down twice when the ground beneath my feet slipped out from under me, and when I couldn't get up fast enough, I pounded the dirt with my fists. Before the backhoe could return, I had built up the little hill just enough to see out of the grave.

That was when I realized that my plan—brilliant as it was—was just a tad lacking. Had I built up the hill closer to the rim of the grave, I might have been able to pull myself to safety. The way it was, I was in the center of a pile molded like one of those cone-shaped bullet bras Madonna is famous for wearing. Too bad the pointy part of the cone was smack-dab in the center of the grave.

I didn't have time to try to reconfigure my escape route. From here, I could see the backhoe chomp into what was left of the waiting dirt pile. It backed up, turned, and headed my way. This time, I knew the load would be its last. There were no corners left for me to hide in.

At least I would be buried with my peep-toe pumps.

I was just thinking that it wasn't much of a consolation when a couple things happened.

Number one, I got a look at the man operating the backhoe. Tall, skinny, young. He had a wild mop of dark curly hair, and I knew I'd seen him before. Somewhere. If I wasn't so freaking scared, I might have taken the time to figure it out. But I was. Scared, that is.

At least until a sleek black hearse rolled around the corner and stopped nearby.

The funeral had arrived.

My attacker saw the procession just as I did. The motor still running, he jumped off the backhoe. The last I saw of him was his back as he ducked into a dense planting of rhododendrons.

And me?

My knees were knocking so loud, I'm surprised the funeral director didn't hear them when he got out of the hearse and came over to the grave to give it one last look-see before he had the pallbearers bring the casket over.

"If you wouldn't mind." I stuck my hand out, and honestly, I couldn't say what the poor man was thinking when his mouth fell open. Maybe he was wondering what he was going to do with the deceased now that the hole was nearly filled. Or maybe he'd just never seen a redhead in very dirty clothes rising from the ground before. I was hardly in the mood to quibble. Speechless, he offered me a hand and more gratefully than I can say, I accepted it and climbed out of the grave.

* * *

What's a girl supposed to do in a situation like that? I don't know about anybody else, but this girl is no fool. There were a couple of those carry-along reusable shopping bags (that I never use) in the trunk of my car, and I got them out so I could sit on them and keep my car seat reasonably clean, then I drove like a bat out of hell, all the way home.

Once there, I did a couple things, not necessarily in this order:

I locked the door behind me and checked the lock three times to make sure it was secure.

I looked inside every closet and under my bed just in case someone was lurking.

I took a shower.

In fact, I took two showers.

And promised myself before the afternoon was over I'd take another one.

Just to make sure all the dirt of the grave was washed away.

That done, I called Ella and told her I wouldn't be back at Garden View for the rest of the day. She, of course, was in that board of trustees meeting, which meant all I had to do was leave a message. By the time I saw her the next day, I'd come up with some plausible reason that explained my absence and didn't involve nearly getting buried alive.

Buried alive.

Just thinking about it made a shudder shoot up my back.

I also called Quinn, and him, I didn't want to leave a message for. I wanted to tell him the story of what happened back at Garden View. Right now. When I got his voice mail, I didn't bother to leave a message. Somehow, "Someone tried to kill me" just doesn't pack that same punch when it's left as a message.

After my second shower, I'd put on flannel lounge pants (they were decorated with palm trees and pink flamingoes, a present from my mom in Florida) and a long-sleeved T-shirt and now, I wrapped my arms around myself in an effort to stop my shivering and held on tight. Sure, I considered calling Quinn again—who is, after all, mighty good in the hold-on-tight department himself—but decided against it. I was fine, if a little shaken, and I'd see him later that evening and tell him what had happened.

I'd also tell him about the kid on the backhoe. The one with the shaggy hair.

A kid I knew I'd seen somewhere before.

Maybe with a little time and the chance to think, I could remember who he was and how I knew him. Then, maybe I could also figure out why he wanted to kill me.

The knocking inside my ribs started up again, and I knew there was only one thing that could calm it down. Bad news, not a scrap of chocolate anywhere in the apartment. I should know. I looked through every drawer and cupboard. I settled for second best and poured myself the last of a bottle of pinot noir that I'd opened a week before.

One gulp and some of the ice inside me uncurled. Another, and a blanket I pulled off my bed and wrapped around my shoulders when I sat down on the couch, and I found myself letting go the breath I'd felt as if I was holding since that first load of dirt rained down on me. A third . . .

And I swore I heard someone in the hallway outside my door.

"You're imagining it, Pepper," I told myself.

But I sure wasn't imagining the shadow that slipped by out in the hallway.

Imagining? Oh, I was imagining, all right, and right about then, my imagination pictured the kid with the shaggy hair, come to finish what he'd started back at Garden View.

The ice was back, and its cold made me shiver. Knees knocking, I dragged myself off the couch and into the bedroom. Once upon a time, Quinn had given me a baseball bat and insisted I keep it around for protection. I, bright girl that I am, had informed him that it was never going to happen. Messy, for one thing. And for another, I'd have to get too close to a bad guy to actually use it.

Now, I felt around under the bed for it and dragged out the bat with trembling hands. By the time I got back to the living room, I knew I'd done the right thing because somebody was jiggling the door, trying to pop the lock.

One near-death experience a day is enough for anybody, thank you very much.

I closed my fingers around the bat in a death grip just as the door shot open.

Deep breath.

Tense muscles.

I raised the bat over my head, all set to swing, and it was a good thing the fear subsided just for an instant. Otherwise, I might not have registered the faces of the two people standing out in the hallway with their mouths open, looking from me to the bat and wondering what they'd just walked into.

All the terror washed out of me and I was left there, bat in hands, in complete and utter astonishment, looking from one of them to the other. "Mom? Dad? What the hell are you two doing here?"

11

I was too stunned to invite my parents in, but hey, they were my parents after all, and a little thing like an invitation never stopped Barb and Gil Martin. So busy laughing they didn't even notice me stashing the bat behind the table near the door, they looped their arms together and breezed past me and into my apartment.

My mother looked around and crooned, "It's so nice, honey," but don't think that fooled me. I recognized the appraising look she swept across the apartment. Quick, yes. Thorough, absolutely. Nobody could size up a person, a place, or the retail cost of furniture and accessories as well as Mom. Nobody could bullshit like she could, either. Not when it came to things like this. Oh yeah, there was a sweet smile in her eyes, but I knew what it really meant. She was well aware of the fact that the family had fallen on hard times. She'd just never imagined I'd hit bottom so hard.

Don't get the wrong impression. It's not that Mom is snooty or anything. Mom is . . . well, it's a little hard to explain. Let's settle for particular (at least when it came to clothes, home furnishings, and jewelry). While I'm at it, I might as well point out that she's got terrific taste and a great sense of humor. And she's kind to small children and animals, too. It's just that Mom is used to the best. Back in the days before Dad got sent to federal prison, she always had it, too. She wouldn't have settled for anything less.

Federal prison.

The words flowed through my veins like ice water and I raced forward, slammed my apartment door shut, flattened my back to it, and looked at my dad in horror.

"You escaped!"

I got my height from my dad's side of the family. Like Grandpa Martin, Dad was over six feet tall, slender and handsome enough to be appreciated by the tony clientele who used to worship his skills as a cosmetic surgeon. But then, even features, a firm chin, and dark hair touched with silver at the temples does that to a lot of women. When I'd visited him in prison in Colorado, I also realized that like so many of the other prisoners I saw, he had a sort of lean and hungry look. Wary. Like I could blame him? Word on the street is that federal prisons are a whole lot like country clubs. Don't be fooled. Prison is prison, and when it came to prisoners, Dad was an aberration. Gen pop is not made up of Harvard-educated doctors who've given in to temptation and gotten caught red-handed.

When my dad looked down at me, he was smiling. But the smile didn't quite make it all the way to his eyes.

"Don't be silly, sweetheart. You know I'd never do anything as foolish as that." Dad folded me into a hug and held on for a long time. I didn't complain. It beat the hell out of talking to him on a phone with a heavy plexiglass window between us.

When he was done and he held me at arm's length, there was a sheen in his eyes. "I got early release," he announced. "You know, because of my good behavior. I just got back to Cleveland this afternoon."

This was good news. Better than good. But let's face it, this whole family reunion thing came at me out of the blue. And on top of nearly being buried alive.

I was at a loss for words.

Not so my mom. Never one to keep still, she was already fluffing the pillows on my couch, grinning at my dad, and blushing like a sixteen-year-old every time their eyes met. My coloring came from the women on Mom's side of the family. Redheads, all, with porcelain skin and the God-given gift of knowing how to take advantage of their looks. At sixty, Mom was slim, and wearing yellow capris, a sleeveless top the color of limes, a kicky cropped cardigan in a sunshine-y shade, and a dozen gold bangle bracelets. It seemed a couple years in Florida hadn't changed her taste in jewelry.

"Here's how it works," she said, tossing the pillow back onto the couch. "When a person gets released early, that person has to have somebody to vouch for them. You know, somebody who will keep an eye on them. Day and night."

There was that blush again, along with a giggle that made me wonder what Mom and Dad had been up to since she collected him at the airport.

Not something I wanted to think about!

"I had to prove that I had a stable place to live, and they'll want me to find a job." Dad was grinning, too.

"So you're . . ." Dad was on my left and Mom was over in the other direction, and I looked back and forth. "The two of you are heading back to Florida?"

"That's the really good news!" No one had ever accused Mom of a lack of enthusiasm. She raced over to give me a peck on the cheek. "I bought a condo, honey. About ten minutes from here. Dad and I are back for good!"

"This calls for a celebration!" Dad took hold of my hand. "How about we head over to Lolita's? That was always your favorite. We'll get a bottle of champagne and—"

"I'm not exactly dressed for Lolita's," I said, glancing down at my flannel pants and the pink flamingoes on them. Better that than reminding my own father that he was an ex-con who'd lost everything when the federal government swooped down on what it called his illegal enterprise. No way he could afford one of the priciest restaurants in town.

"But we can celebrate. Right here." I raced into the kitchen. Thanks to Quinn teaching me the finer points of wine drinking (okay, yes, he'd taught me some other things, too, but that's not what I'm talking about), I always kept a couple bottles around. I'd finished my glass of pinot, so I uncorked an Argentine Malbec and grabbed two more glasses. I wasn't expecting company, but I managed to scrape together some munchies, too, in the way of Cheez-Its, dry roasted peanuts, and grapes.

Weird.

It was the first word that popped into my head when I walked back into the living room and saw my parents sitting side by side on the couch. They were looking into each other's eyes, holding hands. And it was weird.

And pretty darned terrific.

For the first time since that backhoe had dumped the first load of dirt on top of my head that afternoon, the ice inside me melted and I grinned.

Maybe getting stuck in a grave isn't such a bad thing after all. After all, I managed to crawl out alive. And found my family waiting for me.

"So, they said I was a model prisoner and they saw no problem with me getting out." Dad divided the last of the bottle of wine between the three of us and sat back against my lumpy couch cushions. He popped a handful of peanuts in his mouth. "I think I'm going to like being on the outside again."

"I know I'm going to like having you here." My mom ran a hand up and down his thigh.

He leaned over and gave her a kiss.

It was gross and disgusting to watch them act like lovesick teenagers.

And as cute as can be, too.

Of course, cute or not, there's only so much any one person can take. I was saved from watching any more of the billing and cooing by a knock on my door.

It matched the one that started up inside my ribs when I remembered that just a few hours earlier, someone had tried to kill me. If that same someone followed me home . . . And if now, my parents were in danger, too . . .

My wineglass halfway to my lips, I froze.

"Well, go on, honey." The bracelets on her wrist jingled when Mom waved me toward the door. "See who it is. The kind of day you're having, you never know what other surprises might be in store for you!"

She had no idea how right she was.

Or how terrifying that thought was.

Good thing my flannel pants hid the ways my knees knocked. At the door, I thought about grabbing the bat I'd dropped behind the table and decided if I did, Mom and Dad would start asking questions. Besides, there were three of us there. Three Martins. So I might be deluding myself. I took comfort in the thought that we could handle whatever the Universe decided to throw at us.

I yanked the door open.

And breathed a sigh of relief.

It was Quinn.

"I'm interrupting something."

No doubt he heard the sounds of my mother's laughter. She was, after all, nuzzling her lips against Dad's ear and that sort of sound carries. Especially in an apartment as small as mine.

"Interrupting? No, not at all. It's just . . ." Yeah, I thought about making up some half-baked excuse and sending him on his way. But let's face it, this moment was bound to happen. Sooner or later. I might as well get it over with.

I stepped away from the door and used a Vanna-like gesture to point him toward the couch. "My parents," I said.

Quinn is not easily surprised. Cop, after all. But the way he pursed his lips, I could tell even he wasn't expecting this.

"Oh, this must be your policeman friend." My mother jumped off the couch and hurried over to pull Quinn into a hug. "We've heard all about you," she told him.

"You have?"

Quinn was looking at me when he said this.

I was looking at my mom when I said this.

Predictably, she took our collective astonishment in stride. "Not from Penelope," she told Quinn. At the risk of sounding like I'd fallen under the spell of the superhero mojo that seemed to surround me these days, I've got to admit that her sudden use of my real name rather than my nickname made my Spidey sense tingle. The last time Mom had called me Penelope was when she yelled upstairs to let me know my date had arrived for the senior prom.

"We haven't had a chance for a little heart-to-heart. Not yet, anyway. I heard from Ella, of course, and she described you to a T." She swung her gaze around to me. "She's a wonderful woman, Ella. I'm so glad you've had her here to help you while we've been gone."

It must have been the wine. Or that last handful of Cheez-Its. My stomach wasn't feeling so good. I sat down in the chair opposite my dad and though I was pretty sure I didn't want to hear it, I waited for my mother to explain.

She did. With a smile.

"Well, you didn't think I'd just be sitting down there in Florida and not thinking about you, honey." On her way by, she touched a hand to my shoulder. "I got to talking to

Ella a couple years ago. You know, just by way of finding out what you were up to and if you were okay. We email each other every day. She's the one who told me. You know . . ." She looked at Quinn who was standing behind my chair. I didn't have to look to know his hands were bunched against the cushions. I could feel the tension clear through the fabric. Like he actually couldn't hear her, Mom leaned forward and lowered her voice to a whisper. "About him."

What had Mom said earlier? About more surprises that day?

This was one I didn't need, not a discussion of my love life in the presence of a man who was . . . well, whatever the hell Quinn was to me, I didn't need to discuss it with my parents.

I popped out of my chair. "I'll get another bottle of wine," I said.

"And I'm going to order a pizza," Dad called out. "Still like double pepperoni, sweetheart?"

Since I grabbed Quinn's hand and dragged him into the kitchen with me, neither one of us had a chance to answer.

"Sorry," I said, reaching for another bottle of wine.

"About what?"

Yes, I rolled my eyes. It was an appropriate moment if ever there was one. "My mother and Ella. They've been gossiping about us."

He lifted his shoulders. He'd obviously just come from work. He was wearing a killer navy suit and a shirt the color of pomegranates. Needless to say, the tie complemented both, and somehow managed to bring out the emerald green of his eyes, too. Some people are Gifted one

157

way, some are Gifted another. Quinn's Gift for choosing clothing was equal to mine. Lucky him, though, he didn't have the annoying ghostly Gift to go along with it. "Your mother and Ella, they care about you."

"They need to mind their own business."

My mother giggled, and Quinn looked past me and back toward the living room. "He didn't escape, did he?"

I didn't bother to point out that it was the same question I'd asked. "Don't be ridiculous. He got released early. You know, for good behavior."

"And now?"

I handed off the bottle to Quinn so he could open it and got another wineglass down off the shelf.

Since I didn't know the answer, I ignored his question. Good thing. No sooner were we back in the living room than Mom answered it for me. Sort of.

"So . . ." Her chin quivered with excitement. "We've got something to show you." She reached for the Marc Jacobs bag I remembered as being one of the few things the feds had allowed her to keep from our old life and came out holding a business card. I was curious. More than curious. But rather than hand the card to me, she glanced at Quinn.

"This is perfect timing," Mom said. "You being here and all. Because Ella explained. You know, about how you and Penelope work on so many cases together."

Damn Quinn for looking amused. I was pretty convinced there was nothing funny about this. Not only had Ella and my mom been talking about my love life, they'd apparently been discussing my professional life, too. Good thing neither of them knew about my connection with the Other Side. No good could come from two middle-aged women speculating about that.

Dad and Mom exchanged looks. "We knew the day would come," Dad said, and I swear, if he mentioned me getting married, I was going to run screaming from the apartment. "That's why we weren't surprised when Ella mentioned your . . . well, you know what we're talking about, honey. When Ella said you were getting mixed up in some odd things, your mother and I, well, we never batted an eyelash. The investigating, it makes perfect sense."

Another look back and forth between Mom and Dad. I was feeling like I was watching a tennis match. "It does?"

"Well, of course." My mother's gentle laughter filled the room. "It was bound to happen sooner or later. You know, because of the ghosts."

I don't know how long I stood there with my mouth hanging open.

I don't want to know.

It is, after all, a bad look for me, and rather than think about it, I'd prefer just to pretend it never happened.

I might have had the chance if Mom and Dad weren't sitting there on the couch looking so darned pleased with themselves.

I do know that Quinn finally took my arm and escorted me back to the chair I'd gotten out of just a short while before. He handed me a glass of wine. I drank it. I held out the glass, he refilled it, and I drank half of that, too, before I found my voice and squeaked. "The ghosts? You know about the ghosts?"

"Well, we didn't. Not for certain. Not until right now." Mom's laugh was merry. She scooted forward in her seat. "But of course, we suspected. The look on your face is priceless, honey, it confirms everything!"

Remember what I said about Quinn not getting surprised often? I take it back. For the second time since he walked into the apartment, he looked as if someone had landed a solid sucker punch to the stomach. There wasn't another chair for him, so he dropped onto the arm of the one I was sitting in.

For all her flightiness, Mom is not without a conscience. Her mouth pinched and her cheeks went pale. "I hate to admit it, Gil, but I think you were right all those years ago when you said we should have had the talk with our little girl. Then maybe she wouldn't be sitting there looking like she'd just sucked on a lemon."

"I do not—" There was no use protesting. I had no doubt that's exactly how I looked. "Somebody better explain," I said instead. "And fast."

"Sure. Of course." Dad sat back. For exactly three seconds. That's when there was another knock on my door. "The pizza!" he said.

Call me paranoid. I made Quinn go to the door and since he had way more money than the ex-con, my mom, or me, I let him pay for the pizza, too. He came back carrying two boxes, double pepperoni and the works. That gave me a chance to duck into the kitchen for dishes and napkins and while I was at it, I tried to process everything that had just happened. Too bad it didn't do anything to help settle the sudden thumping in my chest. I returned to the living room, passed around the plates, and made sure my voice was no-nonsense when I said, "Explain. Now."

My mom had just bitten into a slice of double pepperoni and she had a string of cheese on her chin. With one finger, my dad flicked it away.

"It's like this, honey," Mom said, providing the explanation so Dad could wolf down a slice of the works. Something told me quality pizza wasn't one of the amenities offered in federal prison. "It's a family thing. You know, the Gift."

I had yet to reach for a piece of pizza. Good thing. I'm pretty sure I would have choked on it. "You're telling me you—"

"Oh no! I'm not nearly that lucky." Mom had taken another bite of pizza and she washed it down with a sip of wine. "But your aunt Charlotte, and Grandma Martin, of course. Grandma Martin was always chatting it up with ghosts."

Dad nodded. "As kids, we always just accepted it. It was what Mom did."

"But—"

"Well, we didn't want to say anything when you were young." Finished with her pizza, Mom sat back and eyed the box, deciding if she wanted another piece. "You know, in case you didn't get the Gift. We didn't want you to be disappointed."

"But—"

"But when Ella started telling us about all the strange things you were involved with, well, it just made sense." My dad offered a piece of the works to Quinn, but since

161

he was sitting on the arm of the chair looking just as stunned as I felt, he passed. Dad ate the pizza instead. "Mom and I compared notes, and that's when we figured out what was happening," he said between bites. "You see them. You talk to them. Just like my mother used to do."

"But—"

"Oh, I know what you're going to say!" Mom grinned. "You're going to tell us that you thought it started when you hit your head on that mausoleum a couple years back. No doubt, that's exactly how it feels. But think about it, honey. Don't you remember, when you were a little kid, you had invisible friends."

I did. I just never thought—

I swear, my entire Little Italy neighborhood heard me gulp.

"And even when you got a little older . . . well, you did sometimes tell me that you'd had strange dreams. About people you didn't know."

It was true. I just never imagined—

I didn't realize I was trembling until I felt Quinn's hand on my shoulder trying to keep me still.

"Drink some more wine," he advised, pouring.

He didn't have to tell me twice.

"So, like I was saying . . ." When the pizza had arrived, Mom set down that business card on the couch cushion next to her. Now, she picked it up again and handed it across the coffee table to me. "What do you think?" she asked.

The card was tasteful yet eye-catching.

Black, with one bold graphic, a sort of silvery smudge that suggested something mysterious.

The lettering was simple. *GBP Investigations*, it said. Along with my cell number.

Mom was so excited, she could barely sit still. "Don't you just love it?"

"It's . . ." My voice wasn't working. But then, that hardly mattered. My heart was pounding so hard, I was pretty sure nobody would hear me, anyway. I handed the card over to Quinn.

"GBP . . ." Quinn was a good judge of people. It was part of his job description. Knowing he was more likely to get a straight answer from him, he looked at my dad.

"Gil, Barb, Pepper." My dad swallowed the pizza he was chewing and grinned.

"Investigations?" Yes, this was me. Who else's voice would come out so squeaky?

"Isn't it just perfect?" Mom was too jazzed to keep still. She jumped to her feet. "Your dad learned a lot of things in prison."

"Some of them good, some of them not so good," Dad chimed in.

"He's only going to use the good things," Mom added quickly for Quinn's benefit. "But he really can be a great deal of help when it comes to following people and ferreting out information. And me, well, I know I wouldn't be very good at undercover work or anything, but I could answer the phones and keep the files in order. And I could help in the field, too, if I had to. You know, once in a while."

"Help?" Was this a question, or my cry for assistance? Even I couldn't answer that one. "What are you going to help with?" I asked my mother.

"Why, with your private investigation business, of course." She answered so matter-of-factly anyone just walking in on the conversation would take it for normal rather than for the madness it really was. "Your dad and I . . . well, we decided it would be perfect. He needs a job and no doubt, you could use a little help, what with your day job and investigating for ghosts. We've lost so much time. Family time. But this will give us a chance to reconnect. It's a win-win situation. For all of us. We're all going into business together!"

"Well, this is perfect."

I knew Quinn didn't mean that. He couldn't. The pizza and the wine were gone, and I'd made coffee and now, he was seated at my dining room table with me, my mom, and my dad. Perfect? This was nobody's idea of perfect, especially since I didn't know what other big family secrets my parents might blurt out, or how they might start grilling Quinn about things I would rather they didn't discuss even more than the family propensity for chatting it up with ghosts.

Like me and Quinn.

And what was happening between us.

And where our relationship was headed.

Hey, why should Mom and Dad get answers? I'd known the guy for years and I still had no idea.

"I brought some stuff over for Pepper to look at and as long as you're all going to be working together . . ."

Oh yeah, I nearly slapped that smug smile right off his face.

Since I am not a violent person (at least not unless it's absolutely necessary), I pasted on a sweet smile of my own.

"No one said we were going to be working together," I said from between gritted teeth. "If you've got something to tell me about the case—"

"Oh, did you hear that, Gil?" My mom bounced up and down in her chair. Not a good idea considering that the chairs, along with the table, had come from the nearest Salvation Army store and there was no telling what kind of abuse they were able to withstand. "We just opened our doors for business and we've already got a case."

"I have a case," I reminded them.

"Which makes it our case, too," my dad pointed out.

Quinn's lips twitched.

Since he was sitting next to me, it was easy for me to lean to my right and whisper, "Why are you doing this? Why are you encouraging them?"

Quinn had brought a legal pad to the table and he scrawled *cute* on it.

I was pretty sure he wasn't talking about me.

Quinn moved his cup out of the way so he could put his elbows on the table and lean forward, the better to pin Mom and Dad with one of his bad-cop/bad-cop looks. "Let's get something straight. There are a couple things I want to discuss with Pepper and since you're here, I'm more than willing for you to listen and give me your opinions. But this is my case." He glanced at me when he said this. Message received loud and clear.

Which didn't mean I had to listen to it.

"I'm not asking you to get involved," Quinn continued. "And there's no way I want to put you in danger. Gil, you've got keep your nose clean; you can't get mixed up with anything that can jeopardize your release. Barb, it's great to read about mysteries and watch them on TV, but that's not how things work in real life. Pepper . . ."

He didn't bother to finish.

Just as well; I'd already scooted my chair forward so that I could take a closer look at the evidence bags he pulled out of his pocket.

"The postcards from Jack." When Quinn didn't object, I lifted each bag and the postcards in them. Four postcards, four bags. To bring my parents up to snuff, I explained how the cards had apparently come from Jack Haggarty except that we knew Jack Haggarty was dead.

"And you know this because you've seen his ghost, right? You've talked to this Jack fellow." Mom sat up tall. No easy thing for a woman who barely scraped five feet "You're using your Gift. Honey, we're so proud."

"I've seen him," I said. "We haven't exactly talked." I debated about whether to get into the gory details, then decided that if they were going to play detective for this one evening, they might as well know the whole truth and nothing but. I described how Jack looked, how he'd been bound and tied and, apparently, drowned. I told them how difficult it was to communicate with Jack.

Then I figured I might as well go for broke. Well, go partway to broke, anyway.

"We don't seem to be getting anywhere as far as figuring out what happened to Jack or who he wants us to save," I said. "But we've apparently touched a nerve." Along with this information, I gave Quinn a telling look.

He gave me back a blank stare.

"Touched. A. Nerve," I said again. How much clearer could a girl be?

"We really haven't." He shook his head. "There's not much we've found out and—"

Good thing I was sitting next to him. It gave me a perfect opportunity to give him a kick.

"Ow." Quinn winced. "What's that—"

"I think what she's telling you . . ." Across the table, my dad's expression was thunderous. It took him a moment to gather his composure and switch his gaze to me. "Has someone threatened you, sweetheart? Because if they did—"

"Threatened?" Quinn sat back, his arms crossed over his chest. "Why didn't you tell me?"

"It wasn't exactly—"

I might have finished my half-baked explanation if my mother actually waited to hear it. She was as pale as a sheet and she clutched one hand to her neck. "Someone tried to kill you! Oh my goodness, Gil." With her free hand, she grabbed my dad's arm in a death grip. "We need to do something about this. Now."

"Nobody needs to do anything!" I was already on my feet before I was even aware that I'd jumped up. "I'm fine. Look. Fine."

"But . . ."

That from Quinn, of course.

I plunked back down in my chair. "But someone tried to kill me," I groaned.

The new uproar is best left undescribed. Mostly because it was just like the last one. Only longer. And louder. Suffice it to say that when it was finally over, Mom fell back in her chair, Dad was so red in the face, I thought his head was going to pop off, and Quinn was really quiet.

I knew what that meant, and I braced for the lecture.

"Why didn't you—"

I defended myself instantly. "I tried to call. Obviously, you were busy."

"Yeah, if you call talking to Vincent Bagaletti busy." Quickly, Quinn told my folks about the crazy security guard at the hotel and his delusions about the morgue. "You're more important than that looney." It would have been a nice compliment if Quinn didn't growl at the end of it.

I was glad to hear it, but that didn't change a thing.

"I'm fine. Obviously. Jack, the ghost," I added for my parents benefit in case they were so focused on the Pepper-as-dead-person scenario they'd forgotten. "Jack showed me how to save myself and I—"

A thought hit out of the blue and I sucked in a breath.

"Do you think that's it?" I was so excited, I grabbed Quinn's sleeve. "Jack said the only way to redeem himself was to save somebody. Do you think . . . maybe that somebody was me! Maybe we've taken care of his unfinished business and he can rest in peace now." Another thought occurred and I looked across the table at my parents. "That means the case is closed. Thanks for your help."

"Except . . ."

Quinn's objection rumbled through the room.

I grumbled right back at it.

"We still don't know the truth about Dingo," Quinn reminded me. "Or what happened to Jack."

"Because Jack got murdered, too." Thinking this over, Dad shook his head. "We need to review the clues."

"There aren't any," I started to say, then thought about the guy I'd seen jump off the backhoe. "The guy who tried to kill me had dark shaggy hair," I said, turning in my seat to Quinn. "Curly. I swear I've seen him before."

"The comic book shop."

As soon as the words were out of his mouth, the pieces fell into place. I would have slapped my forehead, but since I was trying to convince my parents I was the consummate professional PI, it didn't seem like the best move. "He was at Dick's with that other guy."

"Five-ten, two-sixty, earring in his left year." Quinn didn't give me a chance to tell him his powers of observation were as awesome as his abs. "I'll go over there tomorrow and talk to Dick again. Maybe he knows who those two guys are."

"So we do have a clue." Yeah, it cost me nearly getting killed, but Mom was right, and this was good news.

Not just one clue. Quinn tapped his finger against those evidence bags as a way of saying so. "Somebody's been sending postcards and signing Jack's name," he told my parents.

"To make you think Jack was still alive." My mother had watched her share of old *Murder, She Wrote* episodes and obviously, she'd learned a thing or two. "So the postcards—"

"Must have come from the killer," Dad said.

"Or someone who the killer asked to send the cards for

him, and that person—the sender, I mean—might not know why he's sending the cards. He's just doing a friend a favor. Or he's getting paid to do what he's doing." This, too, from my mom, who was on a roll.

"So the killer . . ." Dad drummed his fingers against the tabletop. "He wanted you to think Jack was still alive. Why?"

"Well, for one thing," Quinn said, "so we didn't go looking for him."

"And find his body. Bound and gagged! Oh, and Penelope, honey, you could have been next!" Mom waved a hand in front of her suddenly pale-as-ashes face.

"For another," Quinn continued, "there are some people in the department who think Jack might have been involved in the murder of a guy named Dingo. Maybe our bad guys are the real culprits and they figured that as long as we were looking for Jack in connection with the murder, they didn't have to worry that we might stumble onto them."

"You're not one of those people who think he's guilty." Dad always was good at reading people. But then, that's how he was able to tap into their cosmetic surgery fantasies. A couple minutes with a patient, and Dad could always put a finger on their body image (figuratively speaking, of course). It looked like a few years behind bars hadn't done anything to blunt that talent.

Rather than answering, Quinn took a drink of coffee and while he was doing that, I took a gander at the postcards.

"Las Vegas, Seattle, Chicago, New York."

Dad reached across the table and slipped the postcards

in front of him. "The first thing we should do," he said, "is look at the postmarks and arrange the cards in the order in which they were mailed."

Hey, he wasn't a Harvard graduate for nothing.

"Seattle first." My dad laid that card (still in its bag, of course) out on the table. "Then Las Vegas. Makes sense."

"Because whoever sent them," Mom chimed in, "was in that part of the country."

Dad nodded. "Then Chicago." He set out that card, too. "And finally, New York."

"So what does it tell us?"

Mom was looking at Quinn when she asked the question, and for all I knew, he was trying to come up with the answer. I hardly noticed. Something about the litany of cities struck a chord.

"Seattle, Las Vegas, Chicago, New York." I mumbled the mantra. "Why does that list of cities sound so familiar?"

"We've vacationed in all of them," Mom put in. "Remember that time you jumped in the pool in Vegas, Penelope, and your swimsuit top came off and floated to the surface? Good thing I was right there to help you put it back on again!"

I refused to look at Quinn. I was doing a pretty good job of imagining his smile without seeing it.

"It's more than that," I said, some memory tap-tap-tapping on my brain. "Something recent. I saw the names listed and—"

The truth struck like the proverbial bolt out of the blue and I jumped up. "It's the comic book store again," I said, racing into the living room and retrieving my purse. "The other day," I said to Mom and Dad, because of course, the other day, they were still long gone and didn't know any of this. "When we went to the comic book shop. Dick, the owner, he gave me a flyer."

I pulled it out of my purse where I'd stuck it after I gave it a quick once-over. I pointed to the list of cities on the back.

"Seattle, Las Vegas, Chicago, New York," I read.

Quinn plucked the flyer out of my hands and turned it over. "All cities that hosted a comic book convention like the one coming to town here." His eyes flickered to mine. "Good catch."

"But what does it mean?" Mom asked.

"And how is it going to help us find Jack's killer?" Dad added.

"We're not—" I bit off my objection. There was no use even trying, not when Mom and Dad were looking as if they'd just been handed the winning lottery ticket. After Dad's years in prison and Mom's years of missing him, this was the first something they had to get excited about. To do. Together.

I swallowed my pride along with my objections. "What do you think it might mean?" I asked them.

Neither of them had an answer, but of course, Quinn did. "It's not coincidence," he said. "It can't be. If the killer sent these cards—"

"Then the killer was in those cities for the comic book conventions," I added.

"And if there's a comic book connection—"

"Then it might have something to do with the fact that Jack took Dingo away from the comic book store but never officially arrested him."

"And that kid with the shaggy hair who we saw at the comic book store . . ." Quinn gave me a hard look, waiting for me to finish the thought, but I held firm. This was not the moment to freak out my parents with talk of backhoes and holes in the ground.

"Which might mean . . ." he egged me on.

It's a good thing Mom and Dad were watching Quinn and me go back and forth. Watching them bob their heads one way, then the other, gave me some time to try and figure out where we were headed with this argument.

"The whole thing's got to be connected with comic books," I said, my voice tentative at first, but gaining traction when Quinn didn't tell me I was way off base. "The comic book Dingo took at the shop was valuable. Dick said so. And if he had it with him when Jack took him away—"

"And it was never turned in as evidence," Quinn reminded me.

"Then maybe Dingo took *Superman* seventy-five because Jack wanted it?" I saw my argument fall apart right in front of my eyes and flopped back down into my chair. "That doesn't make any sense. Why would Jack want a comic book?"

"You could ask him," my mother suggested.

"Or we could find out what the guys in Seattle and Las Vegas know." Quinn pulled out his cell and walked into the living room with it.

"Oh, honey!" As soon as Quinn was out of earshot, Mom leaned closer. Her cheeks were pink. "He's dreamy."

"Mom," I groaned.

"Oh, I know. You're an adult and you don't need your mom and dad telling you what to do about your love life."

I didn't even need my mom saying the words *your love life*.

"He seems like a fine man." At least Dad's comment skirted the issue.

"And dreamy," Mom added, but mostly, I think, because she knew it would drive me crazy.

Quinn stuck his head back in the room. "There was a burglary during the convention in Seattle, all right," he said, then talked back into the phone. "What's that? That's all they took?" He clicked off the call and dialed another one, pacing back into the living room.

"One in Vegas, too," he said in a couple minutes when he was done with that call. "And our thief is very selective."

My mother didn't raise any fools. And remember, I'm an only child. Even I knew where this was headed. I looked at Quinn, Quinn looked at me, and we spoke at the same time.

"Superman."

He stuck his phone in the holder clipped on his belt. "I'll wait until morning to call Chicago and New York. Bet they've got the same story."

"All valuable stuff, right?" I asked.

He nodded. "Rare and valuable. Our thief is very selective."

"And I'll bet that means the goods haven't come back on the market."

Let's face it, a Harvard-educated guy shouldn't know stuff like this; we both turned to Dad.

He shrugged. "Makes sense. If you've got a punk who's that selective when it comes to swag, he's not going to fence it. If he was, he'd just grab anything he could get his hands on. But you said this guy is particular. He's not doing this for drug money. Or for kicks. Somebody's paying him to go shopping."

I nodded. "Shopping for Superman memorabilia."

"Which means we need to tap our Superman connections."

I knew Quinn was talking about Vincent, the crazy security guard.

Me?

I had other ideas.

And no way I was going to share them with my new "partners."

13

"I have to admit, I was a little surprised when you called." Milo Blackburne delivered the comment along with a smile and the martini he'd just made for me. "I could have sworn you were playing hard to get."

"I don't play." It might be the only true thing I was willing to tell him that evening, so my smile matched his. "I just thought—"

"That you'd butter me up to write that big, fat check to the cemetery." He sat down in the chair opposite from where I was sitting on a cushy couch, and he laughed, so I guess he didn't really hold it against me.

Which is why I figured I could continue with the whole truth and nothing but. At least for now.

"Well, it would be nice if you'd make good on your promise," I said. The martini was icy cold and perfectly blended and I sipped, and nodded my appreciation. "The board of trustees, they're kind of holding it over my boss's head. You know, the whole thing about getting more and more people to become patrons."

He raised his eyebrows. "Your boss is worried?"

"She'd never admit it."

"But this could jeopardize her job?"

"She'd never admit that, either. Not in so many words. But she's new to the job and she is on probation."

"So you're worried for her."

Not a question, but hey, Milo had been nice enough to invite me to his place for a drink so I guess I owed him an answer. Yes, yes, I know . . . I'm not naive. Not when it comes to men, anyway. I knew he wasn't being a nice guy just because he was a nice guy. He had a thing for me. I also knew I was never going to let him get close enough to demonstrate. He was reasonably young, reasonably good-looking, and if what I'd seen of the house meant anything, more than reasonably wealthy. That didn't mean I was interested. I may have lost a lot of things when my dad's practice went under and I was relegated to a life sentence working in a cemetery; my pride wasn't one of them.

I snapped out of this thought to find Milo watching me carefully. "I'm worried about Ella," I admitted. "She loves Garden View, and she's the best person in the world to be administrator there. She's got years of experience and lots of terrific ideas and more energy than any middle-aged woman should have. But none of those are reasons for you to decide to become a patron or to not become a patron. I'm not trying to make you feel guilty or anything. It's just the truth."

"It's also true that you are a loyal and good friend."

Believe me, I hadn't explained about Ella's problem to try to impress him. But it looked like that was exactly what happened. When he looked my way, Milo's expression was all mushy.

Mushy, I didn't need. Just like I didn't need the look he skimmed from the top of my head and along my sleeveless black sheath dress (not to worry, it had a vee neck, but not too deep of one, and it hit just above my knees). I'd even thought of the whole sexy, tousled curls thing before I left the house; my hair was wound in a fat braid. Neat. Modest. No way did it say *come and get it.*

None of which kept Milo's eyes from glittering from behind those tortoiseshell glasses of his. I knew it was better to keep the subject on cemetery finances.

"As for you becoming a cemetery patron . . ." I began.

"Not another word." He leaned forward and pressed one finger to my lips, and I was so stunned, I froze. Fortunately for me, he didn't go any further. Before I could find my voice and tell him it was inappropriate—not to mention off limits—he got up, strolled out of the room, and left me with a few burning questions. Like, where was he going? And what was I going to do if he tried another move like that when he got back? And who the heck has enough money to live in a place like this, anyway?

When I called him and asked if we could get together, Milo was more than a little surprised. When he said he'd rather host me at his house than meet in some impersonal restaurant and I said yes, I think he was more surprised. When I told him I couldn't wait to see his collection of Superman memorabilia . . .

There's nothing like knocking a guy's socks off.

Especially when you're hoping that the guy in question is going to spill the beans about what he knows about the market for Superman goods.

For my part, I was just as surprised, too, when I arrived at the address he gave me. Yeah, I'd heard Milo had more money than God, but I wasn't expecting anything quite so . . .

I glanced around the living room with its oak paneling, marble fireplace, and killer view of Lake Erie. Everything about the place said Old Money. Fabulous oriental rugs. Paintings that were the real things, not cheesy reproductions. Furniture that glittered from a good application of lemon wax.

My mother would more than approve.

Precisely why I didn't tell her—or anyone else—that I was coming here.

First I'd find out what Milo could tell me about his Superman contacts.

Then I'd let Quinn in on what I'd done.

By then, it would be too late for him to tell me I was taking chances I shouldn't be taking. Besides, I didn't need to hear it from him. I already knew that.

"This should keep your boss happy and in her job." Milo sailed back into the room waving a check. Once he sat down in the plush wing chair across from me, he handed it to me.

And I looked at the string of zeroes behind the "one" he'd scrawled on the check and nearly choked on a sip of martini.

I swallowed. Hard.

"You can't—"

"Of course I can. Although thanks for thinking enough about me to worry that I might be doing something foolish. That just proves what I said earlier—you are a good friend. You care about people. That's not . . ." His breath escaped on the end of a sigh. "That's not a quality I see in most of the women I meet. But then, I suspected that right from the start. You're special."

I took another gander at the check. "Look who's talking!"

He shrugged away the compliment. "I've got plenty of money and I can do whatever I want with it. If that means supporting a cause I think is worthy, then that's my business. Besides . . ." The orange light of the setting sun winked off the lake and reflected in his glasses. "If my little gesture to Garden View helps impress you, Lana—"

"Pepper." I didn't want to take money under false pretenses so I figured I'd better make that clear.

He didn't hold it against me. "You know I'm just kidding." Milo grinned. For a date with a woman at home, most guys I know would have gone casual. Jeans, T-shirt, sneakers. Not so Milo Blackburne. He was wearing a gray suit that cost more than my entire outfit. Jimmy Choo pointy-toed ankle boots and Juicy Couture purse included.

He settled in, completely at home in our magnificent surroundings. "What do you think of my little place?" he asked, apparently reading my mind.

I sat back, too, but not before I tucked that check in my purse before I could lose it. Or Milo could come to his senses and ask for it back. "It's not exactly little. It is . . ." I remembered the sweeping drive where I'd parked the Mustang, the wide veranda outside the front door, the im-

181

peccable landscaping. Just to make sure I wasn't dreaming, I took another look out the floor-to-ceiling windows on the far side of the room and the sweeping panorama of Lake Erie beyond. The house was west of downtown in an area of the city long known for big houses and bigger fortunes. It was built on a rise and beyond the wide veranda and the gardens that bordered it left and right, the lake was a shade of grayish blue that matched the slate roof on the Tudor-style mansion.

"Your home is impressive," I told Milo. "Beautiful."

"Not nearly as beautiful as you, Lana."

There it was again. That slip of the tongue that sent tingles up my spine. And not the good kind.

I actually might have pointed this out if Blackburne didn't sit up fast and reach across the mahogany coffee table that separated us to take my hands in his.

"It could be yours," he said.

It took a couple seconds for my brain to catch up with the conversation. "What are we talking about?"

His smile was indulgent. "What *were* we talking about?"

"We were talking about the house. I said . . ." A couple seconds. And it was a couple seconds too long. Had I realized where this was headed before he latched onto me, I would have beat a hasty retreat. Too late now, so I went for logic instead. "You hardly know me."

"I know enough to know what my heart is telling me is true. You're intelligent. You're kind. You're loyal. You're gorgeous. Of course, I knew you would be all those things, Lana."

Enough was enough. I smacked his hands away and jumped to my feet. "It's Pepper. Pepper, Pepper, Pepper.

If you think I'm so fabulous, you should at least remember my name."

"Of course." Mr. Unflappable. When he rose, he left his martini on the table. That gave him two free hands. Don't think I didn't notice.

I took a step back.

Milo stepped forward.

I was all set to give in to the panic that thumped through me when I saw a bird swoop by outside the windows, and beyond it, the streak of a plane's contrail in the quickly darkening sky.

"It's a bird. It's a plane," I whispered. And reminded myself that nervy guys were nothing new. Not in my life. I could take care of myself; I'd always been good at that. What I couldn't forget was that I had a case, and a ghost who might be depending on me to come through for him. Unless, of course, I was the person he was supposed to save and he'd done that back at Garden View and had already gone to his happily ever after.

Since I couldn't be sure, I had to stay focused. I glanced around the stately appointments of the stately room of the stately mansion.

"Where's Superman?" I asked.

Milo's shoulders shot back. "You are interested!"

"You know I am. When you mentioned your collection the other day—"

"I was afraid you were just humoring me when you said you didn't think it was foolish. You know, so I'd donate to the cemetery."

"But you've already donated. And I still want to see it. Come on." It was one of those all-encompassing phrases.

If Milo took it the way I hoped, it would tell him that he'd been reading me wrong, that I was interested in his Superman stuff. It was also cool and light and airy, and it gave me a chance to sidestep away from him. "I'd never think a hobby you love so much is goofy. Like I told you on the phone, I'd love to see your collection."

I swear, I thought he was going to salivate.

"Well, come on." Before I could stop him, he looped an arm through mine. "You've got a real treat in store for you."

Side by side, we walked through wood-paneled hallways, past a winding staircase and even a suit of armor. We finally stopped in a room at the opposite end of the house. More windows, and another fabulous view of the lake. But there was something weird about this room . . .

I twitched my shoulders, ridding myself of the uneasiness that did its best to creep up on me. While the room where we'd left our drinks was wide and spacious, this room was narrow and out of proportion. The walls were painted a vivid blue that made them feel like they were closing in. The valance above the windows was red. And everywhere I looked . . .

"Superman." I closed in on the framed picture on the wall closest to me.

"Autographed," Milo said, pointing to the picture. "By George Reeves. You're far too young to remember. Well, so am I!" He laughed. "He played Superman in the original TV series. That was back in the fifties. And this . . ." He stepped back and waved toward a bigger framed display next to the picture. Blue tights. Red shorts, a red cape. And a blue shirt with a yellow emblem and a big red *S* on it.

"Reeves's original costume," Milo said.

"I'm impressed." Another truism. "It must have cost—"

"A fortune? Absolutely." One hand to the small of my back, Milo strolled to the next exhibit in his little museum, an arrangement of Superman comics in different languages. "All first editions," he explained. "As is this one, of course. My pride and joy!"

He took my hand and we walked across the funny, narrow room. On the opposite wall and above another marble fireplace was a comic book displayed in an elaborate gilt frame. The cover proclaimed it was all about Superboy.

"I will confess, this is not a recent addition to my collection, but I just recently hung it here. The day after the patron cocktail party at the cemetery, in fact. Until then, this place of honor went to a comic titled *Superman: The Wedding Album*. You know, the story from 1996 when Lois Lane and Superman get married. But at the cocktail party . . . well, that's when I met you, and realized the error of my ways. This comic . . ." Milo gestured toward the book, "features a story called *The Girl in Superboy's Life*. It's the first story in which Lana Lang appears."

"Who I'm not," I reminded him.

"But you are a beautiful redhead," he countered, looking into my eyes. "Just like Lana."

I wasn't about to argue.

No, not because I'm conceited. Because it was time for me to close in for the kill.

"It's all wonderful," I said, maybe a little too breathlessly, but hey, I don't think Milo noticed, anyway. "How did you find all this great stuff?"

"Conventions. Collectors. Auctions." He took my

question at face value. "There's always someone, some-where who's willing to sell."

"Always?"

A spark lit his eyes. What it meant, I didn't exactly know.

"Come on. Spill the beans!" I gave him a playful poke on the arm. It gave me a chance to keep the mood light. "I'm not saying you would ever do anything dishonest, but hey, there have to be people—"

"Who says?" There was a sharpness to his voice I hadn't heard before and I flinched.

He darted forward and cupped my hand in his. "I'm sorry. I didn't mean—"

"Well, neither did I. But I am curious." Playing to the lie, I strolled around the room, looking at his treasures. "It's amazing," I said and hoped the whole breathless thing didn't come across as too phony. "Too amazing to keep to yourself. You should open a museum or something. So any-body who loves Superman could enjoy your collection."

"There you go, worrying about other people again." The sun had slipped below the horizon and that crazy or-ange glow had faded from the lake. The light was soft and gray and when Milo put his hands on my shoulders, I couldn't see his eyes behind his glasses. "I'm so glad you're interested in my collection. In fact, next time you come to visit—"

It was a pretty big assumption to make so I was glad when from somewhere far off in the recesses of mansion, the doorbell rang.

His mouth pulled into a thin line, Milo dropped his hands and backed away.

"What, no butler to answer the door?" I asked.

"His night off," Milo answered, and since he'd already turned and walked out into the hallway, I couldn't tell if he was kidding or not.

Quickly, I glanced around, wondering what else I could see or learn before he returned. But hey, curiosity is a weird thing. When I heard the irritated rumble of Milo's voice at the front door and the reply of not one, but two other voices, I scooted to the doorway of the museum room to try to hear what was going on.

The foyer of the house was directly to my left. About a million feet away, but directly to my left. From there, I had a perfect view when Milo's visitors stepped into view.

One of them was a heavyset man a whole head shorter than Milo.

The other was younger, taller, skinnier. He had a head of wild, dark curls.

The instinct for self-preservation is a funny thing.

Except mine wasn't laughing.

The men were the ones who were in the comic book store when Quinn and I went there, and the kid?

The last time I saw him, he was hightailing it through the rhododendrons at Garden View after he jumped off that backhoe.

He was the one who tried to kill me.

I darted back into the museum room, and I hoped I did it fast enough that neither of the visitors saw me. While I was at it, I looked for a way out of the room, and the house.

It wasn't the windows. The glass was thick and there was no way to open them.

The blood pounding in my head, I raced back the other

way. I wasn't imagining it, the men's voices were getting closer. Trying to think, I put my hand on the corner of the marble fireplace.

That was when the wall opened and spun and I spun with it.

The next thing I knew, I wasn't in the museum room anymore.

No wonder the museum room seemed so misshapen! The room I suddenly found myself in was parallel to it, just as long and nearly as wide.

No windows. No doors. Just the weird spinning wall like something out of a sci-fi movie.

Or a superhero comic.

My heart beating fast and my breaths coming just as quickly, I stepped away from the wall and looked around. The secret room had an chilly feel, but then, that was no surprise. The walls were made from brushed stainless steel. So were the tables, a desk that held a computer, and the chair in front of it.

The silvery color of the steel and the lights recessed into the ceiling made the whole room look as if it had been carved from ice.

Suddenly shivering, I wrapped my arms around myself and went over to examine a larger-than-life statue near the far wall. No, not Superman. Not this time. The statue was of a man and a woman and whatever it was made out of, it was just as cold and silvery as the rest of the room. They were standing side by side, his right hand and her left on a globe.

"Weird," I told myself. "Way weird."

So was the contraption at the center of the room.

Squinting, I closed in on it at the same time I tried to figure out what it was. It looked like a Plexiglas box, big enough to hold a person and suspended between two stainless steel chains that hung from the ceiling.

It was empty.

As empty as Milo would find his little museum room if he got back there and I was nowhere to be found.

Jolted by the thought, I took out my cell phone and snapped a few quick pictures of the strange room, then hurried back over to the wall and pressed my hands to it until I found the spot that made the secret door swing open.

Luckily, when Milo Blackburne returned to the museum room just a minute later, he was alone. He found me admiring his display of Superman comics in French. Hopefully, he didn't notice that I was breathing just a little hard.

But then, I had a pretty good excuse, didn't it?

Not only had I just taken a walk on the really weird side, but I had more questions now than I had when I arrived at Blackburne's.

Like, who were those two guys who'd come to the door?

Why did they want to kill me?

And what connection did they—and the attempt on my life—have with Milo Blackburne?

14

New bar?

I hit the reply button on my phone to return a text message to Quinn and started typing furiously.

No. Not a bar, I told you—

Before I could finish, another text from him arrived.

Didn't tell me u were going out.
New partners with you?

Like anyone could blame me for grumbling? Not only was he assuming I was actually going to go into business with my mom and dad, he obviously hadn't paid enough attention to the first text I sent along with the pictures of Milo Blackburne's secret room.

Not a bar. Told u. Blackburne's house.

My phone rang instantly.

"What the hell—"

"If you read your texts, you'd know this already. And besides, I was going to tell you as soon as I got back. I knew he was a Superman collector, see, and—"

"And we've got one, maybe two murders that have something to do with Superman collectors so you just thought you could run out on your own and—"

"It's not like anything happened. Well, except for the fact that two guys showed up at Blackburne's and one of them was the one who tried to kill me."

To this, Quinn didn't bother to reply. In fact, he hung up. I wasn't surprised when within fifteen minutes, he was pounding on my door. Even with the traffic gods smiling on him, he shouldn't have been able to make it to the other side of town that quickly. Something told me the portable flashing police light and siren he stored under the front seat of his unmarked car had been put to good use.

"I told you, I'm fine," I said, opening the door and stepping back to let him in because really, he would have just run me down to get past me, anyway.

"The two guys. Give me descriptions."

"I don't need to. They were the ones—"

"At the comic book shop." He pulled out his phone, and I think he would have called right over to Dick's and demanded a list of customers, a complete log of every sale made over the last year and footage from Dick's security cameras if there were such things. That is, before he realized how late it was and how there was no way Dick was still hanging around the comic book shop. He covered by shoving his phone back in its holder and reminding me, "That was stupid."

"Not completely." I pulled out the check Blackburne had written to the cemetery and waved it under Quinn's nose. "I can be very persuasive."

"And very stupid."

"I'm alive, aren't I?" Frustrated and tired of standing at my door and arguing, I spun around and headed for the couch. "The two guys who came to see Blackburne never saw me."

"But Blackburne and those creeps, they're connected."

I shrugged.

Quinn wasn't about to take that as the final say on the subject. "Which means Blackburne—"

"It means he *might* be somehow connected with the attempt on my life, not that he definitely is. Besides . . ." I thought about the way Blackburne had looked into my eyes, and his offer to make his casa, *mi* casa. I thought about his obsession with Lana Lang, too, and a shiver skipped up my spine. "He'd never hurt me. He likes me."

Quinn's eyebrows slid up.

I protested instantly. "It's not like that."

"What is it like?"

"Well, it is like that." My shoulders slumped. "I think . . . that is, he sort of . . ." There was no use trying to sugarcoat the truth so I just blurted it out, "I think he sort of asked me to marry him."

Up until then, Quinn was still near the open door. He slammed it shut so he could march over and plunk down beside me. "What did you tell him?"

"Are you kidding me?" It was my turn to jump to my feet. Fists on hips, I glared down at Quinn. "You can't possibly think I'm that shallow."

"I didn't say you were."

"But you did think it. You thought there was the remote possibility that I'd say yes to a marriage proposal from a guy I barely know just because he's rich. And nice-looking. And he's got this house that's so incredibly gorgeous and—"

I didn't need Quinn to interrupt me, I stopped myself. Before I could say anything else that would make him actually believe his half-assed theory.

"That's not why I sent you the pictures," I said.

"The pictures of the bar."

Screeching is so unladylike.

Good thing Mom wasn't there to remind me.

I threw my hands in the air. "It's not a bar. It's a secret room. In Milo's house. I got to the secret room through a secret door."

"And Blackburne showed it to you. Even though it's secret."

"Not exactly. I sort of stumbled into it by myself. Because I didn't want those two guys from the comic book shop to see me. But that's not the point. The point is, it's weird enough to have a secret room in your house. It's weirder when the weird secret room is . . ." It was hard to explain so I grabbed my phone and scrolled through until I found the pictures I'd sent to Quinn earlier. "Weird."

It says something about technology and our dependence on it that rather than looking at the pictures on the screen of my phone, he pulled out his own phone and looked through the pictures I'd sent him. He paused on the one I took that showed a wide view of the room, stainless steel walls and all. "The Fortress of Solitude," was all he said.

I slumped back onto the couch. "The Fortress of—"

"Solitude. Yeah." Quickly, Quinn rolled through rest of the pictures. "In the comic books, and in the movies, and even in the Superman shows that have been on TV, the Fortress was the place Superman went to be alone. The way I remember it, it was made out of ice, or crystals or something."

I sat up. "That's exactly what Blackburne's room looks like." I shot through my pictures until I found the one of the statue of the man and woman. "And this?" I tipped my phone so that Quinn could see the photo.

He scrolled through and found the same picture on his phone. "Jor-El and Lara." Quinn glanced over at me. "They were Superman's parents. At least his parents on Krypton, his home planet. When he came to Earth, that's when he was adopted by the Kents. According to the Superman stories, he kept a statue of his parents in the Fortress. See?" He pointed. "They're holding a globe of Krypton."

Okay, call me slow. It wasn't the first time I'd heard him spout super-facts, but it was the first time it struck me as odd. I leaned forward to pin Quinn with a look. "And you know all this . . . how?"

He set down his phone on the cushion next to him. "Come on, I read Superman comics when I was a kid. Most boys do. And I've seen the movies. I guess we can say that Blackburne has, too. That room is an amazing reproduction of the Fortress of Solitude."

"Yeah. Amazing. And it's in the guy's house. Don't you think that's a little weird?"

I'm sure he didn't need to look, but Quinn scrolled through the photos again. "It's kind of cool," he admitted.

"But it's in his house. And it's not like it's a bar or anything and he takes his friend in there and they have a couple beers and laugh about the Superman stuff. It's secret. I only found it because I leaned on this spot on the fireplace and the whole darned thing spun around, and spit me out into this Fortress thingy."

He glanced at me out of the corner of his eye. "He doesn't know you were in there?"

"When he got back to the museum room where he keeps all his Superman stuff and where he left me when he went to talk to those two guys we saw at Dicks's, I was right back where he left me, looking around like nothing had happened."

"And those two guys?"

"No sign of them. Believe me, I checked and double-checked when I left the house."

"Which was . . . ?"

Another not-so-subtle comment that did—or didn't—call my integrity into question.

"What, you think I stuck around after I found out Milo was friends with some guy who dropped me in a hole and did his best to cover me with six feet of dirt?"

Maybe Quinn's first clue that I was telling the truth was that my hands started shaking when I thought about my close call back at Garden View. Then again, he might not have noticed if he didn't grab them and haul me back down to sit on the couch next to him. He slipped an arm around my shoulders. "I'm sorry. I didn't mean to make you think about it."

"I'm fine." I took back a hand long enough to brush the tears off my cheeks. "It's just . . . well, it was pretty scary."

"And you were pretty brave. Not to mention resourceful."

"Yeah, thanks to Jack." I glanced around the apartment, but there was no sign of my newest client. "Maybe now that he saved me, he's crossed over."

"Maybe." Quinn drew me closer into the circle of his arm. "And that would pretty much prove he didn't have anything to do with Dingo's murder, wouldn't it? I mean, if he was guilty, he wouldn't go to the light or wherever it is that spirits go."

"Is that where you were headed?"

I asked the question and held my breath.

Seemed to me, Quinn did, too. He went very still. At least until he said, "There was a light. I know that sounds goofy, but . . . well, I really did see it. Like a pinpoint. Really far away. And I didn't see anyone, so I don't know who I was talking to, but whoever it was, I told that person I wasn't heading for the light." He turned to look at me. "Not until I stopped to see you first."

This time, the tears that slipped down my cheeks had nothing to do with reliving getting tossed in that grave.

"You saved a lot of lives by telling me where the cops

could find the guy who shot you," I told Quinn. "He was one bad dude. He would have killed again."

"Hey, I was just doing my job." He twitched away the compliment before he crooked a finger under my chin and tipped my face up to his. "But that's not why I insisted on coming here to see you. I know it all happened fast. Faster than it takes to tell it. But in that instant when I realized I'd been shot . . . well, damn, Pepper, I also realized that I didn't want to die. Because I'd really messed things up with you, and I wanted—no, I didn't just want it, or need it, I knew I had to—I had to get another chance. I was about to melt into that bright light for all eternity, and the only thing that mattered to me was that I wanted to make things right with you."

He leaned closer, his lips a hairsbreadth away from mine. "I'm going to try, Pepper. I swear I will. If you'll give me a chance."

It was a sweet and noble declaration, and a step in the right direction.

I never had a chance to reply to tell Quinn that, because his cell rang.

"Doesn't it figure." Quinn sat back, took one look at the caller ID and rolled his eyes. "Vincent," he grumbled.

I sat back, too, and listened while he tried to be the voice of patience. Someday when he was in a really good mood, I would break the news that when it came to that particular virtue, Quinn needed lots more practice.

"It's late, Vincent," Quinn said. "And—"

He listened to whatever Vincent had to say, and although I couldn't understand the words, I could hear the staccato tempo of Vincent's voice.

"Yes, sure. Yes, Vincent, I understand about the morgue and the people who are going to break in. We're going to talk about it some more. How about tomorrow? I'll stop by the hotel and— Now?" Quinn held the phone far enough away to check the time display. "Like I said, it's late and—" Another roll of those emerald eyes. "All right. Give me your address. Yes, yes, Vincent. I'm on my way."

He puffed out a breath of annoyance before he turned back to me. "Where were we?" he asked.

"You were heading over to Vincent's, and as long as you are . . ." I popped off the couch. "You're going to take me along, right?"

Quinn dragged himself to his feet. "Because . . ."

"Because Vincent's as crazy as a loon, but he's talking about something happening at the comic convention and we know things are getting stolen from comic book conventions all over the country, and we know that someone's sending postcards from those same cities and signing them with Jack's name even though we know Jack's dead, which means—"

"I know all that." He already had his car keys out. "What I'm asking is why I should—"

"Take me along?" I opened the door and stepped into the hallway after him. "Thanks, I'd love to come."

As it turned out, Vincent the hotel security guard lived in a three-room rental at the back of a beverage store in a part of town that had been down on its luck practically since there was a Cleveland. Steel mills, highways, boarded-up buildings. In the name of an investigation, I would have made the trip on my own if I had to. But I was glad I had Quinn and his big gun with me.

Quinn knocked and got no answer. He called out to Vincent, and there was no reply. I, sensible person that I am, was just a tad annoyed. Yes, I'd been anxious to tag along, but that was when I thought there was actually something to be gained from it. Now that I knew Vincent was just being Vincent and as flighty and strange and as all over the place as ever, our little visit to the hood wasn't looking like the best way to spend the night. It was late, remember, and as I recall, just as Vincent's call came in, Mr. Tall, Dark, and Grumpy was about to kiss me. Call me crazy, but that seemed a better option than standing out on a sidewalk littered with broken glass, a couple beers cans, and—

Something moved in the weeds near the street and I scooted closer to Quinn.

That was the first I realized he had his gun out.

With his free hand, he reached for the doorknob. It turned easily. "Stay here," he told me.

Yeah, right.

When he slipped into the house as quiet as a shadow, I slipped in after him. Of course, he noticed, but honestly, he didn't try to stop me. We'd stepped into the kitchen, and there was a light on over the sink. Quickly, Quinn scanned the countertop where dirty glasses and dishes were piled high and the two-seater table where a few days' worth of newspapers were piled. Through a doorway directly in front of us was the living room, and he leaned in, took a quick peek, and seeing that it was empty, he pointed to a closed door over on my left.

He motioned me to stay put, kicked open the door, and—

"You don't want to come in here, Pepper," Quinn said.

Too bad I was already on my way when he gave me the warning.

If I had waited, I wouldn't have seen Vincent the crazy security guard, his face bulging and blue, a rope tied tight around his neck until the life had been choked out of him.

"Well, Vincent did say the morgue."

We were standing in the waiting room of the county medical examiner's office, so Quinn's comment, while appropriate, wasn't exactly funny.

Then again, I didn't think he was trying to be. After an hour waiting for a patrol car to show up at Vincent's and another half hour hanging around until a group of Homicide detectives got there, Quinn wasn't in what anyone would call a cheerful mood. Oh, it wasn't like all those other cops weren't glad to see him. It was obvious even to me, outsider that I am, that most of his fellow cops liked and respected Quinn. It was just as obvious that now that he wasn't a part of the Homicide team, they would have preferred if he was anywhere but the scene of a murder.

For his part, Quinn had watched his former coworkers go through the motions and treat him like any other witness. He was friendly. He was professional. And I could tell it was just about killing him (no pun intended considering the situation) to be odd man out.

He glanced down the hallway and the room to which

Vincent's body had been taken a short while earlier. "What I wouldn't give to be in there," Quinn grumbled.

Me? Not so much. My arms had been wrapped around myself to control the rumba rhythm pounding inside my ribs that had started up the moment I set eyes on dead Vincent.

"It's got to have something to do with the convention," I said.

"And the morgue at the hotel?" That wasn't humor I heard in Quinn's voice. It was sarcasm, pure and simple.

"But it's not a coincidence," I insisted, keeping my voice down so the man stationed behind the front desk wouldn't hear. Talking through the situation helped calm my nerves. So did pacing. I walked to the far wall where a picture of roses hung in a silver frame. I walked back the other way. "Vincent's been calling you. He's been warning you that something was going to happen at the convention. Now he ends up dead? At just about the same time we figure out that valuable memorabilia is getting stolen at comic book conventions? Even you have to admit it's—"

"Fishy."

I thought so, too, so Quinn didn't have to demonstrate by sniffing the air.

"I get it," I said. "It's fishy. You don't have to be so—"

I didn't finish. That's because the odor assaulted my nose like a whiff of off-brand perfume. Fish. And not fresh.

When I looked into the farthest corner of the waiting room, I saw a puddle on the floor, a dead carp lying in it, and Jack hovering above.

"So you didn't cross over."

Jack shrugged.

"Which means I'm not the one you were supposed to save."

He nodded.

"So somebody else is going to die?"

Another nod.

"And it all has something to do with Vincent."

"Hmhm Mmm. Mmmmnm"

"Jack's here?" The question, of course, came from Quinn, who looked where I was looking, squinted, and looked some more. "Ask him about Dingo. And Superman."

"Superman, isn't that the only thing you're supposed to be worried about these days?"

The question came from behind us and Quinn and I both spun away from the puddle and the fish and the ghost and found ourselves face-to-face with a heavyset African American with sleepy eyes and a unlit cigarette between his teeth.

"Anderson." Quinn's nod was brusque enough to tell me they were acquainted, but not old friends. "You caught this case?"

"And you didn't." Anderson stepped forward and I stepped aside. "I got a copy of the statement you gave to the cops who got the call. If I have any questions, I'll be in touch. You're over in the Second District now. Am I right?"

Personally, I was glad Anderson didn't pause long enough for Quinn to answer. Something told me it wouldn't have been pretty.

He took the cigarette out of his mouth, looked at the end of it as if he was surprised it wasn't lit, then shoved it back in his mouth. "Heard you were working with the school guards," Anderson said, that cigarette spinning when he spoke. "That's great, Harrison. It's real important for the police to keep up ties with the community."

Even before the last words were out of Anderson's mouth, Quinn had a hand on my arm. "Come on," he said, tugging me toward the exit.

All well and good. Except we were forgetting what we were there for. Which was solving Vincent's murder. And putting Jack to rest. And figuring out why someone was trying to kill me. And . . .

"But what about the Super—"

Quinn's fingers closed around my arm. Yes, theoretically, that shouldn't have clipped off my words, but the pain that resulted did a pretty good job.

It wasn't until we were outside that I untangled myself from his hold. It was just after sunrise and cool. The sidewalk was damp from a sprinkling of overnight rain and the clouds hung thick over the building that housed the morgue.

"What was that all about?" I demanded.

"Anderson's a fool. Always has been, always will be. In case you couldn't tell. There's no use handing him our case and all our evidence."

"But it's not our case, it's his. And if we tell him what we know, it might help him find who did that to Vincent."

If looks could kill, I suppose I would have keeled over right then and there.

Then again, Quinn didn't exactly have a chance to make the look stick.

That was because a car pulled up next to us, the passenger window rolled down, and my mother stuck her head out.

"Yoo-hoo!" She waved and from the driver's side, so did Dad. "It's so lucky you told Ella you'd be late this morning and that you were here. Otherwise, we wouldn't have been able to find you. We've been talking it over, Dad and I."

"Talking what over?" Excuse me for being the voice of reason.

Since my dad had put the car in park, he was able to jump out and come around to the other side of the car so he could answer my question.

"Our case, of course, honey." He gave me a peck in the cheek. "We've been thinking about everything you said, you know, about the ghost and how he drowned and how he can't tell you anything because of that duct tape over his mouth."

"And that's when we decided," my mother chimed in. "You know, about what we have to do next."

A muscle jumped at the base of Quinn's jaw, but hey, he was a better detective than I; he dared asked the question. "And what's that?"

My mother's mouth puckered. "Well, it's obvious, isn't it? I mean, it wouldn't be. Not if Penelope didn't have her wonderful Gift. But she does, have the Gift, that is. And we can use it to our advantage."

"That's right." Dad nodded. "We've decided what we need to do is find this ghost's body."

Quinn slid me a look. "It's crazy," he said. "So crazy, it's really, really smart."

15

"There's nothing in his locker."

Quinn slammed said locker door shut and aimed a look at it that in the Superman universe would have melted the gray metal. "What kind of guy doesn't keep anything in his locker at work?"

"The kind of guy who maybe did keep something in his locker but then someone got here before us and took out whatever it was Vincent did keep in his locker."

This, of course, though slightly convoluted, was not only logical, but brilliant, and if Quinn wasn't in such a crappy mood, he might have realized it. And acknowledged it. Instead, he scrubbed his hands over his face and looked around the tiny employee locker room at the hotel where Vincent worked when he was still alive to work.

"Your fellow cops could have already been here." I ventured the guess because let's face it, Quinn's angry-detective persona might have scared some people into silence, but I wasn't one of them. "Or the murderer might have taken anything worth taking. Maybe even before he killed Vincent."

"Maybe." The single grumbled word was the equivalent of a *wow, you're right, and aren't you a genius* from any lesser person, and with it, Quinn spun around and headed out of the locker room. "Let's take another look around the hotel."

We did.

Just like we'd done when we first arrived there an hour earlier.

We talked to the front desk clerk. Again. We stopped in the gift shop. One more time. We did a turn around the ballroom where workers were scrambling to set up vendor booths and put the finishing touches on a life-sized model of Clark Kent's office at the *Daily Planet*. The comic book convention was slated to start in just two days and it was obvious there wasn't a moment to spare. Guys in hard hats raced around us and there was so much hammering, it made my head hurt.

Each person we talked to told us the same thing—a detective named Anderson had already been there and asked all the questions we were asking.

This did not improve Quinn's mood one bit, and that was bad enough, until every person we talked to added that even if we had gotten there first, there wouldn't be anything to tell us, anyway. Vincent was crazy, and he kept to himself. Friends? As far as anybody knew, Vincent didn't have any. Enemies? It didn't seem likely. The kid did his job (such as it was), ate lunch by himself, hopped on the bus, and went home. It wasn't that he didn't have time to make enemies, it was more like he had so little personality, nobody would have noticed him enough not to like him.

"Except that he did a lot of crazy talking." This was me, always the voice of reason, and I threw out the comment to the guy supervising the building of the Clark Kent office. "Maybe somebody didn't like what Vincent said about the comic book convention."

The guy's mouth twisted. "Vincent said something about the comic book convention? What could he possibly say except that it was scheduled to take place? That is, if we get this damned construction finished. Hey, Mario!" The supervisor waved his arms to get the attention of a guy who was attaching a door to the back of the office set. "Not that way, you idiot. The other way! The other way!" He used his hands to demonstrate and once Mario got the message and started installing the door with the hinges swinging in the proper direction, the supervisor turned back to us. "What were we saying? Oh yeah, Vincent. Who would listen to a nutcase like him, anyway?"

"I guess maybe we should have," I mumbled once the supervisor hurried away. "Quinn, what about—"

I was going to suggest talking to the cleaning ladies I'd seen out in back where employees smoked, but Quinn mumbled something about security tapes and walked away.

I was not overly disappointed. For one thing, being on my own gave me a break from the bad mood that had been hanging over him ever since the day before when we'd visited the morgue (the real morgue) and Detective Anderson had reminded him that these days, Quinn's job pretty much consisted of community relations and nothing else. For another, it gave me a chance to do a little investigating on my own, and that is never a bad idea.

At least it never had been before my parents popped back into my life.

Oh yeah, that was them all right. Walking into the ballroom of a hotel where they had no business and knew nobody. Except me.

"Yoo-hoo! Honey!" Mom waved and made a beeline for me. Dad followed, looking around as he did. "I called Ella and she said—"

"It really is amazing." Dad gave me a good-morning kiss on the cheek. "This is going to be some fancy convention, huh? I might have to come check it out. And you know what else is amazing?" He gave me the once-over. "Ella can't say enough good things about you and all the wonderful work you do, but honey, it sounds like you don't even go in to the office every day. Shouldn't you be there now? It's not that I don't think your investigations are important. And it's not that I don't understand that when Mom and I are officially on board, we'll all be doing this full time, but for now you should probably make a better show of it. You do have benefits, don't you? I'd hate to see you lose them before we can figure out if joining the chamber of commerce can get us a good rate on our own."

I told myself I would explain about my ghostly peeps some other time. For now, the only thing that came to mind was, "What are you two doing here?"

"Helping you investigate, of course." Mom smiled at each workman who scuffled by. "You are here about the . . ." She leaned in close and whispered, though how anybody could have heard her over the sounds of a table saw that started up was anybody's guess. "M-U-R-D-E-R, right?"

"We are. I am." It never hurts to make this sort of thing clear. "But there's nothing going on. Nothing I need help with, anyway. I'm just asking some questions. In fact, I was just leaving. There's nothing to see here and no one to talk to and—"

"Pepper! What a wonderful surprise!"

Surprise, yes. Wonderful? I would have to think about that. Right after I got over the shock of turning toward the sound of the voice.

"Milo!" I wondered if my smile looked genuine or slapped on and decided it didn't matter. One look at me and Milo Blackburne's chest puffed out. His smile was genuine enough for the both of us. "What are you—"

"Just checking on the construction." His cheeks turned a dusky shade that matched my mom's raspberry-colored sweater. "I'm financing it. The *Daily Planet* part of it, anyway. Not the entire convention, of course." He tipped his head in the direction of the set we'd seen being built. "Just my way little way of helping out and paying homage to the greatest of the superheroes."

It was all Mom needed to hear. No, not the superhero nonsense, the financing part. She skimmed a look over Blackburne, assessing his charcoal suit, his wingtip shoes, his haircut, even his glasses. Oh yeah, I could practically see the dollar signs light up in her eyes. Like I said, Mom isn't as shallow as she's just downright practical. She knows a good thing when she sees it—moneywise—and one look, and she knew Blackburne was the real deal.

"Is this a friend of yours?" She stepped forward and had her hand out even as she asked me the question. "I'm Barb," she said, pumping Milo's hand. "And this is Gil. We're Penelope's parents."

"Well, this is perfect!" Blackburne turned to my dad. "I was hoping to talk Pepper . . . er . . . Penelope . . . er, Lana . . ." His blush deepened. "I was hoping to talk to her and arrange something so that I'd have the opportunity to meet you one of these days. And now the pieces have all fallen into place. But what . . ." He looked my way. "What are you all doing here?"

"Investigating, of course." This was Mom. Even as I tried to shush her with a laser look of my own, she rambled on. "We're joining Pepper's firm, Gil and I. GBP Investigations." She whipped out a business card and pressed it into Blackburne's hand. Amazing that I noticed since I was so busy cringing. "Getting ready to put the shingle up. A family business is something we've all always dreamed about."

Except that we hadn't. Not ever.

Before I could point this out, Milo glanced at the business card, then looked over at me. "Investigations. Pepper, you never told me you were a private investigator. Not that I'm surprised. It only makes sense that you'd be engaged in something so interesting." He turned a smile on my parents. "Your daughter is very smart, but I'm sure you already know that. She's also very clever. But she never told me about this." He aimed an admiring smile in my direction. "Tell me, what are you investigating here at the hotel? It doesn't have anything to do with the convention, does it? I'd hate to hear there's anything fishy up. I'm so looking forward to spending the weekend with other aficionados!"

"Coffee." I looped one arm through one of Mom's and the other through one of Dad's and managed to get them both pointed toward the door before either one of them could open their mouths to contradict me. "There's been coffee missing from the employee break room," I told Milo, careful to keep my voice low, like it mattered and we had to keep it under our hats. "They asked us to stop by and ask a few questions, you know, to try and get to the bottom of things."

This whole fabrication might actually have sounded convincing if Quinn hadn't picked that particular moment to join us. He had yet to meet Milo Blackburne, but I knew he knew who we were talking to the moment he set eyes on Blackburne. Then again, Quinn has a way of sizing someone up in an instant and deciding just as quickly that he likes—or doesn't like—that person.

Want to guess which decision he made about Blackburne?

Quinn's nod was barely perceptible. "You're Milo Blackburne."

Blackburne's smile didn't make it all the way to his eyes. "I can tell Pepper's been talking about me. And you're—"

Quinn provided the information. Don't think I missed the look he slid my way while he was doing it. It was one of those what-the-hell-is-going-on-here glances anybody else might have mistaken for casual. Me? I knew Quinn was as serious as a heart attack. And pissed, too.

"Barb and Gil tell me you're investigating," Milo said.

"I have to admit, I didn't think it was anything important until I realized the police were involved. Whatever's going on, I'd hate for the convention to get any bad PR. But then, that's what you're supposed to be taking care of, isn't it, Detective Harrison? If I'm not mistaken, I saw your name on the contact list at the back of the convention brochure. You're our liaison with the city, police protection–wise."

"Nobody knows more about protection than Quinn." I winced even as the words made their way out of my mouth. "That is—"

"Nice meeting you," Quinn said even though he obviously didn't mean it, and since he turned and stalked away, it provided us the perfect opportunity to retreat, too. My arms still firmly through those of my parents, I dragged them across the ballroom and to the door.

Outside, my mother grinned at me. "You didn't tell me you knew the Blackburnes."

"I don't." I couldn't be any clearer. "I only know one Blackburne. Milo."

"And he likes you." Mom stood on tiptoe so she could crane her neck and look back at the ballroom door. It was closed, so I don't know what she thought she'd see. "You're dating?"

"Mom." I would have groaned whether Quinn was nearby or not, so it's not like I was trying to hide anything from him. "He's a cemetery patron," I explained. "He gave us a whole lot of money just a couple days ago."

"That explains why Ella is cutting you some slack about going in to the office." My dad knew a thing or two about the value of friends in high places, or at least in the power of making sure those who could blow the whistle on you were happy. Katherine McClure, his old office manager, had gone to prison for a couple years, too, for helping him cook the books and keeping her mouth shut about it. Katherine wasn't as loyal and she was greedy; a couple thousand extra in her paycheck every month assured her silence.

"What the hell was that all about?" I guess I didn't have to worry what Quinn thought of my mother's blatant admiration of the Blackburne fortune. He wasn't about to start mincing words just to keep her happy. "You're standing there chatting with the guy who knows the guys who—" Quinn realized his anger had gotten the better of him, and he bit off the rest of what he was going to say.

My parents realized that whatever that something he was going to say was, they wanted to hear it, and closed in on him.

I had no choice but to screech to get their attention.

"Are we sure we want to stand here and discuss this?" I was looking at Quinn when I said this because I figured I could count on him to be at least moderately rational. "It's bad enough Blackburne saw us together."

"Why?" my mother asked.

"What does this have to do with our case?" my father butted in.

"And how is any of it going to help us locate Jack's body and find out what's really going on?" Quinn groaned.

His seemed the only question worth answering.

And that would have been great if I had answers.

Which I didn't.

I didn't have any patience left, either, especially when

Mom and Dad walked away and Mom called out a cheery, "Our place tonight for dinner. Seven o'clock. We'll talk more about our investigation then."

"So . . ." I was in the kitchen helping Mom with the salad, but when she slid a look toward the door and the great room beyond where we could hear my dad and Quinn talking over the glasses of Crown Royal Dad had poured when we walked in, I knew what she was getting at.

Exactly why my response was, "So . . . what?"

Mom clicked her tongue. "You know what I'm talking about. Quinn. What's going on between you two?"

"Nothing I want to talk about."

"Or nothing you want to talk about with your mother?"

I wasn't in the mood for subtle distinctions so I grabbed a cherry tomato and popped it in my mouth.

Mom gave her homemade Italian salad dressing one last stir. "He's as dreamy as can be, but he's a cop, after all. He can't possibly be as rich as Milo Blackburne."

I finished chewing and swallowed. "And that matters, why?"

"Oh, I'm just saying." Mom splashed dressing onto the salad and tossed to her little heart's content. "Wouldn't that be quite the coup?"

The quivering feeling in the pit of my stomach told me I knew what she was talking about, but if nothing else, I had been raised to be polite to my elders. I didn't want to hear the answer, but I asked the question, anyway. "Wouldn't what be a coup?"

Mom brightened. "You and Milo Blackburne. That would make our old friends sit up and take notice."

"Mother!" It was all I could take. There were four salad plates out on the counter and I went and retrieved them and marched across the kitchen with them clutched in my arms. "I'm not going to sell myself to Milo Blackburne just so you—"

"I wouldn't dream of it. You know that, honey." The pout that went along with the statement almost made me believe her. "I'm just saying that if it just happens to work out . . . if you just so happen to fall in love with Milo Blackburne . . . and if he just so happened to fall in love with you . . . and if there was a marriage in your future—"

"No." I shoved the swinging door between the kitchen and the great room with my butt. "No and no again."

"You're not disagreeing with your mother?" The question was stern but the look in my dad's eyes was anything but. Dad put down his glass and grabbed the salad plates from my hand, putting them near the four wineglasses and four place settings of silverware already set on the table. "You wouldn't want to upset Mom."

"I would if she wants me to marry Milo Blackburne." I'd already sat down and I flapped open the lilac-colored linen napkin set next to my plate. "No," I said again, glancing to where my mother was sitting on my right. "I'm not going to marry Milo Blackburne."

She had the good sense to be embarrassed to be discussing this in front of Quinn. Or at least the good sense to look like she was embarrassed. "That's not exactly what I said," she mumbled for his benefit.

"Is, too," I mumbled right back.

"Never did." She smiled and passed him the salad.

Quinn is a smart guy. He knew there was nothing to be gained from getting between two Martin women in mid-spat. He took his salad, passed the bowl to my dad, and said the single word, "Jack."

The ploy worked. Mom was so excited, the salad fell off her fork and an olive bounced across the table and landed in front of my plate. "Oh, we're going to talk about the investigation!"

Dad had spent too many years eating prison cafeteria food on a hard-and-fast schedule. He gobbled down half his bowl of salad before he spoke. "So where are we?" he asked Quinn.

"Nowhere if you don't all stay away from Blackburne." I wasn't sure if this comment from Quinn was for my benefit or for my mother's, but just in case, I took offense, anyway.

My shoulders shot back. "He showed up at the hotel."

"And after what happened at his house the other night," Quinn began.

Mom sat up like a shot. "His house? You were there?" It didn't take more than a second before the excitement faded in her eyes and was replaced by worry. "What happened?"

I filled them in as briefly as I could, about the two goons who'd shown up at Blackburne's door, about the creepy, secret room.

All the color drained from my mother's face. "You mean . . . Milo Blackburne . . . he might be . . . not on the up-and-up?"

I couldn't help myself; I pictured the wedding invitation and laughed:

Gilbert and Barbara Martin
Request the honor of your presence
at the wedding of their daughter
Penelope Anne
and Mr. Milo Blackburne,
Bad guy

Oh, what would the old friends think then?

To my mother's credit, I don't think she was thinking about the marriage plans that never would be when her eyes filled with tears.

"Oh, honey, you might have been—"

"I wasn't. I'm fine. But when Blackburne showed up at the hotel today—"

"We almost blew it." My dad groaned and slumped back in his chair. "We told him we were investigating."

"It's a good reason for you both to steer clear." Quinn looked back and forth at both my parents. "I've shown Pepper photos, but she can't pick out pictures of the two guys who stopped at Blackburne's that night. That might mean they're from out of town. Or they don't have arrest records. Obviously, that's not helping us much. Still, we've got a pretty good idea of what's going on. If only we knew the details."

"We know somebody's going to try and steal something at the comic book convention," I said for my parents' benefit. "And whatever it is, somebody thinks it's valuable enough to kill for. Vincent . . ." I didn't want to say too much, so I looked at Quinn, and when he didn't stop me, I went right ahead. "Vincent talked about morgues and such. But apparently, even though he sounded crazy, he knew something. Somebody wanted to keep him quiet."

"Wow," Mom said on the end of a sigh.

"So what do we do?" Dad asked. He'd always been a man of action. So much so, that he answered his own question. "Seems to me, what we said the other day has some merit. It might help figure out what's going on if we can find the ghost's body."

"Agreed." This from Quinn. "The question is how."

We chewed and thought, thought and chewed, and I was just about to admit I was coming up as empty as my salad bowl suddenly was when I felt something cold and wet on the back of my neck.

Drip, drip, drip.

I glanced over my shoulder and up only to find Jack hovering near the ceiling.

"Well, it's about time," I said.

"For more salad?" my mother asked.

My dad is smart; he realized that wasn't what I was talking about. Then again, I was looking up at the ceiling.

"We need to find your body," I said, watching as Jack floated down and settled on the floor. "We figure it's the only way to figure out what happened to you. And how it all ties in with Dingo and Vincent and the comic book convention and that other person who's going to die if we don't do something fast. It is tied in, isn't it?"

He didn't answer.

"What's he saying, honey?" Mom asked, looking

where I was looking and obviously not seeing anything but the quickly growing puddle on the floor. She got up and went to the kitchen for paper towels.

"Can you tell us where to look?" I asked Jack.

He nodded.

"Your body's in water, right?" This went without saying so I wasn't surprised when Jack nodded again.

"There's a lot of water in Cleveland," Quinn grumbled.

Jack looked at him as if to say *no duh*. I did not report this.

"So what we need to figure out," I said to Jack because everyone else was just as clueless as I was so there didn't seem to be any point in addressing them, "is where in the water."

Jack shambled over to the table.

Back from the kitchen, my mother clutched the paper towels to her chest and shook her head at the trail of water on her great room floor, but when she bent to get to work, I stopped her from cleaning it up by reminding her there was no use even trying until Jack was gone.

Mom dropped back in her chair and Jack poked his chin at our salads.

"You're in a bowl." I knew this wasn't right, but he didn't have to look at me like I had two heads. The dead have a lot of nerve.

Jack poked some more.

"Glasses," I told my fellow investigators. "You're in glass? Like in a tub or an aquarium or—"

Jack shook his head.

"Not a bowl. Not glass." I glanced around the table. "Wine? Your body's at a winery."

"Or in a vat of wine." Mom was breathless at the horror of it all.

Jack shook his head.

By now, we were all looking around the table, grasping at straws.

"Butter," Quinn said. "That doesn't make any sense."

"Salt and pepper," my dad chimed in. His head snapped up and he looked at the empty space beside me where only I knew for sure Jack was. "How about the salt mines under Lake Erie?"

Jack shook his head.

I massaged my temples with the tips of my fingers. "Italian dressing," I mumbled.

"Then he'd be pickled, not drowned," Quinn said.

Behind the duct tape, I could tell Jack wasn't amused.

More poking from our ghostly companion.

"The Crown Royal the guys are drinking?" I asked Jack.

This time, he nodded.

"There's a Crown filtration plant," Quinn piped in. "It's part of the city water system."

Jack said no.

"There's a royal . . ." My mother made a face. "Well, there's nothing royal I can think of. Not in Cleveland."

"So what is it?" I wailed. "Crown Royal is a drink. It's a beverage. It's—"

"Whiskey," my dad said at the same time Jack nodded.

Quinn slammed a fist on the table and stood. "That's got to be it," he said. "I know where Jack's body is. In the water off Whiskey Island."

16

As much as it pains me, allow me to provide a little history lesson here.

Whiskey Island isn't actually an island and except during boating season when the marina is hopping, the restaurant is open, and the tiny park is chock-full of sand volleyball players, there isn't much in the way of whiskey around, either. In fact, Whiskey Island is a triangular spit of land just west of downtown Cleveland with Lake Erie on two sides of it and the Cuyahoga River on another. Back in the day (and I mean really way back), the area was settled by Irish immigrants who built a rough-and-tumble shanty community. According to local legend, the Island got its name either because there was a distillery there or because those immigrants built so many saloons.

Smart people that they were, the Irish got tired of the diseases than ran rampant in the swampy area so close to so much water. They moved on, and Whiskey Island turned industrial. These days (even with the marina and the park), there's still a gritty edge to the place.

Of course, the fact that is was late afternoon and raining to boot didn't do much for the ambiance, either.

"This is crazy," I grumbled, casting a sidelong glance at Quinn, who was standing on my left. Over his shoulder and beyond the marina, I could see a giant lake freighter being unloaded at a dock. To my right and across the park was a salt mine and beyond that, I could barely see the outlines of downtown skyscrapers, shrouded in low-lying clouds. Behind us, there were railroad tracks and when a train rolled by, the rumble shook me to the bone. In fact, the only peaceful part of the scene was the narrow strip of beach directly in front of us and the lake beyond where the rain plunked slowly and steadily against the gray water.

The lake where Jack Haggarty's body had apparently been dumped.

I stuffed my hands into the pockets of my leopard-print trench coat. "Don't you guys have some special team of somebodies who look for bodies in places like this?"

"Of course we do." A stiff breeze blew in off the lake and even tucked snuggly in his L.L.Bean Storm Chaser jacket, Quinn shivered. "But I don't want to call them yet. Not until we know if we're really onto something. If I do—"

"Somebody higher up is going to tell you to back off and mind your own business." I figured I'd say it so he didn't have to. "So . . ." I glanced around at the nothingness. Quinn had planned this little foray into the urban wilderness just as evening was falling and though I protested (because that's about when the rain decided to start falling, too), I knew what he was thinking. The fewer people around, the less likely it was for someone to question why we were poking around at the water's edge.

Of course the fewer people there were around, the more desolate the place felt, too.

Inside my raincoat, a cold tingle crawled up my back.

"Told you to dress for the weather." Quinn threw out this comment as if it actually might have helped at this point.

I aimed a smile in his direction at the same time I plucked at the leopard-print fabric. "I am dressed for the weather. Raincoat, see?"

"And the shoes?"

I glanced down at the ankle boots that seemed a perfectly good option before we left my apartment. Bad timing, since that was the same moment the three-inch heels sank a little farther into the mushy ground.

"Come on." Quinn grabbed my arm and dragged me back to his car. He opened the trunk, pulled open a box, and brought out a pair of rubber rain boots. Yellow rubber rain boots.

I looked at the offering as if it were a snake ready to rear up and strike. "You're kidding me, right?"

"I knew you'd pull something like this. That's why I stopped at the army/navy store on my way over to your place."

This was supposed to make me feel better?

I took a step back, distancing myself from the boots as well as the thought of the army/navy store. Any army/navy store.

It would have been an effective maneuver if I didn't squish right into a puddle.

To his credit, Quinn almost controlled an I-told-you-so smile. "You want those pretty shoes of yours to get all wet and muddy?"

He knew me too well.

A minute later, we were walking back to the beach. Well, Quinn was walking in his waterproof boots. I was clumping in the rubber rain boots. And happy to have them (not that I was going to admit it) when we stepped onto the beach and I promptly sank into the wet sand.

I looked to my left, then my right. "The Island isn't very big, but Quinn, where do we even start looking?"

His gaze was glued to the waters of Lake Erie. And here's the thing people who've never seen it don't know. Like the other four Great Lakes, Erie is plenty big. Like hundreds of miles long and way too wide to see Canada on the other side. In fact, looking north the only thing we could see (besides all that liquid) was the stone break wall and a lighthouse, far out in the water. Over on our right on a finger of land that grew out from the main part of the Island was a white building that reminded me of the lighthouse except that it had more style. Tall, round tower, sleek lines. Very Art Deco and if the absence of lights meant anything, very deserted, too.

"Old coast guard station," Quinn said, apparently reading my mind. "Hasn't been used in years."

From this distance and in the gathering darkness, it was hard to tell, but it looked like there was a chain-link fence all around the station and the property that surrounded it.

"Somebody doesn't want any trespassers," I said.

"Or anybody vandalizing the place."

"Or anyone getting close."

What I was saying finally clicked with Quinn. "Which would make it the perfect spot—"

"To dump a body."

Perfectly inaccessible, too.

By the time we walked (okay, I clomped) all the way to where that finger of land stuck out into the water, my hair hung in my eyes and I was sweating. Well, just a little, anyway. As for getting over that chain-link fence . . .

I'd rather not go into details. It wasn't pretty, and it wasn't easy, and by the time we were officially trespassing on what was probably government property and so off limits to civilians, I was breathing hard and my leopard-print coat was ripped in two places.

"Damn!" I fingered the tears caused by rough spots on the fence. "I got this for a steal at a Nordstrom sale. There will never be another one like it."

"Told you to dress appropriately."

Too bad Quinn had already whirled around and started for the Coast Guard station just as he said this. He missed a mighty good glare.

The station itself was actually way bigger up close than it looked from the beach. While Quinn went around to the right, peering into the water and poking around with a stick, I clomped to my left. When I'd finally made it over that chain-link fence, I'd picked up a tree branch and now I poked, too, along the shoreline, half hoping I wouldn't find anything at all.

It wasn't that I didn't want to put the Jack mystery to

rest, but that thought of a body left in the water for a few months . . .

I trailed my stick through the water, and a bicycle tire floated to the surface. I poked again, and this time for my effort, I brought up an old shoe.

Clomping and poking, I walked to my right. The plan was that on the other side of the building, Quinn was doing the same thing, only moving to his left. We would meet at the farthest north point of the station. I only hoped we did it before long. Out there with the cold rain pattering against what was left of my raincoat and in the gathering darkness, I was more unsettled than I ever had been in any cemetery.

It didn't help when a noise behind me brought me spinning around and just as I turned, I saw something small and dark dart into the weeds.

"Cat," I told myself, even though I knew it was too small and not nearly furry enough. I clomped quicker and poked faster, my efforts punctuated by the lapping sounds of water and the noise of a boat motor from somewhere near the marina. Brave souls to be out on the water on a night like this, I told myself. And the reminder was all I needed; I poked even faster.

After twenty minutes or so, I caught sight of Quinn coming around from the other side of the station. He didn't look any happier than I felt, and unfortunately, I knew what that meant. Great theory, I mean about Jack's body being stashed there and all. But a big zero in execution.

Poor choice of words.

Especially when I jabbed the stick into the water one more time and trailed it along the shoreline and a skull floated to the surface, its big, empty eye sockets staring right at me from above the piece of duct tape over its mouth.

I screeched. And jumped back.

Quinn came running.

After that . . .

Well, it's kind of hard to remember exactly. I know he got to me in record time, and that he saw the skull. I know he already had his phone out, too, and I was pretty sure he was going to call those somebodies who take care of things like this for the police department.

He never had a chance.

But then, that was because a whole different somebody picked that exact moment to take a shot at us.

Instinct. It was all about instinct.

My instincts told me to drop to the ground and cover my head.

Quinn had other ideas.

"We're sitting ducks here," he said at the same time he grabbed my hand and yanked me to my feet. By the time the second shot pinged into the worn blacktop too near my yellow rain boots, we were already running for the cover of the Coast Guard station.

"Son of a—" A shot plopped into the building and sent tiny pieces of cement shrapnel flying all around us, and Quinn shoved me behind him. He had his gun out, but I could tell by the way his mouth thinned as he scanned the landscape around us that he didn't know where the shots had come from.

"Somebody followed us."

The perfect moment for a *no shit, Sherlock*, if ever there was one, but I kept my mouth shut.

"Somebody doesn't want us to find Jack's body," I said instead. Not that he heard me, because another shot hit close by. It was followed by another, and another.

My arms over my head and my body folded as small as it was able for a five-foot-eleven woman to get, I listened to Quinn call in to emergency dispatch and report an officer in trouble. That was pretty much when we both realized things had gotten quiet.

Really quiet.

I let go a breath and slumped against the cold cement building. "He stopped. He's gone." My words bumped like my heart. Which at that moment, was knocking around like a clog dancer on steroids. Relieved, I pushed off from the wall of the building. "We can leave now."

If this was such good news, why did Quinn still have his gun out and a steely eyed gaze trained at the desolate landscape around us?

When I moved forward, he stuck out an arm. "He's closing in," Quinn said.

"What? No, no, no. It's supposed to be over now. What are you talking about, he's closing in? He stopped shooting. He's going to—"

"Come around from one of the sides of this building." That big ol' gun of his raised, Quinn pivoted one way, then the other. "If we can hold him off until backup gets here . . ."

We both heard it at the same time. The distant sounds of a pulsing police siren.

Far away.

Too far.

And the put-put of that boat motor, louder now, closer, revving up little by little as if it was sending us a message: run and run fast.

Only there was no place to run to.

"If you have to," Quinn said with another lethal glance all around. "Go into the water."

I looked down at what used to be my adorable raincoat. "Into the—"

"You can swim, can't you?"

"In chlorinated water, yes. When the sun is shining. And the water temperature is a minimum of eighty-seven degrees. But—"

"But nothing. When I tell you, you run and you run fast and you don't look back. With any luck, you can get out of here the way we got in. If not, there's always the water. Got that?"

I actually would have answered if the fierceness in his voice and the heat of his eyes didn't stop me dead.

Okay, okay, so it was a bad choice of words. It wasn't like I had a thesaurus around or anything.

"But, Quinn, I—"

He held up a hand to signal me to keep quiet, and I heard what he heard, the sounds of shoes crunching on pitted blacktop.

"I'm not going to let anything happen to you," he promised.

I was about to tell him I appreciated that when the shooter came around the corner.

"That way," Quinn yelled, pushing me around to the side of the building where he'd searched the shoreline. But then, that's because he was so busy returning fire with our attacker, he didn't see the other guy blocking our exit that way. I tugged at his jacket sleeve, he managed a quick look over his shoulder to see what I saw, and we exchanged glances. There was only one thing to do. Our land exits were blocked; we had no choice but to head to the water.

Maybe it was the sounds of the pinging gunshots that blocked out the noise of the boat motor. Or maybe the police car sirens on the freeway across the railroad tracks did that. Maybe I was just so freakin' scared, I wasn't paying attention to anything except putting one yellow boot in front of the other and being grateful that I was still alive to feel the asphalt beneath my feet. Whatever the reason, I didn't hear the boat slip up to the shoreline or realize it was there waiting for us until we got to where I thought I was going to have to jump.

"Come on, honey, hurry!" My mother looked her usual resplendent self in a hunter green rain slicker and boots that weren't nearly as clunky as mine. Her eyes wide and her voice tight with panic, she offered me a hand and held on tight while I took a deep breath and jumped in beside her. Dad was behind the wheel and he took off the moment Quinn landed on the deck next to me.

"But what . . . how . . . ?" I looked back and forth between my mother (who either had tears rolling down her cheeks of was getting hit with as much rain and lake spray as I was) and my dad, who whooped in triumph and piloted us on a wild zigzag course toward the break wall and the open water beyond.

"It's amazing what you learn in prison," Dad called out.

"Like how to hot-wire a boat. Imagine!" I don't know when she managed to grab the other one, but Mom now had hold of both my hands.

Quinn was not all that into tender reunion scenes. No big surprise there. A hand on each our backs, he pushed us down until both Mom and I were kneeling on the wet deck. His gun still out, his hood back, and his dark hair slick with rain, he angled himself between us and the back of the boat and when one last shot pinked into the water not three feet off our left side, he returned fire.

When the noise of the blast finally stopped echoing in my ears, I dared to look up long enough to cast a glance at my mother. "And you knew we were coming here because . . . ?"

When Quinn sat back, apparently signaling that we were far enough away from shore to be out of danger, Mom did, too. "Don't be silly, honey." She patted my hand. "It looks as if all sorts of people followed you to Whiskey Island tonight."

She was right about that.

All sorts of people. Including the two who had saved our lives. And the couple shooters who wanted us good and dead.

17

What with me being the world's only private investigator to do the dead, you'd think I'd be a little more used to talk of bodies and what happens to them after they shuffle off the ol' mortal coil. Still, my mouth soured when I looked at the closed door in front of us—the one that led to the autopsy room at the county morgue—and asked Quinn, "You think they found all the . . . pieces?"

"The coroner is sure they did." His cheeks were red, but then, my complexion wasn't at its best, either. The mad dash in the boat, the wind, the rain . . . it all added up to stinging eyes, rough skin, and crimson cheeks. Even the avocado facial I'd given myself in the wee hours of the morning when I finally got back home from Whiskey Island hadn't done much to help. "They put the skeleton together," Quinn continued. "You know, like a puzzle."

"And then they'll be able to tell us what happened to Jack."

"Or you could just ask me."

I wasn't surprised by the shockwave of cold or the puddle that suddenly appeared on the green linoleum floor of the waiting room. The raspy voice, though, that was another thing.

Then again, I guess Jack had an excuse, what with not being able to talk all these months because of that duct tape over his mouth.

Now, he popped into the room and stood in front of us, scrubbing his hand over both his mouth and chin.

"No duct tape. He's talking." I tugged at Quinn's sleeve and pointed to the puddle at the same time I wondered what was up. "There's no duct tape because—"

"Coroner took it off, of course." Jack filled me in on the details and tossed a bit of raised eyebrow in, too, for good measure, and to let me know I should have thought of this myself. "About damn time. Plastic ties, too." He held up his hands to show me that his wrists were free and massaged each as if it might actually bring back the circulation. "I was getting tired of playing games trying to communicate with you."

"You're not the only one. But what about . . ." I looked down at the heavy rope around Jack's legs. By the time we saw the police cars with their flashing lights arrive at Whiskey Island and Dad cruised into the marina and dropped us off so we could pretend we'd gotten away from the shooters without any grand theft larceny involved, our attackers were long gone. The good news was that while Jack's skull had sunk back into the murky depths of Lake Erie, it was easy for us to show the cops where we'd seen it and easy for them to locate, too. Big plus, the skull hadn't floated far from what was left of the rest of Jack's body. High-intensity lights were brought in, those somebodies from the elite police diving unit showed up, and before the sun came up over the eastern horizon, all the earthy remains of Jack Haggarty lay on a blanket on Whiskey Island.

When his flesh dissolved or was eaten by fish (shiver!), that rope around his legs went slack, but it never fell away completely.

The cinder block still attached, Jack shuffled around the waiting room. That is, until as if by magic, those ropes snapped.

"About friggin' time!" Jack breathed (I use this word figuratively, of course) a sigh of absolute relief and took a couple quick steps around the room. "I can move again."

"They cut the ropes from around Jack's legs," I said for Quinn's benefit. "And his hands are free and because the tape is off, he can talk."

"Good." Quinn's gaze was so intense, I swore he could see Jack standing there in front of a blond wood table with a stack of old *National Geographic*s on it. "Now ask him what the hell is going on."

I turned to Jack. "What he said. If we're going to help, we need details, and you're the only one who can give them to us."

"You mean Mr. Super Detective here hasn't figured it all out yet?" Jack's top lip twisted. "I thought he'd have all the answers by now."

This didn't seem the time to report this comment word

for word, not when less than twelve hours earlier, Quinn had risked his life to save mine. Not when my parents had taken chances, too, with their own lives and with Dad getting himself in all kinds of trouble if word ever got out about how he'd taken that boat for a joyride.

I decided it was better not to get mired in emotions and stuck with the facts. "Who killed Dingo?" I asked Jack.

"Who are those folks?" he countered, glancing over to where Mom and Dad were trying to get a cappuccino out of the vending machine. If the way they were laughing and pounding on the machine meant anything, they weren't having much luck.

"My parents," I said, eager to keep the explanations short and sweet. "They're sort of . . . kind of . . ." A cup fell into the little receptacle at the front of the machine and frothy faux cappuccino poured down into it, and my parents hooted with delight. "They work with me," I told Jack. "They're helping with this case."

"Not what I expected." He slid a look at Quinn. "Figured he could work this out all by himself. At least that's what he always told me back in the day. Detective Quinn Harrison didn't need me. He didn't need anybody. He had all the answers. Always."

I wasn't imagining it. There was something going on here, and I didn't like being clueless. I turned to Quinn.

"Did you and Jack like each other?" I asked him.

His shrug was barely noticeable. "We rode together for a three years."

"Not what I asked you."

"We always got along."

"Another dodge."

"Look, Pepper, you don't understand cops."

I propped my fists on my hips. "I'm not trying to. Not all cops, anyway. Just two of them. You and Jack."

He pulled in a breath (the *he* obviously being Quinn since he was the only other he in the room who was actually breathing). "We did our job and we did it well. Did I like Jack? That's not the word I'd use. But I always . . . respected . . . him. He got results."

"Respect, huh?" Jack stepped back and crossed his arms over his chest. Since he was still wearing that golf shirt stained with his blood, I was grateful. His arms were beefy; they covered the red splotch. "A cop who respects his partner doesn't walk off and leave him."

"Did you?" I'd already turned back to Quinn when I realized he didn't know what I was talking about. "Did you leave Jack in the lurch?"

"The only place I ever left Jack was in uniform." Quinn stepped back, too. He crossed his arms over his chest. Jack was shorter than Quinn, and broader. His hair was buzz-cut, his nose was wide, his chin was a little too small for the rest of his face. That didn't keep them from looking like twins. Then again, attitude is everything, and these two had it in spades. The raised chins. The stone shoulders. The tight muscles of arms and jaws that told me there had been more to their partnership than either of them wanted to talk about.

I didn't think it was possible for Quinn's chin to come up even more. Shows what I know. "I got promoted to the Detective Bureau. Jack didn't."

"And he thinks I'm jealous," Jack growled and at the same time Quinn chimed in with, "I guess he's jealous."

It was a classic pissing contest. And it was getting us a big ol' nowhere.

"Would one of you like to tell me what this has to do with Dingo's murder?" I demanded.

"Not me." Quinn had been leaning against the wall, and he pushed off. "If I knew that, this case would be wrapped up already."

When Mom and Dad strolled in with their cappuccino, I'd already turned back to Jack. "Time for answers," I said, and because I knew they'd start pestering me and I didn't want to be bothered, I tossed a casual, "The ghost is here," in their direction along with a gesture toward Jack and the puddle.

Eyes sparkling, Mom sat down to watch the one-sided show and Dad took the chair next to hers. He sipped the coffee and handed the cup to her. She sipped and handed it back.

"You picked Dingo up for robbery." I was talking to Jack now, obviously. "But you never filed an arrest report. Come on, Jack," I added when he looked away. "If you wanted to spend eternity with that damned duct tape over your mouth, you could have. But you came to me for help, and we found your body, and now, we're going to find your killer. The least you owe us . . ." I looked at Quinn, and my mom and my dad. "All of us . . . the least you owe all of us is some answers. Why did you take Dingo in and never officially arrest him?"

A muscle bunched at the base of Jack's jaw. "What difference does it make?"

"Because it might help us figure out what happened to you." I shouldn't have had to explain but if there was one

237

thing I'd learned in my time dealing with the dead, it was that ghosts can be a stubborn bunch. "Dingo took a valuable comic book from that shop. And Vincent, the security guard at the hotel, was talking crazy about a heist at the comic book convention that starts tomorrow. And we didn't believe him because he wasn't only talking crazy, but he was crazy, only now he's dead, too, and it's all connected with comic books, so come on, Jack, talk. What's going on? And what do you know about it? You said somebody else was going to die if I didn't help. Who? And are we on the right track? And how can we prevent that from happening?"

Jack flopped into one of the plastic waiting room chairs. "Dingo . . . Kid was a nobody, know what I mean? Small-time punk. I ran into him a time or two, you know, when I was breaking up fights in the park or chasing loser kids who were getting their thrills turning over their neighbors' garbage cans. Never thought he'd amount to anything, and I was pretty much right."

"Except that you arrested him but didn't."

"Yeah, well . . ." Jack settled back in the plastic chair. Not the height of comfort, but then, when you're dead, you don't exactly have to worry about how a machine-molded seat feels on your keister. "I met these guys, see, and . . ." He eyed me carefully, and I don't think it was because he was trying to figure out how I'd react to whatever it was he was going to tell me. Somehow, I knew Jack Haggarty didn't care what the world thought of him. "They were looking for a little protection, if you know what I mean."

I nodded. "Protection. Like they were paying you—"

When Quinn's eyes narrowed and his hands bunched into fists, I ignored him. If Jack could act like he didn't care, so could I. At least until I had all the facts.

"Yeah, that's right." As if Quinn could actually see him, Jack aimed a look in his direction, daring him to criticize. "They were small-time hoods. Breaking and entering, stolen cars. I helped them out with useful information. You know, like when there was a patrol car due in the area. That sort of thing."

"What's he saying, Pepper?" Quinn's voice was razor sharp. "Was Jack taking bribes?"

I owed him this much of the story. I turned to Quinn and nodded.

He grumbled a curse. "That explains the money stashed in his closet."

"Oh, come on!" Jack rolled his eyes. "Tell Harrison he knows what it's like."

I did.

"That's bull," Quinn spit out.

"Yeah, I guess it is if you're Quinn Harrison." Jack's mouth twisted. "That's because he's just a pretty boy who always had more money than he knew what do to with. He never had four alimony payments to make every month." He slid a look over me that made goose bumps pop up on my arms. "Not yet, anyway."

"He needed the money," I told Quinn, who in response, simply shook his head in disgust.

Jack was not fazed. He waved a dismissive hand in Quinn's direction. "I'm not going to start feeling guilty just because Mr. Life of Riley here thinks I should," he said. "You asked for the truth and I'm just telling you.

Yeah, I made a little money on the side. It's not like I didn't need it. And it's not like I didn't deserve it for all I put up with on the streets."

This, too, I told Quinn, who did not look convinced. That was right about when I decided that it was tedious reporting every little thing Jack said to Quinn and my parents, like listening to one of those goofy translators when they show UN meetings on the news. I promised myself I'd remember the highlights and fill them in on all the details later. For now, getting the facts straight was what mattered.

"So . . . Dingo?" I waited for him to explain.

Jack shrugged, and then, because I guess it felt so good after not being able to move for so long, he rotated each shoulder. "Turns out Dingo got connected with the same guys. He started pulling some small jobs for them and they'd give him a cut of the profits."

"Which is why when he took that comic book from Dick's, you never turned him in."

"Or the comic book!" Jack chuckled. "That's what those guys were after. Go figure! But I guess if you know where to sell 'em, that sort of thing brings in a pretty penny."

"And the two guys?" I am not brainless, I already had a suspicion that they were the goons who'd come after me at the cemetery, the ones who'd taken the potshots at us on Whiskey Island.

"Rossetti, husky guy with an earring, and his nephew, Howie. I doubt you know 'em."

"Don't be so sure of that." I could put the name Rossetti to the husky guy who'd shown up at Milo Blackburne's front door. It fit. But nearly being buried alive by a guy named Howie seemed like adding insult to injury.

"And Rossetti and his nephew, Howie . . ." I said this nice and slow so Quinn could get the message and jot down the names. "They were the ones stealing memorabilia from conventions in other cities, too?"

"Got me!" Jack stood up, and left a puddle on the seat of the plastic chair. "All I know is what happened here in town, and what happened here in town was—"

"They murdered you." I felt obligated to point this out since he was acting like it was no big deal. "Why? You did what you were told to do, right? You got Dingo out of that comic book shop and you turned over the comic book to Rossetti and Howie. Who did they sell it to?"

Another shrug.

He was either dodging or he was the most clueless aider and abettor out there. Either way, I was frustrated at not getting any straight answers. Feeling antsy, I paced back and forth in front of Jack, trying to find the words to tell him he was a scumbag. That is, until another thought hit, and I froze. "You killed Dingo."

At this point, I had to excuse Quinn for kicking the wall and swearing a blue streak.

"Jack didn't say he did it," I pointed out, eager to calm him down. "I'm just throwing out the theory."

"And did he?" Quinn turned and aimed a look at the empty space in front of me that would have killed Jack if he wasn't dead already. "Did you, Jack? Because I'll tell you what, plenty of people think you did and I'm the idiot who always stood up for you and told them they were wrong."

"Really?" Jack was honestly surprised. "Tell him thanks for nothin'. And tell him he was right. I didn't have anything to do with Dingo's murder."

"Then why the Topic candy bar wrapper at the scene?" I asked him.

Another shrug. "Just to get my goat. They figured if the cops were busy looking at me as a suspect, they wouldn't look anywhere else."

"Which is the same reason they sent postcards to the cops at the Second District from the cities where they were staking out comic book conventions."

Jack pursed his doughy lips. "Did they? Obviously, Rossetti and Howie didn't think of that. Between them, they don't have the brains. Make the cops think I was still alive and on the run." Jack's smile told me he admired the ingenuity of the scheme. "That, coupled with the candy wrapper at the scene of Dingo's murder would make them concentrate on finding me. And ignore everybody else."

"Only there was no way they were ever going to find you. Because that's when you disappeared."

Jack glanced away. "They killed Dingo. It wasn't like the kid didn't have it coming. He pulled a job for them, some jewelry store robbery. But he kept some of the stuff for himself. Howie didn't much care. But then, Howie couldn't spell *cat* if you spotted him the *c* and the *a*. Rossetti, though, Rossetti isn't the type to forgive and forget. When I heard what happened to Dingo . . . well, you can believe me or not believe me, but I'm telling you, that's where I drew the line. Yeah, I might be okay with taking a little bit of an extra payday now and again from guys who were ripping off comic book stores and rich peoples' houses, but murder . . . I couldn't go along with that."

"And they killed you because they thought you'd turn them in."

Jack scratched a hand over his chin. "It was the same night they killed Dingo, and after they got rid of me, they actually went back to the scene of Dingo's murder and dropped one of my candy bar wrappers there. Rossetti always thought he was pretty funny."

"But now they can be arrested!" Of course, it wouldn't be that easy, not without evidence. I didn't need either Jack or Quinn to point this out, so I was quick to change the subject. "So you think there really is going to be a heist at the comic book convention?" I asked Jack. "And that somebody's life is in danger? Who? If you tell us, we can protect that person."

Jack shook his head slowly. "Wish I knew. I don't. All I can tell you is I've got a real bad feeling about that convention. Rossetti and Howie, they've got something big planned. And, Pepper . . ." He looked around at the little clutch of folks gathered there in the waiting room, at Mom and Dad. At Quinn. At me. "You're going to have to be mighty sharp. Otherwise, somebody's for sure going to die."

18

Comic book geeks get up bright and early.

It was well before noon and already, the ballroom at the convention hotel was packed. Attendees dressed like Batman, and Mario, and Wolverine, and a whole bunch of comic world inhabitants I didn't recognize and didn't want to meet pressed in on booths where vendors hawked books and costumes, games and T-shirts. There was something going on near the Clark Kent *Daily Planet* office, and that end of the room was crowded both with people in costume and folks in regular street clothes.

I wouldn't have gone anywhere near the mob scene if I hadn't see a cop over there, too. One in a killer suit he never should have been able to afford on his salary.

Quinn didn't spare me a look, and it was just as well. Though he was busy scanning the crowd, it was impossi- ble to miss the little vee creased between his eyes. He was pissed about something. Royally. "Don't you ever work?" he asked.

"Took a vacation day. I didn't want to miss any of the excitement. Has there been any excitement?"

His voice was acid. "Only if you count a promotional giveaway of some newly published Superman comic."

That explained the people who hurried around us to get over to the *Daily Planet* set. "Anybody we know?" I asked.

"Not a one."

He didn't need to say more, because, see, I caught that little expelled breath at the end of his sentence, and I knew what it meant. Vincent's crazy talk or not . . . Vincent's murder notwithstanding . . . Quinn knew we were getting nowhere on our investigation.

"And obviously, no morgue." I was sure of it, but I took another look around the ballroom just to confirm. Whatever Vincent knew, whatever he'd been talking about, somebody thought it was important enough to silence him permanently. But whatever he knew, we'd never know. Because there was no morgue in town except the real one we'd been at the day before with Jack. Well, with what was left of Jack. No morgue, no clues to go on, and nothing of interest at the convention, either, unless I counted the host of wild-eyed people, giddy at the prospect of so much geekiness packed into one place.

Darth Vader strolled by, complete with heavy breathing, and I shivered inside the gold sweater I was wearing with pants the color of a Hershey's Special Dark chocolate bar. Outer space villains, superheroes, characters from video games, it was surreal and, "Too weird," I mumbled.

"As weird as a woman who can talk to ghosts?"

I wondered when Quinn would finally say something. After our interview with Jack the day before in the waiting room of the real morgue, Quinn had been strangely silent about all that took place. Mom and Dad, not so much. Later in the evening, they showed up at my apartment with wonton soup, General Tso's chicken, and a big ol' container of shrimp fried rice. They were so thrilled to be part of the investigation and so anxious to show how much they supported me in what Mom somberly called my "Mission," they never stopped asking questions—about Jack, about the other ghosts I'd dealt with over the years, about the cases I'd solved.

Quinn, though Mom assured me she'd invited him, did not join us.

He didn't call, either.

It wasn't hard to figure out why.

Quinn had been brought into my woo-woo world kicking and screaming, and believe me, this, I understood. It took me a long time to get used to the idea of ghosts being real, too. And I was the one who could see and hear them. For a man who thrived on being in on the action and suddenly had to stand on the sidelines and listen to my one-sided conversations, then buy into the whole notion that I was actually talking to someone most people didn't even believe could exist, then to listen to whatever I thought we had to do because he couldn't argue about it since he wasn't in on the conversation in the first place . . .

Yeah. I got it.

Just like I suddenly got what he was so pissed about.

"Ghosts are real," I said in an offhand sort of way intended to make him feel like he didn't have to either defend himself or jump on the bandwagon. I was helped out in conveying my message when the Incredible Hulk strolled by. He was a scrawny guy in ripped pants and poorly applied green makeup. Not so incredible, but big points for trying. I rolled my eyes. "Superheroes, not so much."

"But these people take the whole thing very seriously."

None more so than Milo Blackburne, who at that moment appeared at the ballroom doors and strode over in our direction. He didn't see me. Otherwise, I knew he would have stopped to chat. Instead, he marched into the midst of the crowd and as if by magic, it parted in front of him. The next time I got a glimpse of him, he was clutching one of those new Superman comics and beaming like a kid on Christmas morning.

I turned my back in hopes I wouldn't catch his eye. "Blackburne's got enough money to buy whatever Rossetti and Howie steal," I pointed out, though I was sure Quinn had already thought of this theory.

"Exactly. But that means he's got enough money to buy whatever he sets his sights on. So he wouldn't need somebody to steal the stuff for him in the first place. And he wouldn't need to buy stolen goods, either. Why complicate his life like that and risk getting arrested? Blackburne's loaded. When he wants to buy something, I'm sure he just finds the collector who owns it and makes him an offer he can't refuse."

"Good point." I hated to admit it. "Then who—"

"It could be any one of them." That eagle-eyed gaze of his scanned the crowd as if just by looking, he might figure out what was going on and how it all tied in to Dingo and Vincent's murders. "It could be a dozen of them working together. From what I've heard, there's always a market for stolen collectibles. The more collectors think they can't get their hands on something, the more they want it."

Quinn was wearing an earbud and before he could continue, he put a hand to his ear and stooped his head, listening, then, with a mumbled curse, headed toward the lobby. "Altercation in the parking lot," he grumbled. "Somebody just ran over somebody else's Scooby-Doo stuffed animal."

"Ah, the life of a detective!"

If I wasn't so busy watching the way Quinn moved through the crowd like a panther on the prowl, I might have noticed Milo Blackburne slip up beside me. "Off to take care of business, is he?"

"Something like that."

"And you're here . . . ?"

Don't think I hadn't already come up with a plan to cover this contingency. In fact, the idea had popped into my head the moment I saw Blackburne stroll into the ballroom. "To see the *Daily Planet*, of course," I said, and threw in a smile for good measure. "I know you had more than a little something to do with getting it set up here at the convention."

"Which means I also have special access." He offered me his arm.

In the name of my investigation, I took it.

Milo escorted me over to the area that was roped off to keep ordinary mortals from contaminating it, but hey, he had clout, and money, and a reputation as a collector and a generous donor. One look at him and the burly bouncer type stationed near the front of the set nodded and let us pass.

It goes without saying that I am not easily impressed, especially by all things comic book–like. But I will admit, the moment I set foot in the phony office of the phony *Daily Planet*, I knew a whole lot of thought and care had gone into building it. Along with a whole bunch of money.

This was no chintzy stage set that looks passable from the seats and barely holds together up close. The hardwood floor was genuine. So were the wooden reporters' desks lined up in rows, each with its own typewriter (not even electric) and black, chunky rotary phone.

"It looks like it came right out of that old black-and-white Superman TV show you told me about," I said.

His smile told me that was exactly the point. "We took poetic license with the phone booth," he said, glancing toward the vintage metal and glass booth on the far side of the set. "In actuality in the TV show, Clark usually changed in the storage room of the newspaper office. But the phone booth is such a big part of the mythos, I couldn't resist! Imagine, entering the phone booth as mild-mannered Clark Kent and emerging as Superman."

He sounded so impressed by the concept I didn't have the heart to tell him I figured Superman as being too smart to bother with a phone booth. Glass walls for one thing. Not to mention there wasn't much elbow room. As if confirming this to myself, I sashayed to the back of the office and peeked inside the phone booth, wondering what Clark did with his suit once he ripped it off his muscular body and slipped into tights and a cape.

"So what do you think?" Milo's question brushed against my ear. While I was busy wondering about Superman's habit of scattering his clothes in phone booths all over Metropolis, he'd come up behind me.

"The whole thing is very cool." Truth, and I stepped away, the better to put some distance between myself and Milo Blackburne. "I've never actually been in one, but my guess is this looks just like a real newsroom. Well, a real newsroom from back in the fifties, anyway."

His smile was broad. "I hoped you'd like it. We'll have drinks here tonight, what do you say?" And in response to my blank look he added, "You are coming tonight? To the cocktail party?"

It didn't seem the right moment to tell him I didn't have a clue what he was talking about. "I'm not sure . . ."

"But you have to come. Look. See?" He cupped my elbow and led me to the front of the set. From here, we had a bird's-eye view of the commotion going on in the ballroom. Over on the far side of the room where the crowd wasn't as heavy, workers were putting the finishing touches on what looked to be some sort of special exhibit. They were testing the overhead lighting, switching the spots on and off, adjusting them, putting them on again. "The convention organizers have promised a surprise and they're going to unveil it this evening." Behind his glasses, his eyes glimmered. "You do like surprises, don't you? You wouldn't want to miss this one."

"You know what it is."

His smile widened.

"And you're going to tell me, right?"

Blackburne leaned in close enough for me to see my reflection in his glasses. "But if I told you, it wouldn't be a surprise, Lana."

I bristled and stepped back. "If you think I'm Lana, it would be a plenty big surprise. Because I'm—"

"Pepper, of course!" Blackburne laughed, dismissing the mistake as nothing and changing the subject. "This . . ." He rapped his knuckles against the nearest desk. "This is Lois Lane's desk. What do you think?"

"It looks like all the other desks."

"Well, yes, basically. But just like the eyes are the windows of the soul, I have a theory that our desks give others insights into our personalities. What does the desk tell you about the woman?"

I gave the desk a quick once-over. "She's neat and organized. Oh, and she's got a picture of Superman on her desk!" I picked up the framed photograph of some good-looking guy who'd undergone the ultimate in humiliation and posed in blue tights and red cape for the photo. I only hoped they'd paid him enough to make it worth his while. "From this, I think I know something else about Lois," I said, setting the picture back down where I found it. "She's got it bad for Clark Kent."

"Oh no!" Blackburne wagged a finger. "She's madly in love with Superman. She has no idea they are one and the same person. Pity she loves him so much," he added, turning away. "I feel bad about breaking her heart."

"Which means . . ." I caught up with him and side by side, we walked back to the desk with the Clark Kent nameplate on it.

"Which means Superman has come to his senses, of course." Blackburne made sure everything on the desktop was arranged just so. "He knows now that Lois isn't the woman for him. He knows . . ." He moved in close enough for his words to brush my lips. "He knows Lana is the love of his life."

It wasn't the first time he started talking crazy while he was looking at me and this time, like all those other times, it gave me the willies. I was just about to tell him as much and ask him to please get real when the head of security came bustling over.

"It's here, Mr. Blackburne," the man said, breathless. "You told me to let you know as soon as it arrived."

"Of course." Blackburne dismissed the man with a nod before he turned back to me. "I'll see you here this evening? I can guarantee you'll be impressed."

I kept a stiff smile firmly in place. "Impressed is something I like to be."

With that, he let the bouncer know I could stay on at the *Daily Planet* as long as I liked and disappeared with the head of security.

I waited until they walked out of the ballroom before I hightailed it back to the heart of the crowd.

All those people and I still managed to run smack into Quinn.

"Everything okay with the Scooby gang?" I asked.

He was not amused. I could tell because he growled.

"Lighten up!" I gave him a playful poke. "Maybe you'll

feel better this evening when you get a couple cocktails in you."

Quinn grabbed my arm and his fingers tightened like a vise. Without bothering to excuse us, he dragged me through the crowd and to the doors on the far end of the room, punched one open, and deposited me in a hallway that was empty except for a water fountain, a sign that pointed to the restrooms, and a few pieces of really bad framed art.

"What do you know about the cocktail party tonight?" he asked.

I hate when he gets all pissy like this. Especially when we're working a case we wouldn't be working at all if it weren't for me and my Gift.

I stepped back, refusing to rub the place on my arm where his fingers had gripped it. "I know I've got a special invitation to attend," I said. "And I'm having drinks with Milo Blackburne at the *Daily Planet*."

"No, you're not."

I am nothing if not reasonable. Except when someone tells me *no*.

"And you're the boss of me how?" I asked him, lifting my chin when he lifted his. "This is my investigation and—"

"No, it's not."

There was that word again.

I bristled. "You wouldn't know anything about Jack Haggarty if it weren't for me."

"Oh yeah, that's right. Thank you very much. Thanks to you, I know my former partner was taking bribes. That really makes my day."

"So that's what you're peeved about! You find out Jack wasn't on the up-and-up and you blame me? Not fair."

He didn't confirm or deny. He simply reached for my arm again.

This time, I wasn't about to get dragged around. I swatted his hand away.

"What's the deal with the cocktail party?" I demanded.

"You don't know? I figured anyone who was having drinks at the *Daily Planet* had the inside scoop on that sort of thing."

"You do lousy sarcasm," I countered.

"I wasn't trying for sarcasm, just the truth."

"Which means, what? Are you jealous? Of me and Milo Blackburne?" The only way I could even begin to put the thought into focus was to step back, squint, and give Quinn a careful look. "You're crazy. You know that, don't you?"

A muscle jumped at the base of his jaw. "I'm not jealous."

"Then what is it?"

With one hand, Quinn rubbed the back of his neck. Yeah, I get the thing about male ego. Especially when the male in question is Quinn. It didn't excuse it, but it explained why when he told me what was going on, it was like each word was being pulled out of him with a pair of flaming tongs. "It's this cocktail party," he said. "I knew they had it scheduled. I just didn't know why."

There was no way I could ask more than with one perfectly shaped raised eyebrow.

"They're doing a sort of big surprise unveiling," he said. "And they've been playing this really close to the vest. In fact, I just found out about it this morning. Nice touch, don't you think? I'm supposed to be helping them keep their damned stuff safe, and they never even bothered to tell me. When I asked why, I was told that if the cops knew what was going on, word might get out, and that would have ruined the surprise for everyone."

I have never been known as a model of patience. Red hair, remember. "Tell you what?"

His sigh was monumental. "Tonight, a collector from Canada is going to be here to show off his copy of *Action Comics* number one. The very first comic book Superman ever appeared in."

I think I was supposed to be more impressed.

I think Quinn realized I wasn't. "It was originally published in 1938," he said, filling in what I guess was pertinent information. "At the time, it sold for ten cents. There aren't many around anymore. And that means every person at this convention would probably sell his soul to get his hands on that comic book. The last one that sold at auction brought in more than a million."

"Dollars?" I nearly choked on the word. "For a comic book?"

"Old and rare. That makes it valuable. And tempting."

I shot a look at the closed ballroom doors as if I could see that fancy-schmancy display.

"You think that's what somebody's going to try and steal."

He nodded.

"Tonight?"

"That's my guess."

"Rossetti and Howie?"

"That remains to be seen. I stopped over at their most recent addresses and learned that neither one of them has been seen in a while. They might be lying low, planning a heist."

"So maybe one of them is the one who's supposed to get killed." It wasn't like I'd ever wish bad on anybody, but a girl can't help feeling just a tad bit revengeful what with being pushed in a grave and all. "They killed Dingo. And Jack. That would save the justice system a long trial."

"If we ever come up with the evidence to try them in the first place."

"So we find the evidence."

"No, *we* don't do anything. I told you, you're not coming to the cocktail party tonight." With that, Quinn whirled around and walked away.

Like I was going to let that be the end of the conversation?

I scrambled to catch up with him. "Oh no, buster. You're not going to tell me to get lost and get away with it! This is my case."

"Were you listening to me?" He turned around so fast, I would have fallen flat if he didn't grab my shoulders. "I told you, Pepper, they're exhibiting a million-dollar comic book here tonight. Do you know what that means?"

"It means morgue or no morgue, somebody's going to try to steal it. Yeah, I get that. It's what we want, isn't it? Then we can—"

"No, then *we* can't do anything. Because you're not going to be here."

"Wrong!" I wrenched myself away from him and made

sure to back up a step or two, just so he couldn't grab hold of me again.

Even that wasn't enough to send a message. "I want you out of here. Now." Quinn's order came from between clenched teeth. "And I don't want you anywhere near this place this evening."

"And miss all the excitement? You're kidding me, right? I'm not going to walk away."

"You will if I have anything to do with it."

A woman conference attendee stuck her head out of the ballroom doors, apparently looking for the ladies' room. One glance at the two of us fighting like alley cats and she ducked back into the ballroom.

"Are you forgetting that you wouldn't have a case if it weren't for me?" I asked Quinn.

"Are you forgetting that Jack told us that somebody's going to die?" His breaths were quick and shallow. His face was pale. I think the only thing that helped Quinn hold on to his temper was curling his hands into fists. That, and spinning on his heels and marching away. "There's no way I want you anywhere near here tonight," he said before he slammed through the ballroom doors and disappeared. "Don't you get it, Pepper? I don't want anything to happen to you. I love you too much."

19

I had been waiting to hear those words from Quinn for a long time.

So go figure, rather than racing after him, making him repeat them just to be sure I heard right, and throwing myself into his arms when he confirmed that I had, I stormed out of the hotel.

A girl has her standards, after all, and being told what to do by a bullheaded guy—even one who finally told me he loved me—wasn't one of them.

Outside, I saw that the weather provided a perfect backdrop to my mood, in a poetic sort of way. Overhead, thick gray clouds bunched against each other and the wind whipped trees and tossed fast-food bags across the road along with the pages of somebody's newspaper.

Perfect.

Gray.

Gloomy.

Stormy.

Perfect.

I was still grumbling as I neared home and thought about sitting in my apartment with nothing to do and no one to bitch at, and sad to say, I knew that would make me even more miserable.

Yes, I'd taken a vacation day and yes (again), I knew I was about to set an ugly precedent, but sometimes, these things can't be helped. I was going to explode if I didn't keep busy.

Garden View was my only option.

By the time I parked and dodged fat raindrops to get into the administration building, I had really worked myself into a state. I hurried past Jennine, our receptionist, and fortunately, when I walked by her office, Ella was on the phone and simply waved. So not in the mood to chat. I marched to my own office, threw open the door, and before I had time to slam it shut behind me, a wall of frosty air washed over me.

No big surprise. Chet, Albert, and Jean were hard at work.

"Hey, lookee who's here!" Chet tossed out the greeting from around the cigar clenched between his teeth. There was a pile of papers in front of him and as he read through them, Jean flipped them over. "Did you know you got a dame buried in this place who used to be a burlesque star? That's gonna make one socko article for that there newsletter of yours."

It wasn't like I wasn't grateful, and just a tad intrigued, but honestly at that moment, I really didn't care. I shooed Chet out of my chair and took his place. The seat was icy cold. Across the desk, Albert was adding and re-adding a long string of numbers on a ghostly ledger sheet. His head down and his thin lips pursed, he didn't spare me a look.

"You're not having a good day." Jean reached for the pages Chet was finished with and tapped them into a neat pile. "Can I get you a cup of coffee?"

"No. Thanks." I scrubbed my hands over my face. "I just need to hide out for a while. I figured I could—"

My words were split by a flash of lightning and a crash of thunder.

On the other side of my desk, Albert's eyes flew open and he pressed a hand to his chest.

"I've got that new tour of politicians' graves to plan and I might as well work on it," I said, continuing on as if nothing had happened, because storm or no storm, nothing could compete with the racket going on inside my head. The word *love* featured prominently. As did that deal-breaking *no. No, don't show up at the cocktail party. No, don't think of this as your investigation.* And, of course, the biggie, the one that didn't even need the *no* to give me the ol' symbolic kick in the teeth—*Mind your own business.*

Okay, Quinn hadn't quite put it that way, but admit it, he wasn't far off.

I actually might have gotten emotional about it if another zip of lightning hadn't snaked through the air. The office lights flickered, and Albert jumped out of his chair and scurried into the corner.

I looked from Chet to Jean to Albert, who was shaking like the leaves on the tree outside my office window. "Not passing judgment here," I said, holding up a hand in the sort of universal sign that proved I meant it. "But you're dead, Albert. And you're afraid of storms?"

"Hey, cut the guy a break!" Chet floated around to the front of my desk. "Don'cha know? It's how he died!"

I wasn't exactly following, which is why my question was a bit unsure. "In a storm?"

Chet leaned over the desk and whispered, "Struck by lightning."

I looked over to where Jean was doing her best to console Albert with advice like, "You must conquer your weaknesses," and, "We have nothing to fear but fear itself."

"But . . ." I glanced back at Chet. "That was like a hundred years ago."

He scratched a hand alongside his bulgy nose. "You ain't heard? You don't know? Ghosts . . . we can get dispatched. You know, for good. We can get zapped into nothingness if the same thing happens to us now as what killed us back when we were alive. If Albert gets struck by lightning again . . ." Chet snapped his fingers. "That would be the end of him. Forever."

"I didn't know." I said this to Albert as much as to myself, and just to show him I hoped there were no hard feelings, I went over to the window and closed the miniblinds. "Better?" I asked him, and he nodded, but he didn't get back to work.

At least not until the storm had blown over, the skies cleared, and the birds started chattering outside the window.

By then, I was a couple hours into reading about the local politicians—council members, mayors, a couple governors—who called Garden View their permanent home, and praying none of them would ever show up and start bugging me. Bad enough I had to listen to the live ones and their endless campaign drivel. I'd already investigated a case on behalf of a long-dead president. That was enough for me. If I ever had to deal with another dead politician, I'd have to remember Chet's foolproof way of getting rid of a ghost.

"You're reading the same page. Again."

I hadn't realized Jean was looking over my shoulder until I heard her voice. I slapped closed the book I was reading and tossed down my pen. "Hard to concentrate," I grumbled. "Damn man!"

"You're not talking about one of the former mayors of Cleveland who are buried on these grounds." Jean, always insightful.

"You got that right." Yes, I'd just dropped it, but I picked up the pen again so I could tap-tap-tap it against the desktop. Being bossy! Warning me that it's not safe to do what I'd been doing and doing successfully these past years! Commanding me to stay away from the cocktail party at the convention that night!

Yeah, right. Like that was going to happen!

"It's all because of this stupid investigation," I said. "Because we can't get anywhere with it, because none of it makes any sense. Vincent got murdered, and I'm sure it's because somebody thought he said too much, but all he ever talked about was a morgue. And there is no morgue."

"There's the county morgue not far from here," Jean pointed out.

"Got it," I told her. "But that's not the morgue Vincent

was talking about. At least I don't see how it could be. And there is no other morgue."

"There's a morgue at a newspaper office," Chet said.

My head came up. "There's a—"

"Morgue at a newspaper office. Sure." His head bobbed. "The morgue. That's what we call the room where all the old newspapers and all the reference materials and such are filed. Only these days . . ." When he looked at the computer on my desk, his mouth puckered. "I suppose it's all stored some other way now. But back in the day—"

"Like in the fifties?" I was already on my feet, groping for my purse while I stared at Chet like that would actually make him answer faster. "Did they have morgues in newspaper offices in the fifties?"

"Sure."

It was all I needed to hear. I had my phone in my hand before I hit the door, and when Quinn didn't pick up that call, I called him three more times on my way back to the hotel. When I got close, I saw why he didn't answer. Something told me he might be a tad busy.

Police cars surrounded the place, their lights flashing, and cops and paramedics swarmed around like bees outside a hive.

With all the commotion, I figured nobody would even notice my car in a no-parking zone. I was talking to the nearest uniformed cop before my door was even closed. "What happened? And where's Detective Harrison?"

This cop shrugged and pointed across the parking lot and toward the lobby.

I took that as a sign that I had free access.

There was a detective stationed inside the door. Hard

to miss 'em what with the trench coat, the rumpled suit, the tie stained with what looked like tomato soup. "Harrison?" I said again. "Where is he? I've got something I have to tell him. About the Superman comic book."

This guy was middle-aged and tired-looking. "You're a little late."

My mouth went dry. "Somebody stole it?" I squeezed my eyes shut. "They came in through the morgue, right? The pretend storage room of the pretend newspaper office. And let me guess, they were dressed all in black and with their faces covered. Like ninjas. Damn! I should have paid more attention."

Unlike this cop, who was by this time paying plenty of attention and looking at me with sudden interest. "We'll need you to give a statement," he said. "What did you say your name was?"

Before I could answer, a team of paramedics raced in with a gurney and my heart skipped a beat. Jack said if we didn't work this thing out, somebody was going to die. And now things were out of control. Somebody was hurt. Somebody might be . . .

When the ballroom doors slammed behind the paramedics, I jumped.

"I was working with Quinn Harrison," I told the cop. "I know, it sounds weird, but it's true. You can ask him. He'll tell you. It all has to do with Vincent's murder. Vincent, the security guard? He knew about the morgue, see. He must have overheard someone talking about what they planned to do, and he tried to tell us, but we didn't listen and now . . ." A quivering started up in my stomach and my knees shook to the same beat. "Just ask Quinn, he'll tell you. Where is he?"

The cop's mouth pulled into a smile that was completely devoid of amusement. "That," he said, "is a very good question. For a guy who's supposed to be our liaison with this shindig, he's noticeably absent."

"He's not—" The paramedics raced back out of the ballroom and I held my breath. That is, until I saw that the person on the gurney was an old guy who was pale, but other than that, appeared to be fine. "He's got to be here," I said, turning back to the detective. "He wouldn't leave. Not when he knew there was a chance something was going to happen. And—"

He didn't give me a chance to say anything else. "There's an officer over there named Jankowski," he said, nudging me toward the registration desk. "You go give him your statement."

Sure, I headed over that way, but there was no way I was going to let myself get waylaid by bureaucratic red tape. I waited until that detective turned around to talk to another detective type and ducked into a nearby hallway where I wedged myself between the snack and pop machines. I tried Quinn's cell again.

No answer.

"Damn." I shoved my phone in my purse and decided to take a quick look around and try to figure out what was up. I would have, too, if an arm hadn't snaked around my waist to hold me in place, and a cloth hadn't been shoved over my face. Whatever that cloth was soaked in smelled funny and I tried not to breathe.

Unfortunately, there was only so long I could hold my breath, and only so long I could fight against the weird sensations that skittered through me.

Flying. Floating. My legs were heavy. My arms went numb.

Darkness snuck up beside me and gobbled me up.

Damn! It was just like Jack said. Things were going to go wrong at the convention. Somebody was going to die. I just never realized it was going to be me.

I have no idea how long I was unconscious, I only know that when I finally woke up, my mouth tasted like I'd sucked on an ashtray and my stomach was doing flips. My head, it should be noted, was pounding so hard, I was afraid to open my eyes.

And just as afraid not to.

I spent a couple seconds listening. For the sounds of voices. For some indication of where I was and who I might be with.

The only thing I heard was a silence that pressed against me like hands.

Afraid I'd find them tied, I took my time trying out my arms and legs. When they moved freely, I sighed, then because my stomach lurched, I took a deep breath. It made me cough and choke and I sat up. As long as I was that much in the land of the living, I figured I might as well go all the way. I peeked around through eyes that felt as if they'd been weighted down with bricks.

The first thing I saw was Superman.

Yeah, blue tights, little red Speedo shorts, cape. Superman. Only this time, not a comic book or a picture or a poster. A person.

"Still unconscious," I told myself. "Still dreaming." Let's face it, that would be the only thing that could possibly explain the superhero vision as well as the vivid blue walls that surrounded me, the red touches here and there, the framed comic books, and—

Awareness knifed through me. My spine stiffened and my eyes flew open.

I was in Milo Blackburne's weird little museum room.

Except last time I was there, Superman wasn't in the room with me.

I closed one eye, trying to focus on the blue-and-red blur standing across the room, and when that didn't work, I scrubbed my hands over my eyes and tried again.

"You're not real," I said.

"Of course I am." The Man of Steel stepped closer but since the light was at his back and in my eyes, I still couldn't get a good look at his face. There was a lightweight blanket thrown over me and I plucked it aside and swung my feet onto the floor.

The room pitched.

With one hand, I clutched the arm of the couch where I'd been laying and shook my head. Not the best move. Even after I was done, the room kept shaking.

"Can't be," I said, my voice as shaky as my vision. "You're just a character in a comic book."

His laugh was deep and cocky. Just like a superhero's ought to be.

He held his hands out to his sides and his red cape billowed around him. "Obviously, I'm very much real. And very much in love with you, Lana."

Wide awake now.

I tried to move fast and get off the couch, but let's face it, I was at something of a disadvantage, what with having been knocked out and all. When Milo Blackburne in his weird costume closed the distance between us, sat down next to me, and slipped an arm around my shoulders, all I could manage was to scoot back, and try to smack his hands away. Great plan. Too bad I was as weak as a wet paper bag.

"What are you talking about?" I hoped he heard the disbelief in my voice and not the panic. This was no time to show how freakin' scared I was. "And why are you dressed like that?" I gave the outfit another once-over. In his boxy suits, it had always been impossible to tell just how well built Milo really was. Now, muscles bulged beneath the skintight blue shirt with the giant yellow *S* emblazoned on it. "Is this some kind of joke?"

He took my hand. "You know it's not, Lana," he said. "I've told you before. I love you. I know you weren't listening. But don't worry, I forgive you. You thought I was nothing more than mild-mannered Milo Blackburne. But now that you know my deepest secret—"

"That you're Superman?" Whirling head and flopping stomach aside, I scooted off the couch. When I stood up, it took a couple seconds for the room to settle down. I clutched my hands together behind my back, the better to keep him from holding on to me again. "Stop kidding around. It's not funny. And it doesn't make any sense.

Unless . . ." The truth hit as it often does, like a jackhammer. I pointed one trembling finger at him. "The comic book at the convention. You stole it, didn't you? That would explain the cops scrambling all over the hotel."

He laughed. "It was quite a sight, wasn't it? There were all those convention goers, milling around, waiting for the evening's cocktail party and wondering what was going to happen at it. I saved them the trouble. As soon as the comic was brought into the room, I put my plan in motion. No one ever expected it. No one could stop it. Before anyone even realized what was happening . . ." There was a computer on a nearby desk, and he flicked on the screen.

"Webcam," he explained. "As you can see . . ." Milo put a reverent hand on the screen and on the scene it showed: that big, empty see-through box in the Fortress of Solitude wasn't so empty anymore. I might not be a comic connoisseur, but I was willing to bet the comic book inside it—one that showed Superman holding a car above his head—was *Action Comics* #1.

"But why?" I tried to stomp my foot for emphasis. It was the first I realized my shoes were missing. "You've got enough money to buy whatever you want. You don't need to steal stuff."

He stood, adjusting his cape. "There are some collectors who are simply unreasonable. They won't sell what they have, not for any price. Sometimes, I simply don't have a choice. You understand, don't you, Lana? Of course you do. You know how important it is for me to have these books and these pictures. After all, they are part of my heritage."

"Your kryptonite heritage."

He wagged his finger. "Kryptonian is the proper word. You'll get used to it, don't worry. Kryptonite, remember, is all that's left of my home planet after it exploded."

It was ignore the crazy talk or give in to the fear. I concentrated on the details. "Then you're the one . . ." It was hard to put the pieces together when I was feeling this woozy, but I did my best. "You hired Rossetti and Howie to travel to the conventions all over the country and steal things for you. But they . . ." Milo wasn't wearing his glasses; it was easy to look into his eyes. "How dare you tell me you love me! They tried to kill me!"

"Yes, I know. I'm very sorry." He touched one hand to my hair. "I'm afraid Mr. Rossetti and his associate can sometimes get a little carried away. They realized you were digging around for information about the deaths of that Dingo character and Jack Haggarty, and they thought you were a threat. What they did, they did to protect me. I hope you understand. Believe me . . ." He traced a finger over my cheek. "I've had a talk with them and set them straight. They are never to lay another finger on you. They just needed a little reassurance, but I've taken care of that. I told them you'd never betray me. Especially not now that you know my true identity."

Okay, it wasn't the first time the word *crazy* came to mind when I thought about Milo Blackburne. It was the first time I realized just how serious it was, though. I stepped back, gauging the distance between myself and the door, hoping it wasn't locked. "I won't tell anybody. I promise." Yeah, lying. Like anybody could blame me? "But you're going to get in trouble for stealing that comic book. If you could just give it back—"

Another of those devil-may-care laughs sent shivers up my spine. "Never! I've worked too long and too hard to get my hands on it. Now, my collection is almost complete."

I swallowed hard. "Almost?"

"The only thing I need now is you, Lana." Milo dropped to one knee. "Make me the happiest superhero alive. Marry me!"

"No." Could I be any clearer? I figured it didn't hurt to try. "No, no, no. I barely know you. And you just stole a million-dollar comic book. And you're wearing blue tights, for crying out loud."

"I know, I know." Like I hadn't just crushed his heart into a million pieces, he chuckled and stood up. "It takes some getting used to. I mean, the whole secret identity, the superpowers. Not to worry, my love, after a while, you'll accept it. Marry me, Lana."

I back stepped toward the door. "No."

Truth be told, I don't think Milo Blackburne really had any superpowers. But I do know that I was still feeling shaky and not at my best. When he closed in on me, it did seem like he did it at super-speed. His hand gripped the back of my neck and though I tried to lock my legs and stay where I was, it was a losing cause. He dragged me over to the computer. With his free hand, he clicked a couple keys and that webcam panned the Fortress of Solitude. It came to a stop focused on the far corner behind that statue of Superman's parents.

"See that?" I couldn't, not clearly, anyway, but that was no excuse for Milo to push my face nearer to the screen. "What do you say now, Lana?"

I didn't say anything. Not until I got a closer look.

And then my heart stopped cold and my stomach went numb and I couldn't have said anything if I wanted to.

"It's regrettable," Milo grumbled close to my ear. "But sometimes, even superheroes have to make hard choices. You've given me no other options, Lana."

My mouth filled with sand, I took another look at the screen and at the man tied up and tossed in the corner of the Fortress of Solitude. He wasn't moving.

I ran my tongue over my lips. "Is he . . . is Quinn alive?"

"For now." Milo let go of my neck and still, I didn't move. I couldn't. I stared at the computer screen and at Quinn crumpled in the corner. "He's been drugged. Just enough to keep him quiet. Another dose though . . ." Before, that cavalier laugh had just been goofy. Now, it was terrifying. "If Detective Harrison stays alive . . . that, Lana, all depends on you."

The words barely made it past my lips. "What . . ." I managed to tear my gaze away from Quinn and whirl toward Milo. "What do you want me to do?"

"Oh, my darling! Don't make it sound so serious." He kissed my cheek. "All I'm asking you to do is marry me. If you don't . . ." Milo skimmed his lips to my ear and whispered. "If you don't, I swear by my Kryptonian heritage that Quinn Harrison is going to die."

20

"And do you, Penelope Martin, take this man to be your wedded husband to live together in marriage? Do you promise to love, comfort, honor, and keep him for better or worse, for richer or poorer, in sickness and in health, and forsaking all others, be faithful only to him so long as you both shall live?"

Did I?

I knew I wouldn't find the answers out in the sea of faces watching the ceremony—not the answers I wanted, anyway—but I glanced over my shoulder to where Mom and Dad sat in the first row of white chairs. They were beaming. Ella, who was sitting next to my mother, had tears rolling down her cheeks. The rest of the chairs were packed with guests, some of them I recognized and some I didn't. The entire Garden View staff was there. So were some of our more socially connected patrons. The rest, I assumed, were Blackburne's business associates or relatives. From the murmurs I'd heard as I was getting ready for the big event, everyone had been as surprised by the announcement of our engagement as they were by the fact that the ceremony was taking place almost instantly, but aside from Dad (who kept asking, "Are you sure about this, honey?" even as we prepared to walk down the aisle), my family and friends had apparently decided that I was a big girl, and I could make my own decisions.

After all, Milo Blackburne wasn't bad-looking and he was obscenely rich. What girl could ask for more? Especially when he stood at my side, those bulging muscles of his—and that red Speedo, thank goodness—hidden under a dapper tuxedo, smiling at me with so much devotion, there was no question that he adored me.

Well, that he adored Lana Lang, anyway.

Adored by a crazy person.

A crazy person who was holding Quinn hostage.

A crazy person who was going to kill Quinn if I told anyone what was really going on and didn't go through with the ceremony.

Okay, so this wasn't turning out to be one of my better days.

"Well, do you?"

The minister's question snapped me out of my thoughts. Too bad it did nothing for the panic that beat through me like the bass line on a hip-hop recording. Or the worry that gnawed at my insides. Or the fear—

Honestly, I couldn't think about the fear. I was already headed for a full-fledged meltdown, and no way I was going to let that to happen.

Not when Quinn's life hung in the balance.

"I . . ." My voice broke over the words. "How can I not?" I asked. I steadied myself with a deep breath and put a plan into action that I'd hatched as I was squeezing myself into the wedding gown from hell. That's when the reality of what was really happening finally hit. Namely, that I wasn't going to get out of this wedding. Not if I didn't do something clever, and quick.

Not quick enough? Not clever enough? Heck with me spending the rest of my life as Mrs. Milo Blackburne. The rest of my life wouldn't be worth very much, anyway. Not if Quinn was dead.

As sweet a smile as I could manage pasted to my lips, I reached into the little silk pouch I had slung over my wrist and took out my soon-to-be husband's ring. I cupped it in my palm—the better to keep him from getting a good look at it—and took his hand in mine.

"This is for you . . ." I purred, "Superman," and slipped the ring on Blackburne's finger.

He was so freakin' happy, I thought he was going to pop.

That is, until he looked down at the gold plastic ring with the curlicues on the band and the big green (fake) stone set in the center of it.

When his eyes went wide and he flinched, I went in for the kill.

"It's kryptonite," I said. "And you're powerless against it!"

That happy smile melted from Blackburne's face and he staggered back. Oh yeah, I knew I couldn't get away with the whole fake kryptonite harming the fake superhero for long. That's why I made my move while the moving was good.

"Mom! Dad! Ella!" I turned toward the wedding guests, who at this point, mostly looked confused. "Get up here quick. I need you!"

When they were within a few feet of the makeshift altar, I ducked behind Blackburne and pushed him in Dad's direction. All those years in prison, and he knew exactly what to do when there was a big guy coming at him. Dad grabbed Blackburne's right arm and twisted. Mom stuck out a foot (and how she was able to afford the fabulous lace peep-toe pumps that matched her champagne-colored dress, I didn't know but I intended to find out) and my groom went down in a heap.

Before he could get back up, I whipped the strand of orange beads off Ella's neck. "He's a bad guy," I yelled, but then I really didn't have a lot of choice seeing as how the gorgeous flagstone patio overlooking the lake had erupted into chaos. "He was forcing me to marry him."

Dad grabbed for the beads and cinched them tight around Blackburne's wrists and though she was being foxy and made it look like an accident, I'm pretty sure the way Mom's pump connected with his ribs had more than a little malice in it.

"Call the cops," I instructed Ella. "Tell them Blackburne—"

"Lana!" On the flagstones at my feet, Blackburne squirmed and squealed. "You can't do this. Not to me. I can break my chains." He strained at the beads on his wrists and for all I knew, he would have pulled them apart eventually. That is, if Ella hadn't plopped down right on top of him.

"He stole the million-dollar comic book," I called out,

already racing across the patio. "And he kidnapped Quinn. Tell the cops one of their own is involved. They'll get here plenty quick."

Plenty quick was how I intended to move, too. With that in mind, I ignored the outstretched hands of some blue-haired woman who mumbled something about how I was making the mistake of my life, kicked off my white satin pumps, lifted my skirts, and headed into the house.

"You'll never find him!" I heard Blackburne's voice from outside, high-pitched and strained. But then, as soon as he piped up, Ella jiggled around to squash him a little more. "He's hidden. In my Fortress of Solitude."

"Thanks, Milo," I mumbled and raced into the museum room.

"Fireplace, fireplace," I mumbled to myself, my words bumping around pretty much like my heartbeat. If Blackburne had lied about keeping Quinn alive until we were man and wife . . .

If I was already too late . . .

I punched the wall until I found the magic spot that triggered the secret door and the next thing I knew, I was in the Fortress of Solitude.

"Quinn?" Well, dang, he'd never hear me when my voice was so small and scared sounding. I spun toward the weird statue of Superman's parents. "Quinn, are you in here?"

"Hiya, Pepper!"

The sound of Quinn's voice brought me to my knees. Literally. I dropped down beside where he was propped in the corner and tugged at the ropes around his wrists.

"We've got to get you out of here. We've got to hurry."

My fingers were sweaty, and they slipped over the knots. "Blackburne is crazy. I don't know what he might have had planned." The knots loosened and I breathed a sigh of relief and tugged on Quinn's arm. "Come on."

He brought his arms out in front of him and looked at his hands as if he'd never seen them before. "What's the hurry?" he asked, though in all fairness, it came out sounding more like, "Wha's da huey?"

"Nice here." He stretched out on the floor. "Warm."

"No, it's not nice here." I grabbed one hand and pulled. "And why are you acting so funny and talking so weird?"

Good thing I figured out the answer on my own, because there was no way I was going to get it from Quinn. Whatever drug Blackburne had administered, it was still in Quinn's system. He was alive. He was breathing. I was grateful. But Quinn was as drunk as a skunk.

"You look like . . ." From his spot on the floor, he squinted up at me. "Pepper. You look like Pepper."

"I am Pepper." I knelt back down on the cold steel floor, the better to let him get a bird's-eye view. "And you're Quinn, Quinn Harrison. You don't belong here. We need to get you outside."

"Okay." He didn't move.

"Now."

"Okay." He wiggled his fingers in front of his nose and laughed.

"Quinn." I tugged at his hand again, hard enough to make him slide a couple inches across the floor.

"Whee!" Quinn threw back his head and laughed. "That was fun. Do it again."

I did. In fact, I tugged until I couldn't tug any more, all

the way over to where that million-dollar comic book hung on display in the clear case suspended in the center of the room.

"All right now." I propped an arm around his shoulders. "You're going to have to stand up and walk out of here. Can you do it?"

He looked at me, his nose wrinkled and his eyes scrunched. "You look like Pepper," he said.

Don't ask me how since his legs were Silly Putty, but I managed to haul him to his feet. "I think it's time for us to leave."

"Okay." He didn't move.

"Now."

"You look pretty."

I glanced down at the gown and my bare feet sticking out from under it.

Quinn leaned in to brush my lips with a kiss. "Like a princess. Are you a princess?"

"I am. And the princess gets to tell her subjects what to do."

His eyes sparkled and with one finger, he traced the sweetheart neckline of my gown. "Anything."

"Later." I caught hold of his hand and held it in a tight grip. "For now, the princess wants to take a walk. Yeah, that's what she wants to do. She commands you to come outside with her and take a walk."

"Wanna stay here." He nuzzled a kiss against my neck and his tongue sent ribbons of fire racing over my skin. "My job is to make the princess very, very happy."

"Ah, happy!" Fireworks erupt every place his kisses landed and for one quick second, I tipped my head back, enjoying the sensations. "But we can't—" I stepped back, hanging on to his hand but keeping a safe distance between myself and the sensations he sent skittering through me. "The princess . . ." I wasn't sure when all the air had been sucked out of the room, but I knew I had to fight to fill my lungs. "The princess commands you to stop now. She wants to leave."

"Okay."

"Okay?"

"Okay."

I tried to tug him closer to the spinning secret door, but no luck. He was too busy giving me the sort of careful once-over I'd seen him subject suspects to, only on the job, he was never as googly eyed. "Are you getting married or something?"

"I'll explain. Later. After we're outside."

"No." He locked his legs and refused to move another step. "Need to know. Now." He made an effort to emphasize his point by pounding one fist against the steel desk, but since he missed by a mile and nearly went down in a heap, I don't think it had quite the dramatic effect he'd hoped for.

When I grabbed for him to keep him from falling, Quinn took advantage and wrapped his arms around me. "If you're going to marry anyone," he said, "it's gotta be me."

Not the moment to roll my eyes, but it's not like I could exactly help myself. I gave those broad shoulders of his an openhanded smack. "You're drunk."

"I'm . . . drunk. And serious."

"It doesn't count, not when you've been drugged."

"That doesn't change . . . how I . . ." He hiccuped. "Feel."

"I'll tell you what . . ." I pushed out of his arms. "We'll talk later when you're feeling more like yourself."

"Won't change my mind." He shook his head so hard, his inky hair flopped over his forehead. "I love you."

My heart clutched. My breath caught. I hate to admit it, but I got misty-eyed.

"You look like Pepper," he added and grinned.

So much for a magic moment.

I hung on tight so he couldn't escape and we headed for the secret door.

We were nearly there when it spun open and Rossetti and Howie stepped into the Fortress of Solitude.

M y only choice was to plow past them and run like hell and I would have done it, too, except for the fact that dragging Quinn behind me was like trying to corral a bowl of Jell-O. Oh, and that Rossetti had a gun pointed right at us.

"Boss said if anything went wrong at the wedding, I was supposed to take care of him." With the barrel of the gun, Rossetti pointed at Quinn. "I guess something went wrong. And since you're here, too . . ."

"There's been a delay. That's all." I took a step back and hauled Quinn along with me. "I was just about to head back outside and—"

"It's soundproof in here. Did you know that?" Rossetti moved forward.

I scrambled back another couple steps and when all Quinn did was lean forward, close one eye and look at that big ol' gun like he'd never seen one before, I tugged him.

"Nobody's gonna be leaving here," Rossetti said. "And nobody's going to find you, either. 'Cause nobody knows about that secret door."

It was a classic line from a classic bad guy, and it would have packed a punch if at that second, the door didn't swing open again.

As it turns out, Howie was standing a tad too close. When the wall came around, it clunked him in the head and he went down like a brick.

Mom and Dad raced into the Fortress of Solitude screaming something about following Rossetti and Howie. Rossetti did what bad guys do and took a shot. And me? I didn't have a lot of choice. At the same time I flung Quinn to the floor and threw myself on top of him, I swiped at the box containing *Action Comics* #1. The clear box swayed like a son of a gun. Rossetti's shot pinged, ricocheted, and bounced back at him. It didn't kill him, and there wasn't much blood. Well, not too much, anyway. When he grabbed his shoulder and fell to the floor howling, Dad kicked the gun across the room.

I lifted myself up far enough to make sure Quinn was okay and found him looking up at me, a grin as wide as Lake Erie on his face.

"Hey," he said. "You look like Pepper!"

21

It didn't take much to convince the cops that Blackburne was a bad guy. For starters, there was my signature obviously forged on the marriage license that had been given to the minister. And, of course, the biggie: that stolen comic book hanging in the Fortress of Solitude. I don't know what that display case it was in was made out of, but it hadn't gotten as much as a scratch from the bullet that bounced off it when Rossetti took a shot at us. Blackburne was hauled in for questioning, but not before he looked at me longingly and screamed, "Lana, I love you!" Rossetti and Howie were handcuffed and taken away. The wedding guests were gathered into the big-ass living room and questioned, but since none of them really knew what was up, the cops let them go, one by one, and after a couple hours, there weren't too many of us left out on the flagstone patio.

The minister was one of those left. It should be duly

noted that he looked so panic-stricken that my dad went and got him a scotch, straight up, and his hands shaking as much as his voice, he gave a statement to the cops, swore he was free of any complicity and prayed (I was grateful) that the "poor bride" would not be permanently scarred by this terrible incident.

Mom, Dad, and Ella had plenty of questions of their own, and I sat down with them in the glow of the candles that still fluttered all around us and answered them as best I could. Some poor paramedic (my guess was that he was low guy on the totem pole) had been given the assignment of trying to convince Quinn to go to the hospital, and even from where we sat in those white chairs that had been lined up on either side of the aisle and were now scattered willy-nilly, we could hear his response. I'd better not repeat it word for word. Let's just suffice it to say that Quinn told the man he'd had enough hospitals for one lifetime and there was no way in hell he was going to let them transport him to another one. Apparently, the paramedic knew something of Quinn's reputation; he didn't ask a second time.

Mom and Dad went in search of something cold to drink and I took the opportunity to stroll closer to where Quinn was sitting at a table near the door that led into Blackburne's library. The paramedics had already draped a blanket around his shoulders and given him an IV and about a gallon of coffee to drink when some mucky-muck from the police department showed up who seemed genuinely worried. Worried, schmurried. I didn't care. Not as much as I did when I heard the guy say something to Quinn about what a great job he'd done and how he'd risked his own life to solve the case, and how they would transfer him back to Homicide where he belonged as quickly as they could.

Happy endings.

I like happy endings.

I made myself scarce while they talked details.

"Looks like I missed plenty."

Not to worry, I was half expecting Jack Haggarty to show, so I didn't jump out of my satin gown when he materialized on the stone wall that surrounded the patio.

Not caring what happened to a gown I never would wear again anyway and I never would have even dreamed of buying in the first place if it weren't for the whole Quinn-is-going-to-die crisis, I sat down next to him. "I'll say. We caught your murderers." I slid Jack a sidelong glance only to find that he was staring across the patio in Quinn's direction. "You don't look especially happy about it, and you should, you know. Now that the bad guys are going to pay for your murder, you can cross over. You know, rest in peace."

"You don't believe that bullshit, do you?"

The way Jack spit out the words made me flinch. This time when I looked his way, I took my time, sizing up the way one corner of his mouth was pulled into a thin line, and the lethal set of his jaw. His shoulders were rock-steady and just as hard. His eyes—trained on Quinn— were fiery.

"Something's wrong." Understatement. I mean, after all, my knees were knocking and my stomach was back to doing the sorts of painful triple-axel contortions it had been when I stood at Milo Blackburne's side at the altar.

If there was anything I'd learned over the course of my investigations, it was to trust my instincts. Mine were screaming. Too bad I couldn't understand exactly what they were saying.

"What are you talking about?" I asked Jack. "And why are you . . ." Even when Rossetti had his gun trained on us, I hadn't seen the sort of look in his eyes that I saw in Jack's. Single-minded. Unadulterated. Hate.

I hopped off the wall and stepped in front of Jack so he couldn't aim that dagger gaze at Quinn. "Why are you looking at Quinn like that?"

Jack's lips twisted. He swiveled that heart-stopping look in my direction. "Are you that stupid?"

"No." My shoulders shot back. "As a matter of fact, I'm not stupid at all. I solved your murder, didn't I? And I figured out why the bad guys tried to pin Dingo's murder on you. They didn't want to take the heat and they figured if the cops were busy looking for the Topic candy bar eater, they'd never have to worry. You should be grateful, Jack. And more than a little thankful, too."

"Oh yeah. Grateful." His words were blistering. Still in a seated position, Jack floated up into the air, the better to see over me. "I'd be more grateful if that son of a bitch actually died like he was supposed to."

My mouth fell open and even when I made a concerted effort to snap it shut, it automatically flapped open again. "What are you . . . What the hell . . . What are you talking about? Who . . . ?" I whirled around to look where Jack was looking, even though I didn't really need to.

"Quinn." My voice echoed in my ears. I spun back

around only to find Jack sitting on the wall again. "This is some kind of joke."

"I'm not laughing."

"You mean . . ." I guess when the minister had prayed the poor bride didn't suffer any permanent mental trauma, it hadn't exactly stuck, because I had a flashback to those minutes at the altar. My mouth went dry. Just as it had then. My knees banged together. My blood thrummed so hard and so fast I couldn't pull in a breath. "You mean you knew Quinn was the one who was supposed to die? You were . . ." I ran my tongue over lips that felt as if they'd been coated with sandpaper. "You were counting on it?"

"Damned straight." One look at me, stupefied, and Jack laughed. "Figured the more an amateur like you was involved, the more screwed up things would get. And I was right. Only it wasn't supposed to end this way."

My hands curled into fists. "Why?" I asked. "Quinn was your partner."

"Yeah, a partner who always said he'd never move to the Detective Bureau unless I did, too. We took that pro-motional exam the same day, you know. He passed it. I didn't. And he—"

"That was like, what, five or six years ago? Cut the guy a break, he was young. And probably so excited that he—"

"He betrayed me."

Jack's words stopped me cold.

"Quinn's a good man," I said, and talk about cold, I'm pretty sure my voice qualified. "He's honest, and he's brave, and he cares about the people he helps. He's a great detective. I don't know you, Jack, but I'll tell you what, I do know that's something you could never be. You took bribes. You betrayed your badge."

Jack crossed his arms over his chest. "Hate to tell you, honey, but I'm beyond caring. At least about that. But him . . ." Another look to where Quinn and the police department representative were saying their good-byes. I saw Quinn shiver. "The kid was all full of himself when he passed that exam. He was all full of himself when he started at the Detective Bureau. He's still . . ." The looked he aimed over my shoulder toward Quinn packed so much punch, I'm surprised Quinn didn't topple off the chair he was sitting on. "He's still full of himself."

I wasn't going to let that kind of jealousy keep me from pointing out the truth. "Too bad, so sad. Quinn made it through the investigation just fine. Get over it."

"Yeah, he made it through. This time."

My heart stopped. I swear it did. I had faced plenty of bad guys in my day, but I had never felt the sort of malevolence that rolled off Jack with the never-ending rhythm of the lake waves that hit the rocky shoreline twenty feet below where Jack was sitting. "Are you telling me . . ." The words felt heavy on my tongue. I swallowed and gave it another go. "Are you telling me you're going to try again?"

"To get even with Harrison?" Jack's laugh was anything but funny. "You're damn right. You may have noticed . . ." He leaned in close enough for me to feel the waves of cold that pulsed off his ectoplasm. "Ghosts may not be able to touch things or move things, but we can do all sorts of things to influence the living, and your boy Quinn there, he's got a mighty dangerous job. I didn't get to teach him a lesson this time, but I'll get plenty of other chances. Heck, I'm not going anywhere, I've got all the time in the world to keep trying. Until Quinn Harrison is as dead as I am."

Instincts, remember. Mine told me exactly what to do. It started with keep Quinn safe. It ended with keep Quinn safe. What happened to me in the middle didn't much matter.

Bracing for the freeze, I used every last ounce of strength I had and pushed Jack Haggarty as hard as I could.

He wasn't expecting it. I mean, how could he when he knew that touching him would shoot icicles up my arms and freeze me to the bone?

His mouth fell open when he toppled off the wall, and I can't say for sure since I still don't know exactly how the whole ghostly universe thing works, but something told me that before he hit the water, he knew the drill. Ghosts could die if they were dispatched the way they'd been killed in life. That's what Chet had told me.

I owed the guy a new cigar and the chance to write about all the burlesque queens he wanted to for that little piece of info.

Jack Haggarty tumbled toward the lake, screaming at the memory of the way he'd drowned when he was alive and the realization that this time, there would be no second chances. He hit the water and burst into sizzling phosphorescent fireworks.

* * *

"Were you playing with a flashlight over there?"
Quinn's voice was almost back to normal. But
then, I had a feeling he was riding a caffeine and sugar
high. There was an empty coffee cup on the table in front
of him and about twelve of those little sugar bags. They
were empty, too. When I sat down next to him, shivering like mad and hoping he wouldn't notice, he looked
back toward the wall that overlooked the lake. "I saw a
flash."

"Must be the aftermath of those drugs Blackburne gave
you. How are you feeling?"

When he scrubbed his hands over his face, the blanket
that had been around his shoulders drooped, and I tugged
it back into place.

"You don't need to baby me." He shrugged the blanket
away and heck, if he wasn't going to use it, I knew an
almost-bride who was so cold she was pretty sure she was
turning blue. I grabbed the blanket and wrapped it around
my bare shoulders. "I'm fine."

"It's kind of nice. Babying you, I mean. You're the one
who's usually taking care of me." There was a coffee carafe on the table and I poured another cup for Quinn, who
took one sip and made a face.

"It's ice cold," he said. He sized me up and reached for
my hand. "You're ice cold, too. What's going on? Where's
Jack?"

I shrugged, only since I was wrapped in that blanket, I
don't think he saw. "He said he . . ." It's not like I'd never
lied to Quinn, I just wasn't sure if I'd ever lied to him

about anything this personal. "He had to go." Not exactly a lie. "I won't be seeing him anymore."

Quinn twined his fingers through mine. "You really are ice cold," he said, and he got to his feet, dragged me up beside him, and pulled me into his arms.

"Better?" he asked, wrapping me in a hug.

"Way better." I put my head on his shoulder. And call me crazy, but that's also when I realized something was wrong. I mean, it wasn't like it wasn't a great hug. Or that Quinn isn't a great hugger. Believe me when I say I have experience with these things, and I know quality when I see and feel it. Still, I couldn't help but sense a little bit of hesitation. I pushed away so that I could look into his eyes.

Quinn glanced at his feet.

I bent to catch his gaze. "What's bothering you?"

"It's just . . ." He bit his lower lip. "Back there in the Fortress of Solitude . . . I said some pretty crazy things."

I knew it would come to this.

Which didn't explain why the cold inside me got a little icier.

"Hey!" Was that me, managing to sound like it was the most natural thing in the world to hear a guy take back a marriage proposal? "I get it. You were under the influence of some pretty heavy-duty drugs. I knew you didn't mean it."

"Did you?"

Was that relief I heard in his voice? Yeah, I was pretty sure it was.

Just like I was pretty sure hearing it left me feeling as if I'd been sucker punched.

Before I could find a way to get out of the situation and still save face, Quinn pulled me into his arms again.

"Yes, I was drugged. Yes, I know I was acting like a goof. But believe me, I remember everything I said. And I remember . . ." It was dark there on the patio. All the better to see the fire in his eyes when he looked into mine. "I remember I meant every word of it."

I hadn't realized I was holding my breath until I let it go. "Are you saying . . ."

He looked over my head. "The minister's still here, and you've got the dress."

"Yeah, the dress." I looked down at the gown that had surely come straight out of some warped designer's worst nightmare. When I looked back up at Quinn, though, something in his smile told me it didn't matter. Not really. "I guess wedding gowns aren't as important as the weddings themselves. And they're sure not as important as a lot of other things."

"Like the way you were willing to sacrifice yourself to save me." The wistfulness in Quinn's voice was momentary. He held me far enough away to peer into my face. "Are you crazy?"

I shrugged, then regretted it. That wire in the bodice of the dress, remember. "You keep telling me I am."

"And apparently, all this time, I was right. Still . . ." One corner of his mouth lifted in an irresistible smile. "Your craziness doesn't change the way I feel about you."

I hooked my arms around his neck.

"And the way you feel about me," he added.

I gave him a kiss to prove it.

From across the patio we heard glasses clink and the sound of my mother and Ella laughing.

"Looks like we're just in time for a celebration," I told Quinn, and tugged him toward where Mom, Dad, and Ella were sitting with a bottle of champagne they'd somehow managed to get their hands on.

Quinn didn't budge. "I was just thinking about something else, Pepper. About all this crazy Superman stuff."

I was feeling pretty darned good about life in general. I mean, what with saving Quinn's life, breaking up a major theft ring, solving three murders, dispatching a son-of-a-bitch ghost, and not ending up the day as Mrs. Milo Blackburne. I laughed and closed in on Quinn.

"I have been looking for a man of steel," I said, snuggling up to him.

Quinn grinned and tugged me even closer, the full length of his body pressed to mine.

"Looks like I found him." I smiled, and kissed him one more time.

"Yeah, but . . ." Quinn, never the wallflower, hesitated. "You know," he said, "a while back, there was a show on TV about Lois and Clark."

I'd never watched it, but I'd heard about it. I nodded.

"I've seen a few of the episodes," Quinn went on. "The show, it doesn't emphasize Superman's powers so much as it does the relationship between Lois and Clark."

Another nod, but then, I didn't want to say anything because I didn't know what he was getting at and I didn't want to interrupt the flow.

"The show was really popular," he said. "That is, until

293

Lois and Clark got married. People stopped watching, and the show got canceled. Apparently, viewers were more interested in the romance than they were in the happily ever after."

Pardon me for being slow. My nose squinched, I gave him a look.

"I was just wondering. That's all." Quinn Harrison, mule-headed and ridiculously brave. Sounding just a little unsure of himself.

It made me love him all the more.

"If we were in some kind of TV series," he said, "and if we were about to launch into our own happily ever after, and if we knew that if we did, our series might get canceled . . . Would you still do it?"

Honestly, there are times when even gorgeous doesn't make up for thickheaded. I took his hand in mine and smiled. "There's only one way to find out."